A Reunion
in the Keys

≈ A COCONUT KEY NOVEL ≈
BOOK ONE

HOPE
HOLLOWAY

INTRODUCTION TO COCONUT KEY

If you're longing for an escape to paradise, step on to the gorgeous, sun-kissed sands of Coconut Key. With a cast of unforgettable characters and stories that touch every woman's heart, these delightful novels will make you laugh out loud, fall in love, and stand up and cheer...and then you'll want the next one *right this minute*.

For release dates, excerpts, news, and more, sign up to receive Hope Holloway's newsletter! Or visit www. hopeholloway.com and follow Hope on Facebook and BookBub!

CHAPTER ONE

"*I* said my name is Ava Gallagher, your *granddaughter*." She repeated the words a little more slowly to be sure the lady understood the second time. "My dad was...*is*...your son. You gave him up for adoption?"

The woman just stared back at Ava, silent and blank-faced.

Maybe she couldn't hear over the sound of the Uber crunching on the seashell driveway as the car took off and left Ava on some god-forsaken island halfway to Cuba. Or maybe she was hard of hearing like Grandma Janet, but this woman, this Rebecca Foster, didn't look that old, even if she was a grandmother.

She sure didn't *look* like Grandma Janet, but that made sense. Ava's grandmother had been ancient, almost seventy-nine when she died. But this lady? Ava had done the math on her phone calculator in the Uber. Rebecca Foster had to be around fifty-five if she'd been about Ava's age of fifteen when she had a baby almost forty years ago. Ugh. So much math.

However old she was, a few wrinkles formed in her brow as she frowned, put her hand on her chest, and tried to swallow. "My...but.... How did you find me?"

"You *are* Rebecca Foster, right?" Ava asked, shifting from one leg to the other, uncomfortable in the blazing sun knowing she might be seriously messing with this woman's life. Well, sorry. Ava promised Grandma Janet that she would figure out a way to deliver the letter. So here she was, keeping a promise she made literal hours before Grandma J died.

"I am Rebecca Foster," the woman said. "But...I don't understand. How do you know my name?"

Ava put her hand up to shield her eyes from the sun and spell it out one more time. "Did you have a baby when you were a teenager that was adopted?"

She didn't answer. She tried, her mouth opened and a sound came out with a slight nod. Ava took that as a yes.

"That baby was or, well, *is* my dad, Kenny Gallagher."

"Kenny Gallagher?" She kind of croaked Dad's name.

"Yeah, she said you might not know his name."

"She?"

"My Grandma Janet. That's who sent me. She's the mom who adopted your son." Jeez, it wasn't rocket science, lady.

But Rebecca Foster took a deep breath and looked like she maybe didn't understand English. Or at least she could not process what Ava was saying. "Kenny Gallagher," she whispered again.

"Do you recognize his name?"

"No." She shook her head slowly, like her brain was

only starting to actually work right now. "I wasn't ever supposed to."

"Yeah, my grandma said that, too. A closed adoption, or something like that?"

"Sealed." She reached up a hand toward Ava's face, but Ava tucked her hands in her jeans pockets and inched back. "I can't believe you're here. A granddaughter. How old are you?"

"Almost sixteen." It sounded better than fifteen, maybe easier for Rebecca Foster to understand how Ava managed to get to the middle of nowhere on her own. "So, what should I call you?"

"Shocked," she said. She pressed both hands on her chest now, like she had to hold her heart in place. "But you can call me Beck. Please, just Beck."

"'kay. Hi, Beck."

"I really don't know what to say." She added a little uncomfortable laugh. "I feel like we should throw our arms around each other and hug."

Ava held up a hand. "I'm good. Not a hugger. Anyway, my Grandma Janet made me promise to find you."

"She did?"

"And then she died, so..."

"Oh, I'm sorry."

"Not as sorry as I am," Ava murmured.

"Where do you live?" she asked.

"Um. Atlanta." Like this lady *used* to, and it would have been a lot less complicated to accomplish her mission if Ava hadn't had to haul her butt to a place called Coconut Key just to keep her promise.

"Atlanta?" Beck's eyes widened. "Do your parents know you're here?"

Why was that the first thing grown-ups thought about? "Parent," she corrected. "Just my dad. And, uh, no. He doesn't know. But it's cool." At the slightly horrified look she got, Ava tried to deflect a meltdown with some humor. "Probably Grandma Janet knows." She pointed to the sky and grinned. "And she'd tell me that God will strike me dead if I don't keep a promise to a person who died a few hours after I made it. So...I got here."

"How?"

"I got creative," she said. "Managed to get to South Florida, then took that Uber..." She thumbed over her shoulder.

Beck shook her head. "Okay, but I meant how did your grandmother know my name? Everything about that adoption was sealed and secretive. A lawyer handled it. No one was ever supposed to open up any of the papers."

Ava shrugged. "She must have opened something because she told me your name and address and said I had to find you."

Beck looked totally confused. "But why?"

"To give you this." She dug into her bag for the envelope she'd been carrying around since Grandma died three weeks ago. "She made me swear I would put this letter in your hands in person. That was a huge deal to her. I couldn't mail it, but I had to give it to you. Of course, she thought you lived in Atlanta, which would have been a *whole* lot easier, but..."

"A letter?"

She slid out the white envelope and handed it over. "She also said I had to be sure you read it."

Beck took it, staring at the Birch River Road address

Grandma had written on the front, a house out in the burbs where Ava had started this quest.

"But how did you find me here? I moved from Alpharetta a month ago."

"I know. When I got to your house, the new people were unloading furniture." And Ava had freaked the heck out when she saw the moving truck. "They said you'd sold the house and moved to Florida, which really threw me. But, as Grandma Janet used to say, I'm fast on my feet."

"They gave you this address? Here, in Coconut Key?"

"Yep. I whipped out that letter and said it came to my house by mistake. And the man's wife gave me your forwarding address."

Beck blinked at her. "She did?"

"Well, she was overwhelmed with moving, so I caught her off guard."

Beck ran her finger over the envelope, looking at it. "And how did you get all the way to the Keys?" she asked, looking as if she was more interested in Ava than the letter.

Ava shrugged. "I told my dad that I wanted to go to, um, visit my aunt who lives in Ft. Lauderdale. I knew if I could get to Florida, I could get to the Keys. And I did." She couldn't help smiling, pretty pleased with herself and the fact that she did it without one little moment of panic. That was the real accomplishment, not convincing Dad to let her go see an aunt they both knew she didn't like. He was ready to send her anywhere when the school year ended last week.

"Does your aunt know you're here now?"

Did it matter? Apparently to Rebecca Foster, it did.

Ava hadn't counted on the Spanish Inquisition, she just wanted to deliver the letter and get back to Aunt Katherine before she figured out Ava was not at the mall.

"Yeah." She added a casual shrug to cover the lie. "You gonna open that?"

But Beck narrowed her eyes, the way adults did when they knew they'd caught you. "And she was fine with that? With letting you take an Uber from Ft. Lauderdale to the Lower Keys, which had to have cost a small fortune."

"Actually a big one, but, like I said, I promised my grandma."

"And your aunt..."

Oh, come on, lady. "She knows I went...somewhere."

"Where?"

"The mall." Man, this woman had a powerful stare. It kind of reminded Ava of her mother, who could pull the truth out of a mannequin. "In South Beach," Ava added on a whisper.

"South...like in *Miami* Beach?" She gasped like Ava had said "the moon." "Your aunt thinks you're at the mall and you are well over a hundred miles away *in the Keys?*"

"It's no biggie. I'll get an Uber back, but that guy wouldn't wait. They have Ubers here, right? I mean, I'm still in America, aren't I?"

"Last I checked." She *finally* looked down at the letter.

"Good. Then you read that and I'll blow out. You'll never see me again, I swear."

Her jaw dropped. "I want to...I don't want you to...I think I should..."

"Can you read the letter?" Ava asked, hearing her voice rise in that fine whine Grandma Janet used to warn her not to use. "Please? I promised my grand-mother." When Beck's eyes flickered, Ava added, "My other grandmother. The one who died three weeks ago."

On a deep, sad sigh, Beck turned and looked behind her at the house she'd walked out of when Ava's driver stopped at 143 Coquina Court. Ava hadn't had a chance to look at the house, but now she did.

Three stories with cute windows and a pretty porch. She also noticed that there were a lot of people gathered on a big second floor porch that wrapped around the side and back, and she could hear voices and laughter.

"Are you having a party?" Ava asked.

"I am."

"Oh." Dang it. "Would it be awkward to let me in to use the bathroom?"

"Awkward? It would be..." She let out a little sigh. "You know, it might be a bit uncomfortable to, uh, meet all those strangers. But I have an idea." She gestured them both toward the street. "My mother lives very close in a cottage that's empty right now. Why don't we sit in there and read this and...talk?"

Talk? She didn't want to talk. But...did she say her mother? "Would that mean she's my great-grandmother?"

She angled her head, then nodded. "Yes, I guess she is."

She might really be messing with this lady's whole life. "Does she know you had a kid and gave him up for adoption?"

"As a matter of fact, she does, but I'll be perfectly honest, she's the only person on earth who does know. Oh, besides my soon-to-be ex-husband."

Ava rolled her eyes. "Guess I walked into a little bit of a soap opera," she muttered.

She put a hand on Ava's back and led her down the stairs. "I'm pretty sure you just launched the next episode."

CHAPTER TWO
BECK

*A*s they walked along the shell-covered road to Lovely's cottage, Beck kept trying to think of something to say, but it felt like her brain had shut down. She'd had trouble thinking straight ever since she'd spied this waif of a girl with waist-length blond, pink, and purple hair getting out of a car in front of Coquina House.

Beck had assumed she was here for Lovely's "Celebration of Life" party that they'd been planning ever since her mother got out of the hospital and began walking again after a fall. A fall, Beck remembered, that had happened following a revelation very much like this one.

Fact was, Beck had only learned that her "aunt" Lovely was really her biological mother less than two months ago, and that teenaged Lovely had given her baby to her sister, Olivia, to raise. So not only had Beck, and her family, just recently come to terms with the fact that her *mother* was her *aunt*, and vice versa, she'd also only just revealed her own teenage pregnancy story to Lovely.

No one but the man she was soon to divorce knew that Beck had gotten pregnant in high school, and that her mother had arranged for a private, sealed adoption. Well, scratch that. Someone knew. This somewhat shy but obviously strong-willed teenage girl knew. And her deceased grandmother—the woman who adopted Beck's baby boy—knew.

But did...that boy, who was now close to forty years old?

Beck still hadn't told her own grown daughters, two of whom were in the house enjoying the party she'd just left. She'd planned to tell them, though. She and Lovely had talked about how and when, but they hadn't yet. Mostly because they were dealing with their own major life changes, and the mother in Beck wanted to protect her daughters from more upheaval.

Peyton had recently quit her job in publishing and broken up a serious relationship after being cheated on, moving to Coconut Key to lick her wounds and find her way. Savannah, her headstrong middle daughter, had also come to the island with baggage, almost five months pregnant from a man she refused to say much about.

But now Beck would have to tell them. Unless she put Ava Gallagher back in an Uber and let her figure out how to get back to Ft. Lauderdale. And that, she knew, wasn't going to happen, at least not easily. Now that Beck had seen the girl's green eyes, so much like her own, and knew the son she gave up thirty-nine years ago was a man named Kenny Gallagher? No. Letting go of this new branch of her family tree wouldn't be easy.

Despite the May sun washing Coconut Key in warmth, goosebumps rose on her arms.

"So, just to be clear, your dad doesn't know...about me? Only your grandmother?"

"He knows he was adopted, but I don't think he knows your name," Ava said, looking up so the sun caught the tiny diamond-like stud in her nose. "Grandma Janet told me not to tell him so he didn't get in any trouble."

"But she sent you on the mission?" Beck couldn't hide the disdain in her voice. What kind of grandmother would do that?

Ava's eyes flashed, clearly picking up on the judgment Beck was passing. "She thought you lived in Atlanta," she said. "She died before I could tell her you moved."

But Ava had come anyway, which said a lot about her character. Beck swallowed and changed the subject.

"So, what's he like?"

Ava threw her a look. "Who?"

"Your father." *My son.* "Kenny Gallagher." She liked saying the name. He was suddenly someone, not just a baby she'd cried over when her mother had refused to let her hold him even for one minute.

"He's like..." She lifted a bony shoulder. "He's just my dad."

Well, that wasn't good enough. Beck wanted more, but she knew enough about teenage girls, having had three of her own, to realize that pushing for information wouldn't get her any. She'd have to coax it out of Ava, and she planned on doing just that.

Still holding the letter, Beck gestured toward the hibiscus bush that marked Lovely's property. "It's right here."

"Wow, pretty," she said as they came around and saw

the brightly painted bungalow, on high enough of stilts that you could see under the house to the beach and water on the other side.

"Is that...the ocean?" Ava asked.

"Yep."

"Where are the waves?"

"It's calm and shallow here in the Keys," she said, studying the girl as so many questions rose up.

But Ava was frowning, looking around like someone trying to get their bearings. "But when we came down, the Uber driver said it was the Gulf of Mexico."

"That way." She pointed to the north portion of Coconut Key. "The other side of this island is technically in the Gulf. These islands are where the Gulf and the Atlantic all blend together, which is why the water is calm. Unless there's a storm, then it's anything but calm."

"Huh. Well, it's really pretty here."

It was, but Beck didn't want to talk geography and weather during her few minutes with her granddaughter, so she tried to guide the conversation back to more personal things.

"So, you said it's just your dad raising you? Where's..." Her voice drifted off, not sure how to ask such a simple, but potentially complex, question like *Where's your mother?*

"My mom died five years ago," she said, making it not complex at all, just sad.

"Honey, I'm so sorry." Her heart slipped a little, imagining how hard that must have been for a ten-year-old. No wonder she tried to act tough. "Do you have brothers or sisters?"

She didn't say anything, but stared at Lovely's cottage

for a long moment. "I had one brother," she finally said. "He died, too. It was a fire."

"Oh." Beck put her hands over her lips at the magnitude of what this little girl had been through. And her son! Without knowing any of them, Beck's heart ached. "That's terrible."

"I like the pink door," she said, obviously seizing on anything for a change of subject.

"My mother's a painter and loves her bright, tropical colors," she explained. "Come on, I'll show you."

She guided Ava up the stairs, climbing them for the first time in about seven weeks where she didn't pause and think about how she'd found Lovely at the bottom, unconscious, moments after Beck learned the secret Lovely had been keeping from her.

She hadn't reacted well at first to the news that Lovely was her biological mother...so it was ironic that she was right back here just a couple of months later, already trying to figure out how to get this girl to stay so Beck could meet her son.

Except whoever was responsible for Ava didn't know she was here. And that was

very concerning. Not to mention that Kenny Gallagher might not even *want* to know his birth mother. His adopted mother, this Janet Gallagher, had something to say, though. Beck was holding it, anxious to read.

Inside, Ava seemed instantly enchanted by the beachy beauty of Lovely's colorful home. She walked toward the doors that led out to the patio that ran the length of the house, looking out to the unobstructed view of the water, which was ten different shades of turquoise today.

"Holy cow," Ava whispered.

"I know when you live in Atlanta, it's hard to believe," Beck said, hoping to draw her out a little more. "What part of town do you and your dad live in?"

"Sandy Springs." She turned and made a point of scanning the beach. "Cool hammock."

Sandy Springs? Her son had lived half an hour away and she never even knew it? Beck looked at the mesh hammock, barely seeing it as she processed this news. For some reason, she'd always imagined the people who adopted him lived far, far away. "It's the best spot in the Keys," she said, trying to focus on the moment. "Always has been."

"You're from here?" she asked, barely able to hide the envy.

"I lived in the house we just left until I was ten," Beck told her. "I spent hours in that hammock. Well, ones like it. They are usually replaced every year or so, depending on the summer storms." Good heavens, she was babbling. "So, did you want to use the bathroom? It's right around this corner."

"Oh, yeah, thanks." She disappeared for a moment, leaving Beck a few minutes to try and sort things in her mind.

She had a granddaughter named Ava. A son named Kenny. And a letter from the stranger who'd adopted her baby. She looked down at the envelope with a sense it could all get more complicated when she read this letter, which was why she hadn't torn it open. She needed to be ready.

When Ava came back out, she pointed to the beach. "Can I go down and swing in the hammock?"

The way she asked made Beck remember that the girl was fifteen, still young enough to ask for permission, but old enough to get herself from Sandy Springs to Coconut Key to keep a promise. Something about that touched Beck, even charmed her.

"Of course you may, Ava. I'll be right here on the patio." She lifted the letter. "Reading. Or do you need to watch me read it?"

She shook her head. "I trust you."

The three words made her heart slip around unexpectedly. "Thank you."

With that, Ava slipped out and down the back stairs, leaving her bag on the table, which made Beck feel better. At least she wouldn't bolt back to Ft. Lauderdale.

Beck watched her walk the short distance to where the hammock hung in the shade of the coconut palm trees, squeezing the letter while she stared at the young girl. Her whole body hummed with expectation and anticipation. For the letter? Or for the possibility of getting to know her first grandchild? Or for the chance to meet her son?

All three, she decided as she perched on the edge of a chair, watching Ava's lithe body in tight jeans and a crop top as she loped to the hammock. Her shiny multicolored hair swung in the breeze, like a carefree kid having a walk on the beach...not a runaway teenager who'd come six hundred miles to deliver a letter from a dead woman.

Sighing, Beck slid her fingernail under the seal, taken back to the morning when she'd opened a pink envelope from Lovely Ames who was, Beck had thought at the time, her estranged aunt. The invitation to Coconut Key had changed her life in every imaginable way. In a few months, she'd gone from a broken-hearted woman whose thirty-four years of marriage had been imploded by her husband's infidelity to a soon-to-be B&B owner, forging a relationship with a long-lost mother and two grown daughters.

Was everything about to change again? Part of her didn't want that at all. But another part of her...

Part of her wanted to hold her first grandchild and do nothing but love her. But first, she had to read this letter. Taking a steadying breath, she pulled out a few sheets of folded loose-leaf paper covered with blue ink and stylish penmanship.

Dearest Rebecca,

I suspect that, by the time you read this, I'll be singing with the angels. I have no doubt that's where I'll be, as the Lord above has lived in my heart for many, many years. He has watched over me with a remarkable amount of care, giving me seventy-nine mostly happy, usually healthy, and always delightful years on this earth. It's been a good life.

Much of that, I owe to you. At forty years old, I had given up any hope of ever having a child. I had one, or nearly did, but that sweet baby was lost when he was still in my womb. We'd made a room for him, though, and kept that room waiting in our home, year after year. For me, it was a symbol of our hope that our heavenly Father would give us a child to place in that nursery. But the cradle stayed empty despite our most fervent prayers.

Until one day, our dear Pastor Eugene called and told us his friend, a lawyer, might have the answer to our prayers. There was a young girl nearby who was in the family way, and her mother wanted a sealed, private adoption that would not involve government agencies or any names.

That teenage girl was you, Rebecca. And when the pastor called to say your mother had taken you to the hospital, I stood in that baby's room that I had kept empty for years, and I cried. Tears flowed until I choked on a sob and Jimmy had to come in and calm me down before we went to the hospital where you were giving birth. We waited just outside the delivery room, praying for the baby, with Pastor Eugene.

Just after the baby was born, a very sweet nurse came out to tell us, and she brought me outside the room, so your mother could give me the child and I could hold him before the nurses took him away.

I was shaking, I remember. Right outside the door, I heard crying, but it wasn't sweet Kenny. (He was such a good baby!) It was you. I heard a young girl sobbing the way I had in the baby's room before we left for the hospital. I heard you begging your mother to please let you see and hold the boy. My heart was torn into a thousand pieces and, quite honestly, I almost backed out that very moment. How could I take another woman's baby, even if that other woman was only a child herself?

But the nurse squeezed my hand and promised me this was the miracle and a minute later, your mother came out and handed me the most astonishing gift God had ever made—a perfect, beautiful, dark haired baby boy.

Oh, and that sweet nurse? I don't think she knew she was breaking any rules, but she told me your name, and your mother's. I want you to know that not a day has gone by that I haven't prayed for you.

Beck let out a breath she hadn't realized she'd been holding, lifting her head, almost a little shocked not to be in a hospital ward in 1982, begging Olivia to let her just touch him. Just once. She rarely relived the ache, but there it was, sharp and poignant and as fresh as it had been on that hot summer afternoon.

She cleared her head and caught sight of Ava, still in the hammock. After a moment, she let herself lean back on the chair, emotions and memories rushing through her.

Her baby had dark hair...like the forbidden bad boy named Billy Dobson who'd gotten her pregnant in the first place, then let their parents convince him to sign away any rights or custody. With another slow breath, she dove back into Janet Gallagher's missive.

My son—your son? our son?—has been a source of joy for me and my late husband, Jimmy. Kenny was athletic (such a baseball player!) and has a very intelligent mind. He was raised to love the Lord with all his heart and soul, and although grief has changed him, I firmly believe he still has faith. He just refuses to admit it.

When he was just twenty-one, Kenny married a girl from our church named Elise, who was pure and wonderful. They were such a sweet couple. Everyone loved them. They had a little girl, Ava, when Kenny was twenty-four, and then another angel of a boy, Adam, who had Kenny's dark hair and eyes. Five years ago, there was a terrible house fire that took Adam, who was six at the time, and Elise. Kenny wasn't home. He'd taken Ava to a weekend camping retreat with our church, and they were spared. But he has never forgiven himself for not being home to save his wife and son. And he has never forgiven God, having never again entered the church since the day Adam and Elise were buried, side by side.

Oh, my. Beck pressed her hand over her beating

heart. What a terrible tragedy. No wonder that girl had a bit of a chip on her shoulder. There was something about the woman's words that suddenly made all of these people so real and three-dimensional.

She imagined the writer, Janet Gallagher, as a woman of strength and faith, taking the time to write this whole story to a stranger, knowing she shouldn't really send it— not according to the terms of a sealed adoption. But she'd trusted her granddaughter to get the job done, probably knowing that Ava had the brains and ability to figure out a way to accomplish the task.

It made Beck respect them both, and really made her want to read on, hoping to understand why Janet Gallagher would take this huge risk.

I have known for some time that I would be leaving this world and going to the next, and I am at peace with that. I will be thrilled to see my Jimmy, and Elise, and hold darling Adam again. But I leave behind my two most treasured possessions, Kenny and Ava. I have prayed until my knees bled about what I should leave them in this world. I have asked God to bring Kenny back to Him, and to protect my dearest Ava, who is my whole heart. She is tender and soft on the inside, but since her mother died, she has created a shell around her heart that just can't be broken.

Ava is struggling, though she'd never admit it. Her grades are falling, she has been suspended for doing some not-so-Christian things, and she's threatened to run away from home.

To make matters worse, Kenny doesn't know what to do with her. He's pulled away from her, building a wall between them that breaks my heart. He is a paramedic on call at the fire station, and builds homes, so he works a lot. Ava stays with me, but after I'm gone, she'll be alone. I'm worried about her.

Rebecca, I know nothing about you. Nothing. But I did remember the sound of that girl crying in the delivery room, and that tells me you have a tender heart, too. So, I hired a private investigator to find Rebecca Mitchell, daughter of Olivia Mitchell. The investigator said finding you was quite easy, and I was thrilled you were still in the Atlanta area, married and a mother of three girls! Surely that meant God wanted me to find you. So, as I near my time, I'm writing this letter and trusting Ava to get it to you. And this is what I'm asking:

Will you love her? Will you help break that shell around her heart? Will you take the time to talk to her, listen to her problems and help her solve them? Would you take one more "girl" in your life to be her emotional shoulder that Ava so desperately needs? I'm truly afraid if she doesn't have that in her life, she will be lost, troubled, or worse.

Her aunt is in Florida—she is Elise's brother's ex-wife. She's a soulless socialite who has no real interest in Ava but tries to be nice to her out of pity. She isn't up for the task of loving my sweet granddaughter.

I don't know you. But I heard you cry that day, and we share a connection. We are both Ava's grandmother. One by blood, one by life. I'm writing to ask you to help her in whatever capacity you can or will, and be there for her.

Her father has no idea I've written this and would probably be angry, since he's in deep denial about this. He doesn't know your name and has never shown any interest in learning more about his biological parents. I know he is a good man, but lost. My concern is Ava, who is at a difficult and delicate age, and so desperately needs a good woman to help her navigate the whitewater of life. And who could be better than a woman who is already part of her family?

Could that woman be you? Since you live in Atlanta, maybe, just maybe, you can help her.

And, once more, thank you for your decision to give Kenny up for adoption. He gave us immeasurable joy and made my life complete.

God bless you,

Janet Gallagher

PS. If you can't help, then would you please just convince her to do something about that horrible hair and that thing in her nose?

"Mom?"

With a soft gasp, Beck looked up, yanked from the words on the page. "Savannah."

"We've been looking everywhere for you." Her daughter turned and called over her shoulder. "She's here, Pey."

"Why?" Peyton, her oldest daughter, was a few steps behind. "Mom? Jessie said she saw you leave with someone, but we had no idea you came over here. What are you doing?"

They both came into the house and through the open doors to the patio where Beck sat, a questioning look in their eyes.

"Did the party suck or something?" Savannah asked, her hand absently rubbing her slightly protruding belly.

A frown formed on Peyton's face, her pretty features drawn into a concerned frown. "What's the matter?" Always the more empathetic of the two older Foster girls, and exceptionally close to Beck, Peyton would be the one to smell trouble.

"I'm..." Beck looked down at the letter, then remembered Ava, instantly seeking her out on the hammock.

She was still swaying, thank God, relaxing in the dappled sun that came through the palm trees that held the hammock. Beck's gaze shifted back to the page, landing on the handwritten words.

My concern is Ava, who is at a difficult and terrifying age and so desperately needs a good woman to help her navigate the whitewater of life. And who could be better than a woman who is already part of her family?

Could that woman be you?

She wasn't entirely sure what Janet was asking, and would need to read the letter again and again. *Could* she be that woman? Unlikely it could happen the way Janet imagined, since Beck no longer lived in Atlanta. Frequent visits and long talks with Ava weren't possible. At least, not in person.

And that, she realized with an unexpected thud of disappointment, was a shame. Because, like it or not, that was her granddaughter down on that hammock. And that little girl needed something, and she must have needed it enough that her grandmother didn't mail the letter...she wanted Beck to meet Ava. She probably knew that was all it would take to seal the deal.

"Who's in our hammock?" Savannah demanded, pulling her thick, dark blond hair back to get a better look. "It's not public property, people."

But Peyton's gaze was on the letter. "What are you reading, Mom?"

For a moment, Beck just stayed quiet, the echo of Janet Gallagher's words still in her head.

Could you be that woman?

She didn't know if she wanted it to or not, but her life

had just shifted in a real and dramatic way. She looked from one daughter to the other.

What did it say about Beck that her daughters came straight to her when they faced the hardest challenges of their lives, even when they were twenty-nine and thirty-one? It said she knew a little bit about being there when a young woman needed her.

So, maybe she *could* be that woman. But not until she told her daughters a secret they didn't know.

"Thirty-nine years ago..." She stood, setting the letter on the table so she could hold each of her daughter's hands as she broke the news. "...When I was sixteen, I gave up a baby boy for adoption."

Both their jaws dropped in sisterly unison.

"That boy is a man now, and that girl on the beach is Ava Gallagher, his daughter, my biological grand-daughter."

"*What*?" They both asked the question at the same time.

"You heard me."

Peyton blinked and drew back with a gasp. "We have a brother?"

Savannah's eyes grew wide. "We have a niece?"

Beck just smiled. "And I have another young woman to help bring into adulthood." Still holding their hands, she turned and looked at the lanky girl lounging in the hammock. "I might need your help."

"Oh, Mom. Wow." Peyton slipped closer and put her arm around Beck. "Whatever you need. This is amazing."

Savannah gave her usual wry smile, reaching down to touch her abdomen. "First Grandma Lovely, then you, and now me. We Ames women sure know how to screw...up."

Beck tipped her head toward Ava. "Her late grandmother, who apparently loved her very much, wrote to me before she passed and asked for some help to make sure she doesn't screw up, too. And I for one, want to do what I can." She smiled at them. "Come on, Aunt Savannah and Aunt Peyton. Let's go meet your niece."

CHAPTER THREE
AVA

*S*he could get used to this, Ava thought. Even that shallow water didn't look threatening, not like any ocean she'd ever seen. As long as she was up here, a decent distance from that water, she would be just fine.

Ava sucked in a lungful of beach air and let the sunshine find her face, warming her whole body, thinking about the woman she'd met.

Grandma Janet was right about Rebecca Foster being a nice lady, though Ava had no idea how Grandma J knew that. Ava didn't even know what her grandmother had put in that precious letter, but what did it matter? Ava's work was done. She'd delivered it, going pretty far above and beyond what was expected.

So now...she had to find an Uber and spend the last of the money Dad had Venmo'd her for this trip and go back to Aunt Katherine's house. Her next job? To be such an interminable brat and pain in that woman's butt that when Ava broke down into tears and begged to be sent back to Atlanta, her aunt was all about it.

"Ava?"

She twisted in the hammock, squinting into the sun to see...wait. Who the heck were these women? "Yeah?" She pushed up, a little wobbly in the hammock before she got her feet on the ground.

"I'd like you to meet some very special ladies," Beck said, holding their hands like a trio of cheerleaders marching onto the court.

"Uh huh." Ava tossed her hair back and squared her shoulders, eyeing them as they got closer. One had kind of pale blond hair the same color as Beck's that was pulled back in a ponytail. She smiled at Ava, with warmth in her eyes.

On the other side, the woman was a little taller and seemed more commanding, with a thick head of caramelly-colored waves that fell around her shoulders.

"Hi, special ladies." Ava managed to get up without flipping the hammock and looking like a complete fool.

"Ava, this is Peyton Foster." Beck gestured to the ponytail one. "And this is Savannah Foster. These are my daughters."

"Oh." She inched back, really surprised to be meeting Beck's family. Which made them, in some convoluted way, *her* family.

"Also known as your aunts," Peyton said, reaching out her hand. "It's really nice to meet you, Ava."

Ava gave her what was probably a half-hearted handshake, lost a little in how her eyes were the same color green as her own.

"Nice pink and purple hair," the other one said, also

reaching out her hand. "Maybe you could show me how to do that sometime."

"Oh, I...sure." She looked from one to the other, then back to Beck, feeling that self-conscious warmth on her cheeks that her mother used to call "Shy Ava." She'd never really outgrown it, but ever since her mom died, no one did the talking for her except Grandma Janet.

"Did you, uh, read that letter?" she asked Beck.

"I did." She smiled and it kind of lit up her eyes. "She must have been a wonderful lady."

"The best," Ava agreed.

"And she really loved you."

Like no one except Mom. "Yeah." She shifted from one foot to the other, tucking her fingers in her jeans pocket, the denim tight and hot and making her feel sweaty. "So, then, I'm gonna go now."

"Go?" Savannah took a step closer, her hand on a stomach that looked a little thick for how skinny the rest of her was. "Girl, we just met you. You can't leave."

"Oh, no, you have to stay and let us get to know you," the other sister added.

Ava felt her eyes widen, not expecting this at all. Part of her wanted to say yes, but part of her, the part that would get killed by Aunt Katherine when she got home at nine tonight? That part shook her head.

"I have to get back to my aunt's house."

"Well, I'm driving you there," Beck said. "That will give us a good long time in the car to chat and save you from spending a fortune on a car."

"You...are?" She'd like to save the money. "But my Aunt Katherine..."

"Doesn't know you're here," Beck said. "Let's go back

up to the house and call her. You can put her mind at ease and explain where you are, and I'll talk to her."

Oh, that was not going to be a fun conversation. But at least it would help when she wanted Aunt Katherine to send her home.

"Or not," Peyton said on a laugh. "Mom, she looks petrified."

"Is this aunt scary?" Savannah guessed. "All the more reason to stay with us, the *fun* aunts."

"Girls, hang on," Beck said, holding up her hand. "Ava, you have to tell someone in your family that you are not at a mall in South Beach. Your aunt will be worried."

She gave a slow nod, imagining Aunt Katherine's reaction. "Okay. I'll call her now." She dug into her back pocket for her phone, aware of the three of them staring at her. She tapped the phone.

"Maybe you should put it on speaker so I can assure her you're okay," Beck said.

Fine. She hit speaker and it rang, then jumped into voice mail. Before she could leave a message, Beck waved her hand. "We'll call your dad."

Panicking at the thought, she ended the call. "No, I don't think we should do that." Because he would blow a gasket.

Beck shook her head and gestured for them all to head back up to the house. "Come on. Out of the hot sun and let's figure this out. Honey, you cannot be two and a half hours from your aunt. Your father is trusting her to take care of you, and not—"

"He doesn't care." Why lie? Dad didn't give a hoot if Ava was *ten* and a half hours away.

"I very much doubt that," Beck said.

"You don't know him."

"No," she agreed. "I don't. But I'm going to ask you to please let me call someone and talk to them so they know you're here and you're safe."

"Call Dad then." Because nine times out of ten, it would go to voice mail. "Would that make you feel better?"

Peyton stepped closer to Beck, putting a hand on her shoulder. "Now *you* have the deer in headlights look. You don't want to call him?"

Beck didn't answer right away, thinking for a second. "I do, but...I've never spoken to him in nearly forty years and, well..."

"Look," Ava said, taking a step away from them because all these *feelings* were going to suffocate her. "Just let me get a car and I'm out. No more issues or...stuff."

"No." Beck added a smile to temper the word. "You're a minor, Ava. And you're in my care at the moment."

"I'm not in anyone's care," she shot back, fear rising. "I'm cool and I don't need you. I'm taking off now. Bye."

As she started to walk away, Beck snagged her arm with a gentle but firm grip. "Honey, you're not going anywhere. Your purse is in the cottage."

They faced off for a moment, and instinctively, Ava knew what she was up against and that there was no way to win this one. "Fine. Let's call my dad."

"Let's do that." Beck put a hand on Ava's back, and she instantly shook off the touch.

"Come on, Ava." Peyton came closer. "You're not in trouble."

With a dark look, she stepped away from that sister, but that only got the other one to come next to her.

"Want some advice from me?" Savannah asked. "'Cause I pretty much lived my life on the edge of trouble, right, Mom?"

Ava slid her a look, not seeing much trouble but a little spark of humor in her eyes. "Really?"

"Oh, yeah. Total black sheep. In fact, right now, I'm pregnant without a husband in sight."

Ava choked a little, her gaze dropping to the woman's stomach which now made sense with the rest of her.

"Yep, this is your little cousin, kid." She started walking and Ava, mesmerized by her, came along. "Wanna meet?"

What? Ava had no idea how to react to that.

"Here." She took Ava's hand and placed it on her belly, which was so weird. Also, hard like a little basketball. "I've been calling her Pink Line because that was the first I knew of her. Oh, a pink line. That means..."

"You're in trouble?" Ava asked.

"See, that's just the thing. I wasn't. Not only am I a smart chick who can figure things out, but I have people in my life who love and forgive me. Like I think your dad is about to do."

God, she hoped so.

When they got back up to the colorful little house, Beck walked out to the patio with Ava while her daughters waited inside.

"You want to call him and make the introductions?"

She blew out a breath that might have also sounded like a moan. "Yeah, sure." Taking out her phone, she tapped it, looking up at Beck's green eyes while it rang. *Please be busy, Dad. Please.*

Otherwise, she was about to be grounded for life.

"Hey, A. How's Florida?"

Dang! "Um, fine. It's good." She searched Beck's face, letting it sink in that this lady was Dad's mother.

"Aunt Katherine treating you okay?"

"She is, but, uh, I'm not at her house right now." Her heart hammered and took a slow trip up to her throat.

"Where are you?"

She tried to let out a breath. "In the Keys."

"The Keys?" He gave a low laugh. "She took you down to the Keys? That's cool."

"Actually, I kind of got here on my own."

Dead silence. A good fifteen seconds of it. "Dad?"

"What the hell did you do now, Ava?" His voice was low and harsh.

"I took an Uber to a place called Coconut Key."

"What? Why? Alone? Who are you with? Are you all right?"

She squeezed her eyes as he whipped the questions at her, a little surprised when Beck reached out and closed her fingers over Ava's.

"I'm with a lady named Rebecca Foster."

"Who the hell is that?" he demanded.

She swallowed. "She's your birth mother."

CHAPTER FOUR
KENNY

*P*ressing the phone against his ear, Kenny Gallagher walked a few steps away from the man using a hammer gun so he could hear better. Because what he thought she said was...

Impossible.

"Excuse me?"

"Why don't you talk to her? Here she is. Call her Beck."

What did she say?

"Hello, Ken, is it? Kenny Gallagher?" The voice on the other end was mature but not that steady.

"That's me," he said, leaving the kitchen for the back patio of the job site, away from the flooring he was currently laying, and away from his boss, Bill.

Holy crap, his *boss*—

"My name is Rebecca Foster, but people call me Beck."

He shook his head to clear it. "Is my daughter okay?"

"Oh, yes," she said, the slightest bit of a gush in her voice. "She's more than...she's lovely, Kenny. She's just—"

"What the hell is she doing there?" He tried but couldn't keep the edge out of his voice. Why wasn't she at Katherine's house in Ft. Lauderdale where she was supposed to be spending the summer? How did she get to the Keys, which could be an hour or two away? She couldn't drive and she—

"She brought me a letter from her grandmother, Janet."

A letter from Mom. To this woman, who is... "Did I understand Ava to say that you're..." He actually couldn't form the words.

"I'm your biological mother," she said softly. "I had you when I was sixteen and gave you up for adoption. Your mother, Janet, hired a PI to find me and asked Ava to give me a letter."

How was this even possible? "My mother wouldn't send Ava to the Keys alone." It was the one part of that story he knew had to be wrong. She'd never put Ava in one second of harm.

"Your mother thought I still lived in Atlanta, but she was wrong. So Ava figured it out on her own."

"Why am I not surprised?" he asked wryly. His daughter was too damn wily for her own good.

"I just want you to know that she's safe. I'll take her back to her aunt's house and she won't be any trouble."

Oh, she'd be trouble. She'd been trouble for a few years now, and the only thing keeping her out of worse trouble was his mom. Now she was gone, Ava was wrecked, and he'd hoped to God that a summer with her aunt in Florida would give them both a much-needed break.

"Okay," he said. "I don't really know what to say. Thanks for letting me know. She's okay, then?"

"She's fine, really. Just..." She let out a soft half-laugh, half-sigh. "A wonderful surprise."

He thought about that for a minute, squeezing his eyes shut. How did he get here? How the hell did he sink so low as a father that his fifteen-year-old had basically run away and found his birth mother? If that wasn't a screaming cry for help, what was it?

Well, every one of Ava's antics was a cry for help. Ever since the fire that ended life as he and Ava knew it, she'd done nothing but cry, one way or another. And her grandmother had been such a help. Now, Ava had gone to...find another grandmother.

He was the suckiest dad on earth. If there was such a thing as heaven, which he knew there wasn't, Elise would be looking down in pure disgust with him.

"Well, I don't know how to thank you," he said.

"Actually, I know how you could thank me," she replied, lowering her voice to a whisper.

What could she possibly want from him? Some kind of...reunion? He'd never wanted to meet his birth mother. His mother, his *only* mother, was Janet Gallagher, the greatest human who ever lived. DNA meant nothing to him. Nothing at all.

"What's that?" he asked.

"Give Ava permission to stay with me for a few days," she said, still speaking softly as if she didn't want whoever was around her to hear. "If you could contact her aunt and arrange for it, I would just love to get to know your daughter."

"I don't know. I don't know a thing about you." Not that he'd demonstrated very good control over his daughter, but still.

"Well, what do you need to know?"

About the woman who gave him life? Everything. Nothing. "I guess I just need to be sure she's safe."

"She's quite safe. I'm fifty-six years old and live in a beach house in Coconut Key, which is about twenty-five miles from Key West. Right now, two of my daughters, who are grown women, are staying with me. My own mother lives down the street. We're about to start renovating the house to become a Bed and Breakfast. I'm in the process of getting divorced, have another daughter who is pre-law at Emory, and...let's see, what else? I've never been arrested, never had a driving ticket, and I only drink a glass of wine now and then."

He closed his eyes and let it sink in that his real mother was a person with a life and a family and a world that he didn't know anything about.

"I'm still so...confused. Why would my mother send her there?" The question was as much to himself as the woman on the other end.

"Remember, she sent Ava to Alpharetta, not the Keys. But you should know that Janet's letter was a plea for me to help Ava because apparently, she's struggling."

It hit like a sucker punch to his solar plexus and for a moment, he couldn't breathe.

"Which, I guess, I'd very much like to do," Beck added. "So maybe a day or two? A week? A month? I'll take anything I can get, but I think I love this little girl already."

His eyes were still squeezed shut and, man, they stung. So bad that he actually didn't trust himself to answer.

"Kenny?" she asked after a minute.

"Uh, listen, Beck." He needed to say no. He needed to tell this woman who, despite what the blood might say, was a complete and total stranger, and he wasn't that sucky of a dad that he needed strangers to help his daughter through her teen years.

Oh, for God's sake, Elise, why did you leave me?

"Yes?" she urged.

Just say no. *No, you can't help. No, you can't develop a relationship with her. No, you can't fix my problems even if you are my mother.*

He cleared his throat and looked through the kitchen window, catching Bill's eye and the "what the hell are you doing?" look on the man's face. Oh, Bill. If you only knew.

But then, if Bill knew, he'd tell Kenny to let her stay. Let the girl get to know her biological grandmother. What could it hurt? After all...

"She can stay for a few days," he said. "And I need her to check in with me. Daily."

"Of course!" He could hear the absolute joy in her voice, which only made him feel guiltier. Elise's sister-in-law, Katherine, sure didn't sound like that when he called to ask if Ava could stay with her for a while.

Had Ava pushed for that visit just to get closer to this woman, Beck? To deliver a letter...or what?

"Do you want to talk to her now?" Beck asked. "Do

you want to tell her? She's with my daughters but I can get her."

He didn't answer, but heard a burst of female laughter in the background, and that tamped down his guilt. A little.

"No, it's fine. Please get me your phone number and address, though, and...send a picture. I'm glad she's happy."

"Well, I don't know if she's happy, but she's safe and we'll give her a nice place to stay with a view of the beach. And I'll...get to know her."

Wow. He came from good stock, just like his mother always said even though he'd never asked for details. "All right, thanks."

"Thank you. And, Kenny..." She let out a quick, uncomfortable laugh. "I'm so glad you landed with such a wonderful mother. I loved her letter. I'll save it forever."

"Yeah, she was a keeper."

They said goodbye and Kenny stood stone still for a minute, gathering his wits.

"Everything okay, son?"

He turned and met Bill's dark gaze, seeing the concern on the man's face...a man who almost always called him "son" even though Bill was only sixteen years older than Kenny.

He'd started the day they'd met and had that first cup of awkward coffee, when this man swooped in and had his back. Bill had hired him, helped him, and had been exactly what he needed when he needed it the most. A *father.*

"That was Ava." Sort of. "She did...a thing."

With a quick laugh, Bill stepped closer. "She's a thing-doer, that girl."

"Yeah." Kenny gave him a tight smile, wondering how much to share. Usually, everything. In this case? Well, this was different. "She took off and ended up in the Keys."

"Holy..." His dark eyes flashed. "Is she okay? You need to go get her? 'Cause we can manage without you. You could get time off at the station, I'm sure."

He nodded. He could get time off from his job as an EMT at the fire station. He'd just ask the captain and they'd fill his slots with people eager for the hours.

"I don't know. I could, but maybe she's better off without me."

Bill gave him a look. "What does your sister-in-law say? Is she getting her and hauling her skinny butt back?"

He shook his head. "She's not with Katherine." He swallowed and made a decision. "I don't know exactly how she swung this, but she took a letter my mother wrote to a woman named Rebecca Foster."

Bill's dark brows, still black even though most of his hair had gone silver, drew together. "Who's that?"

"You might know her as...Rebecca Mitchell."

The frown faded very slowly as the name hit his brain and Bill realized exactly what was going on. He muttered a soft curse.

"You do know who I mean."

"Of course I do." A little color drained from his face. "So how did Janet get that name? Through a DNA search like I did?"

Kenny shrugged, not at all sure how an adoption that was supposed to be "sealed" was anything but, since he'd just gotten off the phone with one parent and was staring at the other.

He'd never forget the day this man came up to him at a coffee shop just a few months after Elise died, when Kenny was in the darkest imaginable place. He'd introduced himself as Bill Dobson, his biological father. As he had with Beck, Kenny rejected the relationship at first. His dad had died two years earlier, but James Gallagher had been all the father Kenny needed.

But Bill had shown him the DNA tests his kids had done on one of those ancestry sites and they'd found a freakish match to a local man named Kenneth Gallagher. The connection was real and undeniable.

Kenny had no idea his DNA information was in that database, but a little digging showed that Elise had submitted it as she was searching for Kenny's biological parents, just a few months before she and Adam were killed. The results had been sent to her email, and he never saw them. Unlike Kenny, Elise had been fascinated by the fact that Kenny had been adopted and longed to connect with his biological relatives.

She'd have been happy to know that Bill Dobson had always wondered about the kid he'd been forced to sign over when he was a teenager, and his suspicions that Kenneth Gallagher was his son had panned out. That morning they had formed an awkward acquaintance, but what Kenny needed more than anything in those wretched days was a friend.

Bill Dobson became that friend and mentor and boss. He became "Uncle Bill" to Ava, frequently showering her with too many gifts or slipping her twenty-dollar bills like, well, like a grandfather might.

Bill and Kenny didn't tell a soul about their real connection, wanting to honor the "sealed" adoption and Rebecca Mitchell's privacy. As far as the world was concerned, they were just two men who worked together at Bill's successful contracting business. Two guys who watched football and shot the breeze and laughed a lot. If they shared a resemblance, no one noticed.

"She's having Ava stay there for a couple of days," Ken said. "She wants to get to know her."

"Listen, Ken," Bill said, coming closer. "I've had almost five years with you. That woman, Beck, did all the work and made the sacrifice to give up her baby to strangers. Now it's her chance."

"To get to know Ava?"

He just lifted one brow. "You should go down there."

"Didn't you always say that meeting her could wreck her life?"

"But she's taking Ava in, so I don't think it would be a problem."

Kenny searched the other man's face, remembering— since he so frequently forgot—that this man was his biological father. And Rebecca Foster was his mother.

"What was she like?"

"At fifteen?" He lifted dark brows. "Cute. Young. Very nice. Liked my guitar." He gave a wry smile. "It gets the chicks every time."

"Great. I just said yes to letting my daughter stay with her."

Bill shook his head, laughing softly. "Go down to Florida and meet your mother, son. If she isn't any good, gather up your kid and bring her home. But if she's nice, you should know that." He gave him a nudge. "We can finish that kitchen without you."

Kenny smiled at the man, an unexpected affection rising up. Bill Dobson was one of the finest men he'd ever known. Smart, funny, talented, and highly respected. But more than that, he'd turned out to be one of the most important men in Kenny's life.

Maybe Rebecca Foster would be an important woman.

"All right, you win. I'm going."

"Good call, son."

Kenny grinned at him. "I always listen to my dad."

CHAPTER FIVE
BECK

*B*eck looked at the group gathered around the big kitchen table, just as the sun set outside the western-facing bank of windows. The classic red-orange colors of a Keys sunset cast an ethereal glow over the oversize kitchen, highlighting the ocean view beyond the sliders. The kitchen at Coquina House captured the staggeringly beautiful location that offered both sunsets and sunrises, and the combination of that light seemed to make everyone look like they were in a painting. If Beck had painted it, she would have called it...*Family*.

Not everyone around the table was related, but the sense of family was strong.

As they chatted, sipped on lemonade or something stronger, and managed to easily include Ava in their conversation, Beck let her gaze slip from one person to the next.

Peyton sat across from her, nursing a wine and smiling at something the young man next to her whispered just for her benefit. Her color was high, and not because of the wine. Valentino Sanchez, or Val, as everyone now called him, had that effect on Beck's oldest daughter. On most women, she suspected. A hard-working Keys fisherman with an easy smile, long black hair, and the kind of eyes that could make a woman melt, Val's interest in Peyton seemed genuine.

She just hoped Peyton didn't get hurt again. She'd left a boyfriend in New York because he hadn't wanted marriage or children, and Peyton did. Of course, Greg had iced the cake by having a fling with another woman while Peyton was down here helping Beck, but sometimes that's what it took for a woman to see a man's true colors.

After the breakup, Peyton had quit a dead-end job in publishing and moved out from her high-rise condo with Greg, easing right into a new life in Coconut Key for the last few months.

Not only was she dating Val, but she'd started working for Beck's dear friend, Jessie Donovan, who owned Chuck's, a gourmet restaurant down the road. Peyton was a server when they needed one, and, since she'd discovered a true love of cooking, she'd been an apprentice under Jessie, a phenomenal chef and Beck's childhood best friend. In addition to working at the restaurant, Peyton was using her publishing expertise to help Jessie write and publish her first cookbook, *Cuisine of the Keys.*

"Val, am I getting my tuna tomorrow?" Jessie called down the table. As always, Jessie's brown eyes shined with an inner joy that even losing her husband four years ago hadn't erased. In fact, since Beck had arrived, Jessie seemed even more content, although Beck suspected that it was the friendship and working relationship Jessie had formed with Peyton over these months.

Although she had the occasional bouts of jealousy, Beck was delighted to share her daughter with Jessie, who never had children of her own. Jessie had thrown herself into cooking and running the small, high-end restaurant, although business wasn't that great these days. Maybe it was the coming summer season, which was slow, or maybe it was a competitor who'd come to town.

But they all had high hopes for the cookbook which could drive more customers to Chuck's.

"You will get your tuna tomorrow," Val assured her.

"Great. Then I'm going to have three dishes ready for photography by noon tomorrow." Jessie leaned across the table to look at Savannah, reminding Beck that her middle daughter, a budding photographer, had agreed to take the pictures for the cookbook. "Can do?"

"Can do," Savannah said, glancing at Ava, who sat next to her. "Want to tag along and see a photo shoot?"

Beck's heart swelled with love for her daughter at the invitation.

"Is it, like, work?" Ava asked.

"It's, like, fun," Savannah shot back with an easy laugh. She'd done more than anyone to make Ava feel comfortable, using her quick wit to make the girl laugh even if she didn't want to. "Wait until you see the soft underbelly of food photography. You'll never look at an ad for Burger King the same."

"Why?" Ava looked a little horrified.

"Let's just say those clear dots on the tomato aren't

water droplets and the gooey mayonnaise is literal Elmer's glue. So, no eating the finished product."

"I'll make some you can eat," Jessie said, smiling at Ava. "We need to get some meat on those bones."

She gave herself a little hug. "I like being skinny," she said.

"You'll change your mind when you meet Jessie's Key Lime pie," Savannah quipped.

Next to Beck, Joshua Cross, Jessie's older brother, agreed. "Best in the Keys," he said.

Beck smiled at him, getting a nice jolt when he turned to her to return a smile of his own. The master woodworker with a good heart and an easy smile had been doing that a lot to Beck, ever since she'd arrived. But until the ink was dry on her pending divorce, their mutual attraction had to end with smiles and friendly hugs.

"You okay, Beck?" he asked under his breath, as if he sensed her whole world had undergone a seismic shift this afternoon. They'd all been amazed, amused, and generally very cool about the fact that Beck had a teenage pregnancy, although these were friends and family. Plus, who judged things like that these days?

Ava's attention was currently riveted on Savannah, who described how they would set up a table with a beach view for the photo shoot, but Beck barely heard her daughter. Instead, she drank in every angle and curve of her very first grandchild. She hardly remembered what Billy Dobson looked like, but she did have a vague memory of a cleft in his chin, just like the one Ava had.

"Still getting used to the idea that I'm a grandmother of a fifteen-year-old," she whispered back to Josh. "She's sweet, don't you think?"

He angled his head in a half-hearted nod. "She's shy," he noted. "Maybe a little overwhelmed."

"As I was when I talked to her father."

His deep blue eyes grew serious. "Was it awkward?"

"Not really. Just...weird...but I was very grateful he let her stay for a few days," Beck said as Ava laughed at Savannah's latest joke, and her whole face lost the hardness she tried to wear like makeup and all those little rings up the side of her ear. "I hope this gives me some good, quality time with her."

"Then let's get this place cleaned up so you can be alone with her." Josh pushed back, but she put a hand on his arm.

"Relax, Josh. You don't always have to do the dishes. Finish your coffee. I got this."

With another smile, she quietly stood and gathered up a few dishes, telling everyone to keep talking while she cleared the table.

But the last person in the group ignored that order. Beck's mother, Lovely Ames, pushed her chair up and immediately wore that look of satisfaction she always had when she walked and moved without pain or effort. It had been a long recovery since her car accident and then the fall, but Lovely was almost one hundred percent healed now.

"I'll dry," she said, joining Beck at the sink.

"And just think, when we renovate this kitchen, we'll have a dishwasher."

"We're still meeting with Maggie Karras tomorrow night, right?" Lovely asked, referring to the local designer they'd hired to help them remodel the kitchen. "Or do you want to cancel so you can be with Ava?"

Beck shook her head. "She's going to bring samples. Backsplash. Cabinet ideas. I asked Josh to come because he wants to build a special table for the kitchen, and he wants to get ideas based on what Maggie's thinking."

Lovely leaned against the counter and looked around. No surprise that their conversation slipped to the subject that the two of them loved the most these days: renovating Coquina House so they could open up a Bed and Breakfast this fall. "What Maggie's thinking doesn't matter if we can't get a contractor," Lovely said.

Beck sighed in agreement, reminded of their biggest and most unexpected delay. "I had no idea that every licensed contractor in the Keys would be booked until September," she said.

"I guess if we were gutting the entire house, we'd have more pull," Lovely said. "But with just a kitchen and the upgraded bathroom on the third floor—"

"And maybe a second bedroom and bath up there," Beck added. "Plus a refresh of the other bedrooms."

"Even so, it just doesn't seem to be enough to get the attention of a good GC."

"I know," Beck agreed. "So, I'm worried about a fall opening since it's already May. I really don't want to miss that busy season."

At the sound of a burst of laughter, Beck glanced over her shoulder at the table, so happy to see Ava relaxing.

"Savannah's magic," Lovely whispered. "She just makes people feel good."

Beck nodded. "I love having her here."

"Savannah or your new granddaughter?" Lovely asked.

"Both." Beck rinsed a sudsy plate, unable to fight a smile. "I still can't believe it."

"The story you told me outside, before? So sad."

While Savannah had given Ava a tour of the house and showed her the third-floor room where she could stay, Beck had filled Lovely in on a little of the girl's background and how she'd lost her mother and brother.

"Absolutely tragic," Beck said. "I wonder how her father's handled it."

"He's your son," Lovely whispered. "And my grandson. So he's strong."

"My son," Beck smiled at her mother. "Those are two words I never thought I'd utter." Then she laughed. "Dan didn't talk much about the fact that I'd had a baby at sixteen, but when he did, you know what bothered him the most?"

"The fact that you had a son and he didn't?" Lovely guessed, giving the face of disapproval she always wore when they talked about Beck's soon-to-be ex-husband.

"Exactly. He wanted Callie to be a boy so bad, he used to do 'boy incantations' over my belly. And then, when we found out the baby was a girl, he was mad at *me*. Like it was my fault."

"Study biology much, Dan?" Lovely joked.

"Right?" A little bolt of resentment slid through her. "That divorce cannot be final soon enough for me."

"Or for Josh," Lovely whispered.

Beck threw her a look. "I know. I can feel that."

She shrugged. "He likes you. I've known that man since he was knee high to a grasshopper and even when he fell for Lily, he didn't seem quite like this."

"Lovely! We're just friends. We've kissed exactly once

and that was when I was so happy that Dan was going to give me the money we needed for the B&B, I just...celebrated."

"Yes, I know you two are friends, but...there's something there."

Something. Beck still wasn't sure what. "I want to take it slow. And I really will not let myself get involved with a man until that paper is signed as a matter of principle."

"I know, I know. But I want to dance at your wedding."

Beck fought a smile and jabbed Lovely with a playful elbow. "You can dance at Peyton's. Do you think we should get excited about Val?"

"Who wouldn't get excited about Val?" Lovely teased. "I'm in my seventies and I get excited just looking at him. He's gorgeous."

Beck laughed. "And he seems really down to earth and unaware of his gorgeousness."

"Well, he's a Keys fisherman. They're a humble and kind breed of men."

"But he hasn't lived here that long," Beck said. "I was surprised when he said he'd only moved to the Keys two years ago."

She shrugged. "And considering how much he loves his Cuban-American family, I am surprised he left Miami."

"I just hope he doesn't hurt Peyton. I do not want that girl to get hurt again," Beck said softly. "She's bruised from her cheating boyfriend and if anyone knows what that feels like, it's me."

Lovely dried a plate as she looked at Beck. "You've healed, though."

"Thanks to discovering my real mother." Beck leaned

over and planted a kiss on Lovely's cheek. "You've healed, too. Not a bruise on your face and the scars are almost gone."

"They blend in with my wrinkles," she quipped, holding Beck's gaze. "I can't imagine where I'd be without you, Beckie."

"We don't have to find out. But, we do have to find a contractor or we are never going to open our B&B." Beck rinsed a dish and looked around. She'd spent so much time with Maggie Karras on the layout of this kitchen and the way it could work to accommodate guests but not lose one inch of the stunning water views.

But the most beautiful view in the room was at the table. Family. As much as she wanted to get moving with the B&B, she had to remember what mattered most. Her daughters and now, her granddaughter.

CHAPTER SIX

AVA

*N*ot long into her first full day in Coconut Key, Ava realized that she did not hate the place. In fact, she kinda *loved* this quirky little island.

From the minute she woke up, looked out the window, and saw a literal dolphin jump, she was a smitten kitten. Then she went downstairs, and Beck gave her coffee that tasted better than anything at Starbucks and didn't blink an eye when Ava said she wanted to take a walk on the beach.

The sand was soft under her toes, and she didn't even mind all the brown stuff that looked like seaweed everywhere. Everything smelled so good, like it had been dusted in salty, clean air. The sun felt hotter but not like a miserable summer day in Atlanta. This sunshine just managed to make the world glittery and bright. There was nothing scary or out of control here, even that ocean that barely had as many waves as a bathtub. Could she brave it?

She headed closer, letting her feet touch a lapping

wave, standing there for a moment with her eyes closed. Not too scary, even though water terrified her. While she walked, she thought about the people she'd met last night.

The sisters, as she thought of them, were kind of wonderful. One was hilarious and snarky, the other like a Mom-in-Training. She even liked the old lady with the spectacular name of Lovely, who reminded her an awful lot of Grandma Janet.

And then there was Beck, who was bright and blonde and down to earth, a little like Ava remembered her mother. Beck was what Mom would have been like if she'd made it to her fifties, Ava thought. Pretty and joyful and ready to help anyone.

She eased the thought of her mother away, since it always made her sad. Even though, five years later, she could think about Adam and even smile just picturing his cute little self. But when she thought for more than three seconds about Mommy, Ava wanted to cry.

But these people sure were nice. Maybe they wouldn't make her feel bad when she had one of her "panics."

She didn't know what else to call what happened to her periodically and at the most awful and unexpected times. But "panic attack" was the phrase the school nurse had used on that horrible day in fourth grade, about two months after Mom and Adam died, when she had the first one.

She'd never forget that day. She'd been listening to her teacher talk about how hard the test on fractions would be, and all of a sudden it felt like someone was sitting on her chest. She couldn't breathe. No matter how hard she tried, she couldn't open her mouth and take in air. Then she started to shake...and everyone looked at her.

And Ms. Wimbley had to walk her down the hall to the school nurse and all they could do was tell her to drink water and breathe and lay down, but she couldn't stop shaking.

Dad had to come and get her, and he was...nothing. He wasn't mad. He didn't hug her. He was just Dad, as lost as she was.

Then it happened again, one night in bed when she thought she smelled smoke. And another time when she was riding her bike and almost fell on a hill. And then when her friend Liza got her license and thought it would be fun to go ninety miles an hour on a deserted road at night and Ava actually lost it with the worst panic ever.

Ava shook her head and bent over to pick up a shell. After that, the panics started to get predictable. They happened when she felt out of control or very, very scared.

Like the time she'd skipped school and the kids she was with smoked pot. She didn't

even try it, knowing that would bring on a panic. So she went to the mall and got her nose pierced because it was wild, but still in her control. And she dyed her hair a bunch of different hair colors for the same reason.

And even getting in an Uber and going hours to some strange place in the Keys to deliver Grandma Janet's letter wasn't scary because she was in control.

At the sound of a loud string of barking, she turned to be greeted by the three dogs that had never been far from Beck's mother, Lovely, yesterday. Two of them launched right at her, kicking up sand. The little white and tan one came right up to Ava and started licking her bare leg, making Ava squawk with a laugh. The other, all brown with pointy ears, was staring up with genuine concern in big, sweet eyes that looked like someone had colored them with eyeliner.

"You have been greeted!"

She looked up to see Lovely, her third white dog trotting along next to her.

"Oh, hi." She glanced behind her and noticed the colorful cottage where she'd come with Beck the day before. "Am I trespassing?"

"Pepper might think so," she said as she got closer, pointing to the eyeliner dog. "She's my guard dog."

Ava had to laugh because the dog was stout, short, and looked like she couldn't hurt a stuffed animal. "She doesn't look very threatening."

"Don't tell her that. And Basil thinks it's his job to welcome you to the neighborhood."

Giggling a little at the tongue-lapping Basil was giving her ankles, she bent over to pet him. "Thanks, Basil. I feel very, um, wet and comfortable now."

"Are you comfortable?" Lovely asked. "That's all we want."

Smiling, she reached Ava but stopped and scooped up the little white dog next to her. "And Sugar just wants to love the world. She's my little hippie."

Lovely was the one who looked like a hippie. She wore a swishy, see-through skirt that only the coolest chick in the world could pull off, and a top with puffy sleeves. Her long hair, mostly gray, was braided down her back, held back by a headband that looked like something Ava made in summer camp.

"May we walk with you?" she asked. "The dogs need a little air."

"Um, sure. It's a free and open beach."

"But I only walk with people who want me."

Ava gave a shaky smile. "It's fine."

"Thank you." She put Sugar back down, but the dog never left Lovely's side. "She's a Westie," Lovely explained. "Very attached."

"And the other two?" Ava asked.

"Basil is a Jack Russell, who is one hundred percent committed to getting his work done, whatever it may be. And sweet Pepper is a Cairn, my protector. They are my three terriers, and I love them desperately."

Pepper plodded along ahead of them, literally waddling on what looked like two-inch legs. But Basil led the way, stopping occasionally to turn and make sure they were behind.

"Slow down, Basil," Lovely called. "You know I'm learning this whole walking thing all over again."

Ava slowed her step, too, and took a look at the woman, once again reminded of Grandma Janet. Not that they were anything alike, except both in their seventies.

Grandma had been a classic church lady with puffy white hair, and she never wore anything but knit pantsuits and pajamas. Certainly not a maxi skirt in the morning.

"But I'm getting better," Lovely said. "Walking a little more every day."

"I heard you had a bad accident." Ava almost didn't

want to know, because she hated picturing those things, but curiosity got the best of her. "What happened?"

"Before or after?"

She wasn't sure she understood the question. "How did the accident happen?"

"Oh, a dumb left turn."

"Ugh," Ava said, dropping her head back. "I dread those things." In fact, she'd skipped most Driver's Ed classes for that very reason. "It must have been bad because I heard you were in a wheelchair."

"Oh, I was, but it wasn't bad at all. I went to heaven."

Ava froze mid-step and stared at her, mostly because there was no laugh or tease in her voice. She was dead serious. "You did?"

"Well, my version of it. I did see my parents and my sister. That was nice."

"You saw *dead* people?"

Still, not even a single chuckle. "I did, and it was wonderful. Liberating. Informative."

Is that how she'd feel if she went to heaven and saw Mom and Adam? Informed? Or safe? "And when you came back, were you even more sad than when they died?" Ava asked. "Like, did you miss them all over again?"

Lovely thought about that for a moment. "No, not really. I had peace and, in the case of my sister, I had direction. She gave me permission to do something I'd always wanted to do but had promised her I wouldn't."

Ava looked at her expectantly, waiting for more.

"You can ask Beck," Lovely said with a smile. "I've talked enough about me. Tell me about you. What do you young people do for fun these days?"

She shrugged. "You know, the usual."

"Do you have a boyfriend?"

"No. I liked a boy last year, though."

"Oh? What happened?"

They'd gone to the fair, got stuck on the top of the Ferris wheel for what felt like eight hours but was probably two minutes, and he got really freaked out when Ava couldn't breathe and started to cry. "He had no heart," she said simply.

"Oh, darling." Lovely put a hand on her arm. "You are wise beyond your years. I'm so encouraged to hear you say that."

"Full disclosure, Lovely? I didn't realize it. My Grandma Janet did when I told her the story. She said, 'Dump the bum, he has no heart,' and I did."

"I think I would have loved this woman."

"I sure did," Ava said softly, the three-week-old pain still raw.

"What else do you do for fun?" Lovely asked, clearly making an easy change of subject.

"Well, I like to shop," she said. "I like clothes."

"Oh, so do I. And if I had your body, I'd never stop."

Ava smiled. "Well, it does require money, so..."

"What do you like to wear? Shorts like you have on now?"

Ava felt her muscles soften a little as she relaxed with the lady. "I actually like your skirt. The whole sixties vibe."

"You like this?" She fluttered her skirt. "Oh, my gosh, child, I have an attic full and much of it *is* from the sixties."

"Really?"

Lovely stopped—and of course, Sugar did, too—and turned to her. "Upstairs in Coquina House, there are probably two suitcases of my old clothes that are tie-died and flowery and, oh, my, the peasant tops." She touched the little sleeves on her shoulders. "I loved them."

"I love them, too."

"Then you should have them all," she said, her eyes, just as green as Ava's, flashing with excitement. "Let's pluck through the whole lot and find you some clothes. I was about your size back in the day."

"Seriously? We could do that?"

"Let's go right now!" She put an arm around Ava and gave a squeeze, unaware that a touch like that was one more thing that could make Ava panic. Instantly, she jerked away from Lovely's arm so that didn't happen.

"You don't want to?" Lovely asked, misinterpreting Ava's move.

"No, no, I just...I'm not a hugger."

"That's fine, but..." Lovely tipped her head in the direction of the house where Beck lived. Coquina House, they called it. "Let's go shopping. It'll be fun."

Yes, it would. And she'd probably regret this one night when she was back in Atlanta, lonely and scared and sad that people like Lovely were here in Florida and she wasn't.

But she just couldn't resist the offer. "Sure. Let's go."

"Fabulous! Come on, doggies! We're going shopping in Lovely's Attic!"

"That actually sounds like a real store," Ava said.

"Doesn't it?" Very carefully, almost so slyly Ava didn't notice, the woman hooked her arm into Ava's.

"Just for support," she whispered before Ava could slip away from her touch.

"Okay." She couldn't let the old lady walk without support.

But their arms were still linked when they reached the beach house, and Ava wondered who was supporting who.

CHAPTER SEVEN
PEYTON

"*I* have extra spiny lobster that you can make for me." Val walked into the restaurant kitchen with his usual bag of iced fish and a sweet smile and that vague scent of the sea that clung to him after he'd been out on his trawler. "Or would that be shellfish of me to ask?"

He grinned and Peyton cracked up. "Do your bad fish jokes never rest?" she asked.

"Never." He lifted the bag. "Your boss wanted a tuna delivery." His gaze dropped to the black bean relish she was stirring at the prep station. "God, there is nothing sexier to a Cuban man than a woman making black beans."

"File that under things I never thought I'd hear a man say to me."

He notched his head toward the walk-in cooler. "Meet me in the fridge, gorgeous, and I'll say more."

She laughed lightly, but only to cover the decidedly feminine response that Val Sanchez's flirting always caused inside her. But it was just flirting, and she had to remember that. She'd seen him flirt with other women at the restaurant, too. Not overtly, not like a skeevy player, but he was charming and funny and unexpectedly sweet. And so stinkin' handsome.

So, women were drawn to him like moths to light. Peyton sure was, and that was both terrifying and thrilling. But the invitation for a kiss in the cooler was really tempting because she knew exactly how that beautiful mouth felt on hers. The first time he kissed her, pretty much all other kisses—including those of Greg McAllister, the man she longed to marry just a few short months ago—were forever forgotten.

That whole New York existence was pretty much forgotten since she'd moved to Coconut Key. Midtown mornings, the dreary publishing job, and the commitment-phobic millionaire she thought she was supposed to love were all distant memories now. Instead, she lived in an old beach house with her mother, worked in a restaurant kitchen as a junior line cook, and had a crush on a fisherman.

Some might say "how the mighty have fallen." But Peyton just said...this was a heck of a lot better.

"No fridge rendezvous," she teased him. "If I screw up this relish for the photo shoot tonight, Jesse and Savannah will never forgive me. Just leave your delivery. If you're very nice, I might save you some."

"Chuck's is closed tonight?" He gave her a confused look and lowered his bag of fish a little. "I thought Jessie was adding Thursday nights to the schedule. It feels like this restaurant is closed more than it's open."

Peyton sighed and put down the wooden spoon. "Business is down, so…"

"So that's when you stay open and build it up. Simple economics, don't you think?"

"It's not about what I think," she said. "It's Jessie's restaurant. She figures if we're closed, she doesn't have to buy the food or pay the staff."

"But if you're not open, you can't get customers."

She shrugged. "You know what's going on, Val. Coconut Tropics, that new restaurant owned by Tag Jadrien?"

"I know who he is, and I know the restaurant."

"Well, ever since they opened, it's hit Chuck's hard. This is a small market and it's tough for two high-end restaurants to compete."

He nodded. "High supply and low demand. The theory that guides the entire economy."

She was a little surprised that a fisherman in the Keys who made bad puns went right to an economics theory, but Val had built a solid business out of the sea, and she knew he was smart.

"I'm really hoping we can get some marketing traction with Jessie's cookbook, but I don't know if that'll be enough."

He glanced around, as if someone else might hear him. "Coconut Tropics isn't shuttering on weeknights, that's for sure," he said in a low voice. "The inventory manager called me yesterday. Tag heard my catch is the best in the Keys, and so are my prices. They want to become customers."

"Wow, getting that restaurant as a client is great for your business, Val," Peyton said. "But not for this one."

"Get that cookbook done, Peyton, and I'll help you distribute copies to every hotel, inn, and B&B in the Keys. Reaching tourists is going to help build that demand side of the equation."

She nodded and looked back down at the beans, hoping he was right.

"Hey," Val said softly. "No floundering around your fisherman."

She laughed, shaking her head, then her smile faltered as his words hit. "*My* fisherman?" She hated that her heart hitched a little. "Are you saying I've *hooked* you, Mr. Sanchez?" She winked to keep it light with the constant fish banter that had been the thing that first got them laughing when they'd met.

For a moment, he looked uncertain. Just a little surprised, even, by the possibility of it. Then he gave her one of those toe-curling smiles, which was his go-to when he didn't know what to say. "Call me after the photo shoot?" he asked.

She angled her head. "Why do I think you only want me for my black bean relish?"

Laughing, he disappeared into the back, and she uncurled her toes and tried to think straight.

She couldn't do it again. She couldn't fall for another guy who just wanted a good time or even a girlfriend. But asking for more made her feel desperate and there was nothing she hated as much as a desperate woman.

She wasn't desperate. She just didn't want to spend her thirties as a single woman. Was that wrong? Did that make her old-fashioned or lame or pathetic?

Peyton didn't think so. She really thought wanting a husband and family made her normal and healthy. But here she was, starting over. After more than two years with Greg, and a fairly long relationship before that. Why couldn't Peyton find that magic of forever?

When she finished the relish and worked with Jessie on some of the dishes they were going to include in the cookbook, she managed to put Val out of her mind for a while. Focused on a project she really believed in, Peyton joined Savannah, Jessie, and their newest assistant, young Ava, on the "set" that they'd created outside on the restaurant's covered patio.

"The light is perfect," Savannah exclaimed, holding a professional-grade camera at the table they'd set. "Not quite as good as early morning, but this late afternoon works well, too."

Peyton studied her sister while Jessie fussed over the food on the table, resetting the wine and straightening the silverware about six times. Peyton hadn't been thrilled to learn that Savannah was pregnant and planning to live in Coconut Key, especially when this news came as Peyton was telling her mom that she and Greg had broken up.

Of course Savannah stole the spotlight—and Mom's attention—with her pregnancy. Peyton had arrived broken and ready to go head-to-head with her younger sister, which was their usual mode.

But pregnancy had changed Savannah just enough to make her more than tolerable. She wasn't talking about the baby's father, except to say he was "a professional liar" and give the impression he was not going to be in the baby's life for reasons she wasn't willing to share.

That certainly made Peyton less envious of her sister's pregnancy, and made Savannah's situation a little heart-breaking. Add to that the fact that Peyton really needed a cheap photographer for the cookbook and Savannah would work for foot rubs, the co-habitation hadn't been so bad.

"Oooh, look at that shot," Savannah exclaimed, kneeling down to get a close-up of the table.

"That's *Cuisine of the Keys* cover-worthy," Peyton said, putting her editorial hat on.

Jessie looked up, a frown pulling as she brushed back some soft waves that always escaped her ponytail. She was exactly the same age as Peyton's mother, but she seemed younger, somehow. Maybe because she'd never been a mother.

They'd talked a lot about that, and the hole in Jessie's heart when she confessed how much pain infertility had caused her. That conversation had only made Peyton more determined not to settle for less than her dreams of marriage and motherhood, if possible.

"You think?" Jessie asked. "I thought we'd have to do conch on the cover."

"Peyton's right," Savannah said from behind the lens, speaking words Peyton had heard few times in her life. "This is the money shot. Look at this." She gestured for Ava to come closer, and Peyton suspected it was more to include the girl than show her the shot. "Look at the sparkle on that wine glass."

"But aren't you selling food?" Ava asked.

Savannah lowered the camera and shot her a look, fighting a smile. "Yes, little grasshopper, we are, but we are also selling the vibe. The atmosphere and experience. Look at the view in the background and the sunlight sparkling on the wine glass."

"Did you spray the fish with motor oil like you said?" Ava asked.

"She's not doing that to my food," Jessie said. "That's just for ads, anyway. This is a cookbook, and we don't want people to think they failed when their food doesn't look like the picture, right, Peyton?"

"As the editor and recipe-tester of this project, I'd agree," Peyton said. "But as the one-person marketing department of Chuck's Fine Dining? I think it's really important that we remember the reason we're publishing a cookbook. 'Cause we need it more than ever, I think."

"What do you mean?" Jessie asked, concern in her eyes.

And instantly Peyton knew she'd said too much.

"Just, you know. Things are slow. You said so yourself."

Jessie gnawed on her lower lip, stepping away from the table setting to let Savannah take pictures. "What do you know that I don't?" she whispered to Peyton.

"As the low man on the totem pole of Chuck's staff? Not much."

"Tag's hitting Val up for product, isn't he?" Jessie guessed.

Peyton made a face. "He said I shouldn't tell you."

"You didn't. I already knew. One of my friends in the restaurant supply store told me Tag's been spending more time up here than down at his Key West location." She closed her eyes on a sigh. "Just tell him to be careful."

"Of what? Selling to Tag?"

Jessie shot a look that Peyton couldn't begin to interpret. "Never mind," she said. "He won't make that mistake twice."

"What mistake?" Peyton asked.

"Nothing. Just me...worrying, that's all."

"Don't worry," Peyton assured her. "The cookbook's going to be the best marketing you have. And isn't going to cost much at all, I promise."

"Why would he do this to me?"

"Who? Val? He can't turn away business like that. It'll just go to a competitor."

"No, Tag." Jessie shook her head, her dark eyes cloudy as she looked away.

"I doubt it's personal, Jessie. He didn't come to Coconut Key to put you out of business."

Jessie just closed her eyes for a second, silent on the subject.

"I can tell Val you don't think he should take the business, Jessie, but—"

"Don't be silly," she said quickly. "You don't do anything to hurt Val. Ever since he showed up on this island a few years ago, Val has been working his butt off to build his business. I'd never hurt him. It's just I feel like I'm in over my head and with that new restaurant, I'm drowning."

"That's why we're working so hard on this cookbook."

"The cookbook isn't going to save the restaurant," she said glumly.

"It's going to help. Look at that table. Can Tag Jadrien do better?"

Jessie shrugged. "Sometimes I think I shouldn't have gone the fine dining route. It was for Chuck, you know? I just wanted to bake scones and have a café but...Chuck thought I was better than that and I wanted to honor him."

"Really?" Peyton studied her, taking in this new bit of information. "I thought you loved cooking gourmet food."

"I love cooking, but..." She sighed. "When Chuck was killed and I discovered he left me insurance to start my dream restaurant, I wanted it to be what he wanted, and he always thought what Coconut Key needed was a classy, fancy place with me as chef. Apparently, they did. They just want a *famous* chef to go with it." She blinked back a tear and stared at the table. "Can I fix that napkin, Savannah? It's crooked."

"Touch a thing and you're dead."

That broke the tension, making everyone laugh, even Ava, who stood a few feet away, her arms crossed. Peyton took a few steps to join her.

"So, how do you like Coconut Key so far?" Peyton asked.

"It's pretty good," she said, fluttering the bottom of a sweet blue tunic top she wore over skinny jeans. "I went shopping in Lovely's attic today."

"I've never been there...wait. Our Lovely? Her actual attic?"

Savannah lowered the camera and eyed Ava. "You're wearing Lovely's clothes?"

"She took me up there. Beck came, too. I got, like, three tops and two dresses that would have cost twenty bucks in the vintage place in Atlanta that I love. They are, like, legit from the sixties and seventies."

Savannah made a face at Peyton. "She never gave us any clothes."

"Just a gorgeous house to live in," Peyton reminded her.

"True that." Savannah returned to the photos.

"Have you been able to enjoy what makes the Keys wonderful yet?" Peyton asked Ava. "There's incredible snorkeling right on the other side of Coquina House."

Her eyes widened and she shook her head. "I can't swim."

"Take one of the skiffs out," she said. "Those are the boats tied up on the dock on the western edge of the Coquina House property. Or one of the kayaks. We can go tomorrow, if you want."

She looked a little like Peyton suggested swimming with the sharks. "No thanks."

"Well, then how about a tour of town?"

"I guess."

"She sounds thrilled with rowboats and shell shops," Savannah said, throwing a look at Peyton. "Do you not remember being fifteen? How 'bout a trip to Key West, Ava? Now *that* would be fun."

"Key West?" Ava's eyes lit up. Of course Savannah had the magic. "Is it close?"

"Twenty-five miles south," Savannah said. "Let's go tonight."

"Tonight?" Ava's whole body language changed. "We'd be allowed?"

"Contrary to the fact that we actually live with our mother, Pey and I are adults, so yes." Savannah lowered the camera and pointed at the table. "Someone turn the plate about two inches to the left so I can see that gorgeous relish a little more. I say we go tonight so you can tell all your friends you've been to Key West. You up for it, Peyton?"

She was supposed to call Val when this shoot was

over, but maybe it wouldn't hurt to play a little, tiny bit hard to get. "I'm in."

"Jessie?" Savannah looked at her. "You want to bring your cheery mood to Duval Street?"

Jessie smiled because, with Savannah, how could you do anything else? "Sure, why not? I was just going to hang out with Lovely and Beck tonight. They're meeting with the kitchen designer to go over some new kitchen ideas for the B&B, and my brother'll be there."

"Why would he meet with the designer?" Peyton asked.

"Because Mom is there," Savannah shot back with a grin.

"He might be making a piece for the new kitchen," Jessie said.

"And because Mom is there," Savannah repeated.

"Does he like her?" Ava asked. "Are they, like, a thing?"

Peyton, Savannah, and Jessie all shared a look, then started laughing.

"It's too soon to say," Peyton told Ava. "And my mother is getting through a rough divorce, so she's not ready to see anyone."

"But, yes, to answer your original question, Ava," Savannah said. "They could be a thing. Anyone with eyes can see that."

"And Josh is your brother?" Ava asked Jessie. "Sorry, I'm trying to keep everyone straight."

"He is, and he does like her, and she likes him back," Jessie said. "I know this because I'm the best friend who decided those two should get married when we were nine years old, ensuring Beck would be my sister."

"Wait...I'm confused," Ava said on a laugh. "You guys were friends as kids?"

Savannah got a little closer to Ava and put a light arm around her shoulder. "Let's go to Key West, and I'll fill you in on all the Coconut Key dirt. Who likes who, who knows who, who was whose secret baby. Auntie Savannah knows all and tells all."

Ava laughed lightly and gracefully stepped out of Savannah's arm. "Okay, that'd be fun."

"Then count me in," Jessie said. "If anyone is going to give this girl the whole story of all those people, it's me. I'm the one who knows everyone and everything."

"Girls' night out!" Savannah exclaimed, giving Ava a high five and somehow making them all excited the way only Savannah could.

CHAPTER EIGHT
BECK

"*I* can't even put into words how much I love this." Beck ran her fingers over the teal and white scallops on the ceramic sample. "It captures the sea and the color palette and the whole beach vibe I want so much in Coquina House."

"And that's not even the most expensive, so good choice." Maggie Karras, the young, bright, and extremely talented designer, pinned an ebony gaze on Beck. "And I agree that it pulls everything together."

"And you're sure about Shaker cabinets?" At the other end of the huge kitchen table, currently covered with samples of at least four different cabinets, tiles, flooring, and door pulls, Josh looked a little skeptical. "I know it's a clean line, but..." He curled his lip. "Not enough soul."

Next to him, Lovely laughed. "That's our Josh, a man who thinks wood has soul."

Well, he was a "master woodworker," even if he just called himself a glorified carpenter. "Based on his work,"

Beck said, smiling at him, "I think he's right. I could be talked into a different style."

Maggie looked from one to the other, angling her head diplomatically. "The raised crown is gorgeous, and, Josh is right, the Shaker is plain. But, in this kitchen, the view is king." She stood and headed to the sliding doors that went out to the patio, the view of the ocean almost gone in the waning light. "With the French doors we're putting in here, your guests are going to see nothing but amazing sunrises when they come down for breakfast. That's the soul of this kitchen." She crossed the room to the bank of windows. "And, in the evening, sunsets over the mangroves out there. No one is going to think about your cabinets, and honestly, we don't want them to."

She was absolutely right and not a soul in the room could argue with that.

"Then we're done here," Maggie said, turning back to the table. "I'm going to leave these samples because sometimes things look different after a good night's sleep. I'll zip by sometime this weekend and pick them up."

"That sounds great, Maggie." Beck stood and reached for the backsplash sample again, already visualizing how glorious the kitchen would be. And it would be the heart of the B&B she and Lovely wanted to run. "But I don't think my mind is going to change. How about you, Love?"

"I adore every inch of it," her mother said, but then let out a sigh. "But I'm afraid it's going to be next Christmas until it's done."

Maggie grunted softly as she gathered up her bag. "I sure hope you're wrong. But maybe there's some stuff you can start."

"Without a contractor?" Beck asked.

"You could do a certain amount of demo," she said. "With a really good carpenter, you could actually follow my plan and not need a GC. You're not changing egress, windows, plumbing, or electrical, so you don't technically have to file plans with the county. That comes later when you redo the bathroom in the attic."

"I know a good carpenter..." Beck looked at Josh.

"Beck, you know I would in a heartbeat," he said. "But this just isn't what I do. Not well, anyway." He blew out a breath. "I'll help you any way I can, but someone has to know how to gather the right trades or do the work themselves. This is too important to you guys to do half-assed."

Beck nodded, appreciating his honesty. "Well, we're on the waiting lists for four good contractors."

"In the meantime," Maggie said, flashing a smile as pretty as the work she did, "I'll write up the paperwork and we'll get everything ready to order so we can move at lightning speed when we get a GC."

"I'll walk you out," Beck said, standing to join her.

"Please. Relax. I know where the front door is. You guys pour a glass of wine, mull over your decisions, and I'll text you before I come back this weekend." She blew a kiss and added that blinding smile, heading out to the front room.

"I love her," Beck said.

"I heard that!" Maggie called, making them all laugh as she closed the front door behind her.

"She does good work," Josh agreed. "Several of my clients have used her." His work on one-of-a-kind furniture put him in touch with many of the top contractors, builders, and designers in the Keys. And sadly, even he couldn't help them.

"But a designer without a contractor is like having the perfect outfit to wear, but no party to go to." Beck stood and headed to the fridge. "And speaking of party, who wants a glass of wine? And dinner? It's just us since the gang took off to Key West."

"Are you jealous you couldn't go?" Lovely asked, eyeing her with that keen understanding that she always seemed to have.

"Maybe a little," Beck admitted with a smile. "But this meeting was too important, and I'm glad the girls are bonding. Savannah is so great with Ava and..." Beck frowned as she heard the front door open and close again. "Did someone just come in?" She headed right to the dining room and around the corner, coming face to face with Maggie who looked a little flushed.

"Did you forget something?"

"Uh, my name after I met that man down there?"

"What man?" Beck looked beyond her as if someone might come bounding into the door.

"A contractor."

"Seriously?" Beck choked. "One just fell from heaven?"

"He's in a builder's truck with tools and was wearing a T-shirt from a flooring company and he *definitely* fell from heaven, so I think you're off a waiting list and about to hire that GC."

Beck shook her head, completely confused. "I wasn't expecting anyone." Especially not at seven in the evening.

"He's just sitting in his truck down in front of your house, so I asked if he needed anything and he said he was looking for someone named Rebecca Foster. And if he's the contractor?" Maggie flipped some long dark hair over her shoulder with a sassy wink. "Then I'm gonna look my best for every meeting."

Beck nodded toward the door. "Come on, let's go find out what this angel's name is."

"I got his name," she said. "We talked for a minute. I think I talked. I might have just wobbled on knees weakened by attraction. He asked me to tell you he's here."

He did? "I can't wait to meet this guy who makes your knees weak. What's his name?"

"Kenny Gallagher."

"Ken..." Beck could feel the blood drain from her face. "Excuse me?" she barely breathed the word.

"Do you know him? He's not the contractor? Color me disappointed."

"Color me...shocked." *Again.* She tried to breathe, pressing her hands to her chest. "I can't believe he came here. I can't believe I'm about to..." *Meet him.*

"Who is he?" she asked.

Beck blinked, swallowed, and managed to whisper words she never really thought she'd ever say out loud. "He's my son."

🌴

STEADYING HERSELF, Beck gripped handrail as she walked down the stairs from the porch of the stilt house, her gaze skimming the large white pick-up truck parked at the end of Coquina Court. No one was in the driver's seat, and Beck didn't know if that made her disappointed or relieved.

Half of her was dying to look at him, touch him, and revel in this man she'd given birth to nearly forty years ago. Half of her wanted to run, hide, and do what she'd done for almost all of those years: forget he ever happened.

But there was no man down here.

Maggie had kindly suggested she join the others in the kitchen and allow Beck to greet her...guest. No doubt they were filling her in on Beck's teenaged pregnancy, and how his daughter, Beck's granddaughter, had come to Coconut Key yesterday.

Beck turned and peered toward the sunset, which was at its glorious peak now, painting the mangroves and palm trees that lined the canal in shades of peach and orange with streaks of purple. There, she saw the silhouette of a man, gazing out to appreciate what locals never took for granted and tourists paid a lot to see.

That man was her son.

She walked closer and as she did, he turned at the sound of her sneakers on the broken coquina shells along the road. When she got her first look at him, she somehow managed not to gasp.

It was Billy Dobson all over again. She instantly remembered the boy who took her virginity, with his dark hair and dreamy eyes, a cleft in his chin and a strong nose.

This man was taller than the boy she remembered, and broader, and, of course, more than twice the age of the young boy who worked his way into Beck's heart... and jeans.

"Hello," she said, her voice taut. "Are you Kenny?"

He stepped closer, making it even easier to see him. He didn't smile, and his gaze was cool, bordering on cold. Or maybe that was fear.

"Rebecca?" he asked.

She brushed back some hair, vaguely glad she'd put on some makeup and blew her hair dry for the meeting with Maggie. She didn't want his first impression of her not to be a good one.

"I go by Beck," she reminded him as she came closer, surprised at how tall he was, easily over six feet. Not quite sure what to do, she extended her hand. "Nice to meet you."

He hesitated just one second, then lifted his hand, darn near swallowing hers in a massive grip. He opened his mouth to say something, but just let out a little breath and gave her hand more of a squeeze than a shake.

"I've come for Ava," he said.

She let her hand drop with a thud as the real reason for his arrival hit her heart. Of course he wasn't here to meet her. That was just a byproduct. He was here as a father, not a son, and she needed to remember that and not get swept away in yet another family reunion.

Anyway, it was easy to see from his expression that he did not want to be here.

"She's lovely," Beck said, just letting herself be the only thing she could be in this situation—honest. "We've really enjoyed getting to know her."

His eyes narrowed a little as he looked past her. "Where is she?"

Oh, boy. Beck hadn't exactly thought this through, had she? Well, she hadn't expected him to show up out of the blue and unannounced. "Um, actually she's not here."

An imperceptible flash lit his dark eyes. "Where is she?" he repeated with a tinge of impatience.

"She's with my daughters and another woman, a local chef. All very safe and sound, I promise."

This time his eyes shuttered. "Where is she, Rebecca?"

"It's Beck, and she's in Key West this evening."

"What?" He drew back. "My fifteen-year-old is in Key West?"

"It's fine, really. She's with my daughters. They're adults. They're having..." Fun. "Bonding time with their niece."

"Well, we need to get her back here as soon as possible so I can take her home," he said on a slight huff. "It's an eleven-hour drive."

"You can't leave tonight," she said. "I don't know when they'll be back and—"

"Can you call one of your daughters and get them back here, or do you have no way to reach them?"

Beck felt her shoulders square as she looked up at the stranger and tried to remember who was the parent here. "Kenny," she said. "My daughters are perfectly safe and very protective of Ava."

"They met her yesterday."

"They have good hearts and great brains and they won't let anything happen to her." She lifted her chin. "You, on the other hand, shipped your daughter off to an aunt who has so little control she didn't even know that Ava took an Uber two and half hours to meet a complete stranger. So I will thank you not to insinuate that I would let anything happen to that girl who is, whether you like it or not, my granddaughter."

He flicked an eyebrow and almost smiled. Almost. "You just reminded me of her."

"Blood," she said. "It's thick. So thick, in fact, that I'm going to pull the mom card. I'd like very much if you would remove the chip from your shoulder, come into my home, and take some time to get to know me and let me get to know you."

Now he smiled, a slow affair that was probably the reason Maggie had been so flushed. "The chip's permanent," he said as his whole expression softened. "But I see where I get my attitude."

She smiled back at him. "Attitude maybe, but not all that dark hair and..." She gestured toward his substantial body. "And after eleven hours in the car, you must be hungry. If there's one thing a mother can do, it's feed her son. Come on. And, yes, I'll call my daughters and let them know what's going on."

"Are you going to warn Ava that I'm here?" he asked as he walked with her.

"Do you want me to?"

He puffed out a breath. "Oh, hell, with that kid? I never know what to do."

"Well, you came after her. And I'm guessing that's a very strong message about how much you love her."

As they reached the steps, he eyed her, holding back for a moment. "I guess I should say thank you for being so nice to her."

Yeah, he should have. First and foremost. But she'd done enough mothering to this stranger for one night. "It was easy. She's very sweet."

He gave a soft laugh. "Are we talking about Ava Gallagher, here? Did I come to the wrong house?"

"She's a little...shy," Beck said. "Not much of a hugger."

"You hugged her and lived?"

She laughed as they walked up the stairs. "We hugged her. We dressed her in vintage clothes. And now she's doing a little sightseeing with her aunts. It's what families do."

He paused again, closing his eyes as if her words really affected him. "That's what she needs more than anything," he whispered. "Family."

"Well, here you are, *son*." She put a hand on his shoulder and added some pressure. "And you are as welcome as she was."

"Thank you...Beck."

CHAPTER NINE

AVA

*B*y the time they'd walked down Duval Street—and had Key Lime pie *before* dinner—and joined a crowd in Mallory Square to celebrate the sunset, Ava was a goner. For the first time in years, actual, literal *years*, she was having fun. Every minute was better than the one before it.

The whole place buzzed with excitement and color, with wild people and cute little pedicabs and trolleys full of tourists.

Jessie was practically a local who knew everything from where to get a secret parking spot behind a church to how to bypass the tours and see the gardens of the oldest house in South Florida. With just a few hours, she promised a "quickie tour" for Ava, but they were a few hours she'd never forget.

Peyton and Savannah—the aunties, as they giddily called themselves—flanked Ava on every crowded street, making her feel protected and, well, loved. Obviously, that wasn't possible, but it was easy to feel that way tonight. Peyton was like a mother, constantly making sure Ava saw this or noticed that, but gently touching her back before they crossed the street. It was sweet.

And Savannah was more like a fun-loving big sister who never lacked for a joke or line of snark, cracking all of them up with her irreverent comments and observations.

Dressed in her hippie great-grandmother's clothes and hundreds of miles from the sadness that surrounded her in Atlanta, Ava felt happy and free and like she was right where she belonged. And she felt so safe that not for one second did her heart pound or her chest squeeze.

This was the opposite of a panic...this was bliss.

"Oh, and what do we have here?" Savannah stopped them all in the middle of a side street off Duval in front of a big white building with bright green wooden shutters, with tables full of diners on an outside patio. "The restaurant known as Tropics."

"Also called..." Peyton slid a look to Jessie. "Home of the devil."

"I think we should find out what all the fuss is about, don't you?" Savannah asked the group in general, but Jessie was the one who answered with a vehement shake of her head.

"We are not going in there."

"Just to see the place?" Savannah said. "Don't you want to know what you're up against?"

"I'm up against a satellite restaurant in Coconut Key that happens to be owned by the same chef. And I'm not giving him a dime of my money."

"I'll buy," Peyton said, getting a surprised look from Jessie. "I want to know what's so great about this guy's cooking. I want to know why people who used to come to Chuck's are all ga-ga over his new place. And I'm learning to cook as a profession now, Jessie, and I want to experience this guy's menu."

Jessie crossed her arms and took a slow, deep breath. She looked from Savannah to Peyton, giving Ava a chance to study the woman's expression and try to figure out what the heck was going on. She knew it was something about another restaurant, but no more.

Silent, Jessie pulled back a handful of her dark waves, giving Ava a chance to see what a truly pretty lady she was. Even though she was in her mid-fifties, she didn't wear much makeup so you could see she had a light dusting of freckles on her nose. She was what Grandma Janet would call wholesome, the kind of pretty that came from the inside, from being a really nice person.

Best of all, Jessie had a really wide smile that lit up her whole face. But she wasn't smiling now. Not one bit.

"I just can't take a chance of seeing him."

"So you *do* know him!" Peyton seemed stunned by this. "Like you've met him in person?"

"Yes, Peyton, I've met him in person."

"And he knows you by name?" Peyton shook her head. "I mean, all the time we've talked about Coconut Tropics and this famous Chef Tag Jadrien, and you've never mentioned it?"

"What kind of name is Tag Jadrien?" Ava asked, intrigued. "Sounds like a video game character."

"Tag is short for Taggert, it's a family name. Jadrien is

not even his last name. That's his middle name, which is a blend of Jay and Adrienne, his parents. His real last name is Lutwack, I kid you not."

"Wait." Savannah snorted. "Lut...what?"

"Lutwack."

Ava giggled and elbowed her. "You don't even have to make one up for that name."

Savannah answered by reaching up to give Ava a high-five, which felt so much better than it should have because it was like they really were sisters.

But Savannah's real sister, Peyton, was staring at Jessie with her mouth hanging wide open. "You know all of this...how?"

Jessie closed her eyes. "I went to high school with the guy, okay?"

"You did?" Peyton practically choked.

"Yes, so what, Peyton? I know him. We met in Home Ec class." She looked at Ava. "Do they still have that?"

She shrugged. "I've never heard of it, so I'm going with no. Home...what?"

"Economics. You know, where you learn to cook, sew, and balance a checkbook?" Jessie asked.

"I think that's called Family Sciences now," Ava said.

"You went to high school with him?" Peyton was super stuck on this, enough that Savannah just pushed them all toward the door.

"Get over it, Pey. She doesn't tell you everything. And since you're paying, let's go in and get apps. Pink Line is starving, and Ava and I are going to stalk the kitchen to see if we can catch a sight of Taggy Lutwack." She threw Ava a look. "You're right. No challenge."

She managed to usher them all in and they got a booth up front in the bar, which felt incredibly grown up to Ava. She and Savannah ordered ginger ale and then took a walk to the bathroom, but couldn't get anywhere near the kitchen.

"He's probably not here anyway," Savannah said as they washed their hands and talked to each other in the mirror. "But Peyton's sure bent out of shape."

"I guess since she works for Jessie, she thought she should know." Ava shrugged and smoothed her hair, absolutely loving this moment with Savannah, who was cool and hilarious and made her feel so comfortable.

"There are too many secrets in this place," Savannah said. "First we find out my mother had a baby at sixteen and we have a niece." She jabbed Ava's shoulder. "Who rocks purple hair and the Woodstock top. But this is on the heels of finding out my great-aunt is really my grandmother."

"What?" Ava turned to her, trying to figure out who Savannah's grandmother was. "Lovely? You just found that out?"

"Oh, yeah. She gave my mother up at birth to her older sister to raise, and my mom just found out a few months ago."

Ava's jaw dropped like Peyton's had outside.

"Right? And now Jessie knows her competition. And did you see the way her eyes looked? The little flush in her cheeks?"

Actually, Ava hadn't noticed, but she didn't know the lady that well.

"Mark my words, grasshopper, she's hiding more. And

I intend to find out what. Come on." She gestured toward the door. "Let's go see if she'll spill."

Ava didn't know what she liked more—being in on the family secrets or having an actual nickname. Grasshopper. It made her smile.

She was still smiling at the table while they devoured shrimp—not oysters, thank God, because Pink Line wasn't allowed to have uncooked fish. Then Ava had her first bite of a conch fritter and could kind of see what all the fuss was about. Except Jessie curled her lip at the sauce.

"Would it have killed him to use a whisper of horse-radish?" she asked before popping the bite in her mouth.

"Would it kill you to tell us the whole story of your relationship with Taggy?" Savannah narrowed her eyes at Peyton. "Didn't Callie have a stuffed cat called Taggy?"

"A tiger," Peyton corrected. "Mom had to throw it away because Callie kept tearing the seams and eating the stuffing."

"Eww." Ava made a face. "Who's Callie? Your dog?"

Savannah laughed so hard she almost choked.

"Your third aunt, who is almost your age," Peyton explained. "Callie's our little sister. She's nineteen and in college, beating the world, being perfect."

"Except for when she ate stuffed animals," Savannah said. "Which was the last thing she did that was less than perfect, but I love her anyway."

"And she's nineteen?" Ava asked. "She's only four years older than me. How is that possible?"

"She was Mom and Dad's special surprise when I was ten," Savannah said. "And that made her my own personal baby doll."

"Can I meet her?" Ava asked.

"When you get back to Atlanta," Savannah said. "She goes to Emory University but this summer she's working at our father's law firm, where she has worked every summer and Christmas break since her fingers could reach a keyboard. I think she has her own office with a view."

"Oh, impressive," Ava said.

"Everything about Callie is impressive," Peyton told her. "She's drop-dead gorgeous, flat out brilliant, and beyond ambitious. Like, don't get in her way because Callie is on a mission in life. She wants to be on the Supreme Court someday, and I have no doubt she will."

"Wow." Suddenly, the idea of meeting this superstar was a little less appealing. "And she's only nineteen?"

"Going on forty," Peyton said.

"Don't listen to her," Savannah added. "Callie has her weaknesses, too. I know. I'm one of them. She *adores* me."

Who wouldn't, Ava thought.

"She *tolerates* me," Peyton said. "And it's only gotten worse since Mom and Dad split. She's very close to Dad. Very."

"Whereas Mom and Peyton have always been like this." Savannah pressed her two fingers together. "Which left me, middle child, somewhat alone."

"That's sad," Ava said.

Peyton rolled her eyes. "She makes it sound like we left her behind and went on vacations."

"They brought me for comic relief," Savannah quipped. "But now the whole family is broken and I'm sliding into the cracks." She grinned. "You can fit there, too, grasshopper."

Ava smiled at that, still trying to put all the puzzle pieces together. "So was it a bad divorce for Beck and...?"

"Dan," Savannah said. "Daniel Foster, attorney at law, cheater at heart."

"Oh."

Peyton inched forward to explain. "Our dad left our mother to marry his law partner, a woman named Mari Cummings. It really blindsided Mom and broke her heart."

"He did redeem himself, however." Savannah dipped a fritter in the sauce. "He gave Mom all the money from the sale of their house in Alpharetta, which was very generous and allowed her to turn Coquina House into a B&B, so she has a business and a home." She popped the food in her mouth and raised her eyebrows to Ava. "Told you we'd tell you all the scoop tonight. Too much info about your brand-new family?"

"Well, it's a lot," Ava admitted with a laugh. "My family is just me and my dad and the most exciting thing that happens in our house is watching Wheel of Fortune."

"While ours actually spins." Savannah grinned. "What other gossip do you—"

"Jessica?"

They all stopped and looked up, coming face to face with a tall man wearing a chef's apron.

"Jessica? Is that you?"

"Oh boy," Savannah whispered to Ava under her breath. "Taggy."

Across the table, Jessie sat a little straighter, blinked in surprise, and, whoa, even in the dim restaurant light, Ava could see her whole expression turn hard.

"Hello, Tag," she said.

"You're here." He sounded like he couldn't believe it, maybe a little amused, based on the smile that threatened. He looked old to Ava, with long hair pulled back into a ponytail and those wireless glasses that professors wore sitting low on his nose. "How are you?" he asked, the question not casual like you might ask someone you barely know. This sounded like he really cared how she was.

"I'm fine, thank you."

"I can't believe you're here. I mean, you won't walk into my place in Coconut Key, and you come here?" He sounded a little mad, to be honest.

"Blame us," Savannah said, leaning forward. "We heard the conch fritter sauce didn't have horseradish and I prefer it that way. Are you the celebrity chef, Tag....something?"

"Tag Jadrien," he said with a quick nod, his attention back on Jessie. "You never responded to the messages I left at your restaurant. Did you get them?"

She swallowed so hard, Ava could see her throat across the table. "I did, but we've been busy. Let me introduce you to Peyton, Savannah, and Ava, friends from Coconut Key."

"Hello, ladies." He nodded toward them. "Maybe you'll take advantage of my invitation to visit my new location on your island. Dinner will be on me, as I've promised Jessica but...never heard a response."

He looked at her for a long moment, his dark eyes intense.

"Thank you," Peyton said when no one else answered. "I'm working at Chuck's now, so I may take you up on that. Always good to see what the competition is doing."

"Not competition," he said. "Mutually beneficial businesses. Extremely beneficial. And if you'd ever return a call, Jessica, I could explain how."

"I'm so busy, sorry."

He lifted one brow like...like he knew she wasn't that busy at all. "I'll try again in a few days, okay? I do really want to talk to you."

Jessie just gave him a tight smile, silent.

"Enjoy your appetizers, ladies. I'll be sure they're on the house."

"Oh, that's not—"

But he quieted Jessie with a wave of his hand. "It's my pleasure." Then he nodded goodbye and stepped away, leaving everyone at the table staring at Jessie like she had answers to questions they didn't even know they should be asking.

She lifted her hand before any questions came, but Savannah held up her phone. "Hang on, guys. I just noticed Mom has texted me a whole bunch of times and called twice. I didn't hear it."

Peyton grabbed her phone. "Yikes, me too."

Savannah leaned back and looked at her phone, silent for a moment before she put it face down on the table. "We have to go."

"What's wrong?" Jessie asked, but Savannah had reached over and put her hand on Ava's leg, which normally would have bothered her, but Ava just looked up.

"What?" she whispered, sensing this was about her.

"Your father has driven to Coconut Key to get you."

"Of course he did," she said softly as the news hit. "I knew this was too good to be true."

The other women exchanged silent, unhappy looks as they gathered their stuff to leave.

Ava just crossed her arms and did her best to fight the tears. No panic, just big fat disappointment.

CHAPTER TEN
KENNY

*T*he woman who gave him life was nice. Kenny made a mental note to tell Bill when he got back that the girl who liked his guitar was still quite attractive, easy to talk to, and classy. Wonder what Bill would think of that?

And he wondered what Beck would say if she knew that Kenny not only knew his birth father, he considered him one of his best friends. He had no idea, but gut instinct told him there was no good reason to mention it. His parents had signed some waiver and Bill showed zero desire to meet the woman. Kenny and Bill had a friendship and a working relationship and that was all that mattered. These waters were muddy enough.

Happy with that decision, Kenny sipped the cup of coffee she'd just given him along with instructions to relax on her deck while she got a hold of her daughters.

It hadn't taken much to convince him to eat the sandwich she'd made, after the people visiting bid a fairly hasty goodbye. He'd eaten at this outside table, giving

monosyllabic answers to the few questions that Beck
Foster had asked, and stared at the calm water that
stretched to the horizon as darkness fell.

Beck Foster. His mother. Just thinking those words
felt like a betrayal to the woman who raised him. He
loved his parents as much today as he had growing up.
Janet and Jim Gallagher were the finest humans he'd ever
met—loving, kind, grounded in their faith and family.

He shifted on the lounge chair and blew out a breath,
the sting of losing his mother not even a month ago still
sharp. And if it hurt him, he knew it had wrecked Ava,
who had worshipped her grandmother.

"They're on their way back," Beck said as she stepped
outside, holding her own cup. "And I do so hope that you
will reconsider and stay here tonight. I don't think it's safe
to drive another eleven hours."

He slid her a look as she sat down next to him. "I can
handle it." *Mom.* It was almost implied enough that he
had to smile.

"I'm sure you can, but I'm just thinking about Ava."

"We'll stop at my sister-in-law's in Ft. Lauderdale," he
said. "And Ava will just whine the whole time."

"She doesn't strike me as a whiner, but," she added
quickly, "I raised three daughters so I know how capricious their moods can be."

He wasn't entirely sure what *capricious* meant, but he
had an idea she knew that those moods could swing like
monkeys in the jungle. "I admit, it would have been nice
to have my wife around to manage the moods."

"I'm so sorry you lost her." The sympathy was
genuine, and he angled his head in silent acknowledge-
ment. "Ava said it was a fire?"

He clamped his jaw and nodded.

"Would you like to talk about it?" she asked gently.

"I don't talk about it," he said simply. "Just like Ava doesn't hug. We all have our ways of coping."

"Or *not* coping," she said softly.

He let that hang in the air, took a sip of coffee, then set the cup on the table. "When my wife and son died in a house fire, I was away with Ava on a church camping trip. I'm a part-time EMT at the fire department, and my very own crew at the station couldn't save them, despite heroic efforts. Can you spell guilt and blame and debilitating regret?"

"I know."

"She told you?" He found that hard to believe.

"Not about the guilt and shame and regret. The rest was in your mother's letter to me."

"Yeah, that." He shook his head. "I guarantee you that if my mother had any idea her letter would get Ava to pull a stunt like this, she wouldn't have written it."

"Janet seemed pretty determined to reach me. And she must have communicated that determination to Ava, or she wouldn't have figured out how to do it."

"She's wily, that one. Brilliant, like her mother," he told her. "But honestly, to come up with the idea of spending a month with her aunt? I should have seen right through that. Ava can't stand that woman, who isn't really a relative, since she's Elise's brother's ex-wife, but she's the closest thing to an aunt or sister she has."

"Not anymore," Beck said quietly. "But how could you possibly suspect her reason for wanting to stay the summer in Florida? She's grieving and it's natural."

He shrugged, silently grateful for the support and not

a chastising over what a bad parent he was. He already knew that.

"But then she got in an Uber and came here?" His voice rose with disbelief. "That took a lot of nerve. And God only knows how much money."

"It was fearless," Beck agreed.

"And stupid. She had your mailing address. Put a stamp on the thing and call it a day. Why didn't she do that?"

"I think," Beck said, "that deep down, Janet wanted her to meet me and maybe Ava wanted that, too."

He threw her a look, not sure what to say. Why would she want that? Ava had known he was adopted since she was old enough to understand what that meant. No one ever hid the fact, nor did they hide the fact that the records were sealed and he wanted to keep it that way. That was why they never opened up the can of worms to tell her that Bill Dobson was her grandfather.

Of course, Elise died before she could find that out or it probably wouldn't be a secret. His wife had been curious as hell and ran that DNA test that he found out about later, but Ava showed no interest in that mysterious branch of her family tree. So why now?

"What exactly did that letter say?" he asked.

"Do you want to see it?"

And read his mother's plea for help because he wasn't doing his job? "No, thanks."

She let out a soft breath of resignation. "Janet made a request, and if you take Ava away and back to Atlanta, I can't honor that request."

He eyed her, considering what the hell his mother would ask of a perfect stranger—the woman who gave him to her. "You know, for my mother to track you down by hiring a PI, whatever she wanted must have been serious. That was a bold move for a woman who would normally pray for her answer, not pay for it."

"She came to me as a grandmother. She wanted help with Ava. She said there've been problems since your wife and son died, which is understandable, but—"

"So she asked you, instead of me?" He dragged his fingers through his hair, a bolt of irritation ricocheting through him. "What the hell, Mom?" he muttered under his breath, seeing Janet Gallagher's sweet little face and snow-white hair. Who knew she'd be this...devious?

"She died worried about her granddaughter, whom she obviously loved very much."

"They were pals. Like this." He smashed two fingers together and held them up. "So, what did she want you to do?"

"Just...to love her. I think her phrase was 'break the shell around her heart.' And to be a woman in her life to talk to and, you know, manage those moods."

Mood management was not his strong suit. "She does need that," he admitted.

"But, of course, your mother had no idea I'd moved away from Atlanta, so..."

So her request couldn't be honored. "I'm doing my best," he said gruffly.

"I'm sure you are, Kenny. She's not a lost cause, just a lost girl. I'd be happy to...she's welcome here. For as long as she likes, but..." She reached over and put her hand on his arm. "I can't imagine how hard it would be for you to spend time without her after losing your wife and son. You'd be lonely."

But he'd shipped her off to Elise's sister-in-law's house for as long as that could work. Weeks? A month? All summer? "I don't know," he said.

She pushed up as a beam of car lights lit the garden area below. "Well, you better figure it out because they're home. Why don't I send Ava out here so you can talk privately to her?"

Because Beck had to know if he got Ava near his truck, he'd just take off and put this behind them. But maybe that wasn't the absolutely right parenting move.

"Okay. Thank you."

He was surprised his heart rate had kicked up while he waited, not exactly sure what he was going to say to her.

Aw, Elise, baby. Why did you have to leave me alone in this life?

Ava cleared her throat behind him, almost as if she understood he'd left the building for a moment.

"Hey," he said, standing up and turning to see her narrow silhouette in the sliding glass door.

"Hi, Dad." She didn't smile, but then, she so rarely did.

"Come on out here."

She hesitated for a minute, then walked out to the open air, taking the seat Beck had been in, silent, looking at him, waiting for whatever he would say.

How could he do this differently this time? The question plagued him.

Something about the air out here, the nice lady who turned out to be his real mother, and the request that his beloved mother had made took the wind out of his discipline sails.

"So, how was Key West?" he asked.

She blinked, inched back, and searched his face like she wasn't sure she was talking to her father. "It was... amazing. Like, so much fun." A smile pulled at her lips. "The sisters? My aunts? They're hilarious and wonderful. And today I went up to Lovely's attic—that's her real name and it's a legit attic in this house—and she gave me these cool vintage clothes."

Guilt pressed on his heart for wanting to drag her away from this brief respite of happiness with relatives she didn't even know she had.

"They've been nice to you, huh?"

She swallowed and rubbed her hands together. "Yeah. Nicer than Aunt Katherine, who wasn't ever around."

At the mention of his loser sister-in-law, he huffed out a breath. When he called her on the way down, she hadn't been nearly contrite enough for letting a child out of her sight like that.

"I know, Dad. I know," Ava said, fending off the lecture. "I shouldn't have done that, shouldn't have left like that. I just...I wanted to get that letter to Beck for Grandma J."

"Why didn't you mail it?"

"I promised her that I would be sure it got to the right lady and that she read it. Grandma said it was so important that I put it in her hand. I don't know why, but she made me promise. And she died the next day! I couldn't break that promise."

He got that, he really did. And he knew exactly why his mother made Ava promise that—so that Beck Foster would meet Ava and do the right thing. Just reading a letter wouldn't elicit the kind of response she'd gotten. And his mother knew that.

So this request must have been very, very important to her. And she hadn't told him because that's how Janet Gallagher quietly did her magnificent parenting. Couldn't he at least try to emulate her?

"So you've been having fun here?" he asked, genuinely curious and also wanting to keep this peaceful moment going a little bit longer.

"So much, Dad," she whispered. "I feel comfortable here. I haven't had a single moment of, you know, the panic feeling."

Her anxiety attacks. Another thing that kept him awake with worry. "Good, that's good."

"And I even put my foot in the water down there."

Ava? She didn't even want to take baths, let alone go near the ocean, even one that calm.

"And I let someone hug me. Twice." Her voice cracked and his would have too, if he could speak. This was huge. This was unbelievable. She stopped being able to stand physical contact the day after the funeral.

She'd come home from burying her mother and brother and had a complete breakdown, screaming that she never wanted anyone to ever hug her again after all those people embraced her over and over.

"Ava." He leaned forward, but, as always, catching himself before he touched her because she always yanked herself away. "That's amazing."

"I like this place," she whispered on a half sob. "I don't want to go home. Not yet. Not...for a while."

He just stared at her and felt himself nodding.

Exhaustion bore down, along with the right answer. The only answer.

"Beck has offered to let me stay here tonight," he said. "Let's take a look at the situation in the morning, Ava. Maybe we can stay for a few days."

"Oh, thank you!" She popped up and for one crazy minute, he thought she was going to hug him. "I'll go tell my aunts! And Jessie! And Lovely! Is she still here?" She went flying into the house, leaving him in stunned silence.

Maybe Elise had been looking down and handled that one. He had no other explanation, but, for once, he knew he'd done the right thing.

CHAPTER ELEVEN
BECK

*W*hen Beck came into the kitchen the next morning to check on Jessie's scones warming in the oven, she found Kenny on the back veranda, sipping coffee, catching a glorious sunrise over the Atlantic.

"Did you sleep out there?" she called with a laugh as she walked past the open doors, headed for the coffee maker.

He didn't answer, but pushed up and came in to join her. "No, I slept in that cozy room with a view to the other side, which is just as picturesque with all the canals and greenery. Where exactly am I, again, besides paradise?"

She laughed. "Coconut Key is uniquely shaped, like an actual coconut, folklore has it. The main road, US 1, cuts through the heart of the island with half to the south, where we are,and half to the north, with the open Gulf views. Coquina Court is like a little finger that sticks out, offering these amazing views."

"Great fishing, I imagine."

She smiled. Men always want to fish in the Keys. "Great everything. Nature in abundance. And great food, like these scones." She opened the oven and peered in. "They're from Jessie Donovan's restaurant called Chuck's. You passed it on the way in."

He sniffed at the buttery aroma from the pastries. "Don't have to taste them, I can tell they're going to be great." He glanced toward the front of the house. "No sign of Ava yet, I suppose?"

"She's fifteen. Do you really expect her to be up with the sun?"

"I don't know what I expect." He joined her by the coffee maker and set his empty cup down, nodding his thanks when she refilled it. "Fifteen-year-old girls are a mystery to me."

"They're a mystery, all right. And each is totally unique, so if you're looking for answers, I'm not sure I have them."

He took a deep breath and let it out in a sigh, heading toward the table. "You remodeling?" he asked, taking in the samples that Maggie had spread out.

"My mother and I are renovating this house to be a B&B," she told him.

"Really? That's quite an undertaking."

"Kind of. It was a boarding house in a previous life, owned by my grandparents. I lived here until I was ten, with my mother, who is..." She laughed softly. "Not the same mother you met."

"Ooookay." He settled in a chair and gave her an expectant look.

"You're not the first secret baby in the family," she joked, joining him at the table.

While he sipped his coffee, she gave him the pared down version of her story, enough for her to see he was fascinated.

"And now, our next chapter," she said, gesturing toward the samples on the table. "The Coquina House Bed and Breakfast. Step one, a completely remodeled kitchen. After that, we're refurbishing the rooms on the second floor, then upgrading the bathroom on the third floor, and maybe breaking that whole floor into two rooms with a second bathroom. It's all very ambitious and overwhelming."

Quiet, he looked around. "Not to me. I do construction, and kitchens are like second nature to me. If you keep that wall, this is a pretty easy job. But everyone wants open concept."

"Actually, we are keeping it because in a B&B, I'll want some separation between the kitchen and dining room, which will be where guests eat. But I want it open enough that they feel they can use the kitchen when they want to."

He narrowed his eyes, scanning the room. "You're picking the Shaker, I guess?"

She gave a soft laugh. "After some debate, yes. My designer, Maggie? You met her, right?"

"Oh, yeah." His eyebrows flicked. "I met her."

So the electricity went both ways, she thought, hiding a smile. "She thinks we should have all the emphasis on the views from the veranda and that bank of windows to capture the unique one-eighty view. So, you, uh, *do* kitchens?" She tried, maybe failed, to keep the note of excitement out of her voice. "I thought you said you were an EMT."

"That's a part-time gig. Most of my days are spent on a job site. I'm a tradesman for a contractor up in Atlanta, and we mostly do high-end residential work."

She let out a little moan. "A contractor. The Holy Grail that I can't get for love or money. Please tell me he has friends in the Keys."

He shook his head and looked a little...not surprised. More like worried? He probably thought she was going to beg him to stay and renovate her kitchen. And the thought had occurred to her.

"Can't find a contractor down here?" he asked.

"Earliest available is September, maybe, and that's only if I sell my firstborn to get..." She bit her lip and almost laughed, but to his credit, he did laugh.

"I'm not for sale."

Something slipped inside her at that, some tension and discomfort that just disappeared when they shared that one simple joke. "No chance you're for hire, then?" she asked, lifting her cup to act like it was a joke. "But I guess I'd still need a contractor."

"Not for the kitchen, not technically. As long as you don't change electrical or plumbing, or a window, you don't have to pull permits."

"That's what Maggie said last night," she mused. "But I thought I should use one person for the whole job. Wouldn't that save me money and time?"

He lifted a shoulder. "Not if you have to wait a year to get one."

She sighed, running a finger over the scalloped back-splash. "What about this? Too trendy?"

"It's pretty and I bet it looks great in here." He scuffed a boot on the old linoleum floor. "Replacing this I guess?"

"I picked this tile, the kind that looks like a wood plank."

"Very popular," he said.

"Oh, dear. Am I making a mistake with all this?"

He laughed. "The biggest mistake you can make during a remodel is second-guessing every decision. Trust your gut and stick to a budget. And make sure you get someone who won't rob you blind because, man, there are some unethical people in this business."

She took a sip of coffee, nodding that she understood that.

"But the idea of a B&B?" He gestured toward the rest of the house. "With that room I slept in? You'll be booked solid in no time. This is a gem of a piece of real estate. There aren't even that many houses on the beach."

"A lot of that land is protected, thank God, or owned by Lovely, since my grandfather bought it first. All along the north side, between here and the main road, is a warren of canals, with lots of houses and boats."

He stood as she talked, examining the room a little more, no doubt with a professional's eye.

"The house is almost a hundred years old," she told him. "But it's been knocked down and rebuilt after hurricanes several times. Each time, it's safer and stronger than the one before."

"It's beautiful craftsmanship," he noted, eyeing the carved door jamb. "You'll want to keep that Victorian design, but bring it up to date."

"And not follow every trend on HGTV," she added.

He turned and gave her a smile, the first real one from the heart, and she was reminded so much of a boy she knew in high school. Funny, he'd never asked about his father. If he did, she'd tell him the name; if he didn't, well. Some things were better left unsaid.

"So what could I do without a contractor in here?" Beck asked.

"With the right person? Everything, but I'd start with a good inspection of the wiring and plumbing." He walked to the sink to put his cup away. "If they're set, have someone look at your design and give you an estimate."

Just then, they heard footsteps on the stairs and a noisy yawn. "Sounds like one of our daughters is up."

"Two of them." Savannah walked into the kitchen, her hair a tousled mess, a baggy T-shirt over sleep pants. "I slept up on the third floor with Ava, who is on the way, but not a great riser, is she?"

"She's not a morning person," he confirmed. "You're sharing a room with Ava?"

"Just last night so you could have mine. It's fine. We have lovely twin beds up there on the third floor." She brushed by Kenny and poked him in the shoulder on her way to the coffee maker. "Hello again, brother."

Kenny's brows flickered slightly. "Savannah, is it?"

"It is. I'm the funny one. Also pregnant, in case you can't tell." She pressed the T-shirt over her baby bump. "Meet Pink Line."

"A girl?" he asked.

"Don't know, don't want to know, don't care. Although, we sure could use a boy in the estrogen hut." She grinned at him. "Another boy."

He smiled. "Well, congratulations, Savannah. When are you due?"

"October second." She put a cup of water in the microwave for her tea. "So, do you mind if I practice motherhood on your daughter for another day? She's sharpening my skills and, to thank her, I'm taking her shopping, for a pedicure, and...you know. Other girl things."

"Oh?" Beck sat up. "Could I go with you?"

"I'd cry if you didn't, Mom."

"But Lovely has a doctor's appointment this morning and I'm driving her. Could you do the pedicures then, and we'll meet you for lunch and shop with you guys?" Beck stood, thrilled with the idea.

"We'd love that," Savannah said. "But we still didn't get permission from Daddio."

He gave a soft, dry laugh. "I kind of promised Ava we could stay a day or two, so I'm sure she'll hold me to that and not allow me to run off back to Atlanta quite yet."

"Why would you?" Savannah asked. "You're in paradise."

He turned to Beck. "I actually could check out the wiring and plumbing stuff for you, if you want. Once you get that cleared, it might help you find someone to renovate the kitchen without a GC."

Beck nearly hugged him. "That would be amazing. But don't work the whole time. I mean, there's lots to do here. We have a couple of small motorboats you could take out, or kayaks. All the snorkeling you'd want to do."

"Actually, I'm more at home in a kitchen that needs to be renovated than anywhere else."

Beck laughed. "Maggie was right. You *did* fall from heaven."

He turned to her, a little interest in his eyes. "She said that?"

But before Beck could answer, Ava walked in. "Whatever smells so good has to be in my belly right now."

Kenny blinked at his daughter like that comment surprised him, but when Savannah put both her hands on Ava's shoulders, he had an even more surprised look at that.

"Grasshopper clearly takes after her Aunt Savannah."

"Grass..." He just shook his head, laughing. "Yeah. You guys go do girly things and I'll work on the kitchen."

Work on the kitchen. That was music to Beck's ears.

Beck opened the oven and let the warm air blow on her face, but that did nothing to take away her smile. Her son, a daughter, and granddaughter were in her kitchen laughing, eating, and...discussing the renovation she longed to do.

She didn't even know she had this hole in her heart, but today, it felt filled.

🌴

AN HOUR LATER, Beck still felt filled with that unexpected joy as she described the whole scene to Josh at his workshop.

"It was amazing," she crooned. "I still can't get over the fact that I found him."

"Technically, Ava found you." He looked up from the table where he was using one of his zillions of tools to smooth the edges of a breakfront he was making for the lobby of a resort in Key Largo.

"She did." She leaned against the table and checked her watch, not wanting to be late to pick up Lovely for the doctor's, but in no rush to leave Joshua Cross's woodworking shop. She loved the smell of freshly shaved wood, all so solid and comfortable.

Or maybe she just liked to be around Josh, who smelled good, too, and was as solid and comfortable as any man she'd ever met.

She stopped by here frequently when running errands around Coconut Key, sometimes bringing him coffee or some lunch, sometimes nothing but a quick hello to check on the progress of one of the many pieces of furniture he created.

In addition to his sister, Jessie, and, of course, Lovely, Josh had become one of her closest friends on the island. She loved to bounce ideas off him, to talk about their lives, her plans, his work, and the people they both cared about. Today, she'd brought him the last of the scones and coffee, and a lot of questions.

"Do you think I should hire someone to do the kitchen without a general contractor?" she asked, settling on a stool to watch him work. "Kenny thinks it would be pretty easy."

"You can, but if that guy bails on you? Not good." He shook his head. "True, you don't need permits to remodel a kitchen unless you're changing the structure, but you do need some kind of guarantee. A GC can't risk his license by disappearing. Some clown you find off the street might not show up after tearing the place down and leaving you a mess."

"Eeesh. I don't want that. It's bad enough we're going to have to live without a kitchen for a few weeks."

"Lovely's cottage is a few minutes away, and you have Chuck's down the street." He smoothed a corner and drew back, inspecting the work. "Although I guess on nights it's open, you won't want to cook there."

"We'll make it work, if I find someone reputable."

"You'd have to—"

The front door dinged and he rolled his eyes, no doubt because he knew he was being interrupted by someone who thought this was a furniture shop. Yes, he had a few pieces for sale in the front, but mostly Josh worked on straight commission for clients, and rarely had walk-ins to the small showroom in the front.

"You want me to see what they want?" she offered, sliding off the stool. "I can turn away business as well as you can."

"Better," he said with a sly smile. "Have at it, Beck."

She headed out, finding a woman casually inspecting a front door leaning against a wall.

"Hi," Beck said. "How are you?"

"I am in love with Joshua Cross," she cooed, then laughed. "With his work, I mean."

"It's gorgeous," Beck agreed, taking in the attractive forty-something woman with smooth dark hair pulled into a ponytail, and a well-toned body in leggings and a tank top that said "Namastay Awhile."

The woman sighed over a mirror, or maybe her own reflection. Then she turned, her shapely brows lifting in expectation.

"Most of these pieces are done on commission," Beck said. "But were you looking for something in particular?"

"Joshua," she said with a little bit of surprise that Beck didn't know. "I'm looking for him."

"Oh. I don't think he realized he had an appointment."

"Well, it's a surprise, but..." She inched to the side to look back toward the workroom. "A pleasant one, I hope."

"Let me go tell him you're here. What's your—"

But the woman had already brushed by. "Josh!" she called. "I couldn't wait another minute to tell you the news."

"Oh, hi, Gwen."

Beck turned and followed, sorry she couldn't have run better interference when he was so busy. But she walked in just in time to see the woman slide her arms around Josh's in a warm embrace. "Congratulations to Coconut Key's best bachelor."

What? Beck took a few steps backwards and out of the workshop, getting the feeling this was a private moment she shouldn't be witnessing. But who the heck was Gwen and why was she pressed up against Josh?

"What are you talking about?" Josh asked, sounding as confused as Beck felt.

"The bachelor auction!" she said. "Remember, for Habitat for Humanity in two weeks? You're on the roster and I expect you to bring in big bucks, mister."

"A bachelor..." Josh's voice faded away with a laugh. "You asked for my help with a fundraiser for Habitat, Gwen. I thought you needed me to make a door or build someone a table."

"We need money, not fancy doors, Josh. The committee is hosting three events this month for a huge fundraising push. There's a 5K race around Ramrod Key, a spaghetti dinner at Grace Lutheran in Summerland Key, and we landed the bachelor auction. But we're actually holding it at the Marriott on Little Torch Key. Still, it's for my district so I want huge numbers, honey. Huge."

"Can't I run the 5K or eat spaghetti? I do both of those a heck of a lot better than I...bachelor auction."

Listening from the other side of the wall, Beck bit back a laugh, imagining his bewildered expression.

"You'll walk down that runway and you'll smile at the ladies until they empty their pocketbooks, then, I promise, I'll be the last bidder." Gwen let out a little trill of laughter. "You'll be a fortune, but worth it. I will take you somewhere fabulous for dinner."

She laughed again and whispered something Beck didn't catch but it sounded...intimate.

And a little green monster Beck didn't even know resided in her woke up, shook off, and poked at her chest.

But she and Josh were just friends. He hadn't made a move or asked for more, though his interest in Beck had been clear. They frequently took sunset walks if the families had dinner together, and he'd been so helpful in getting her moved in and acclimated to Coconut Key. But...who was this Gwen woman?

"All right, all right," he said. "I'll do it but only 'cause you asked."

Whoever she was...she mattered to him. Beck curled her lip.

"You are a love."

Beck heard lips smack. Had they kissed? She walked further from the workshop, busying herself with straightening some chairs in the show room.

"I'll get back to you with details," the woman called as she breezed into the showroom. "Like what to wear." She winked at Beck. "Or not."

With that, she sailed out the front door, leaving a trail of body spray and confusion.

"Didn't mean to eavesdrop," Beck said as she walked back in. "But a bachelor auction? Is that a real thing?"

He looked up from the worktable, shaking his head. "That woman is a force of nature but, God bless her, she raises so much money for Habitat that they've built about six new houses just in the Lower Keys this past year. She's the first one checking on the lower income families after bad storms and single handedly keeps the food bank stocked."

Oh, great. She was young, pretty, and a doer of good deeds. And very friendly.

"I'd have introduced you, but, trust me, you'll thank me for not bringing you to her attention. If she found out you were opening a B&B here, she'd rope you into giving her money and a shelter for the homeless."

"Wow. She sounds like a very...giving person."

He kind of shrugged, his attention back on the break-front door. "You might look at it that way. She's also kind of needy. For, you know, attention."

"So you think she does these acts of service so it makes her look good?" Which might take her attractiveness down a notch.

"I don't know." He suddenly seemed distracted, bending over to run his finger along the wood. "Something's wrong with this hinge."

Beck swallowed. "She's very pretty."

"She is." He moved the door to a different angle.

"And all that...altruism? It's wonderful." She crossed her arms and came a little closer. "I'm curious, though, about what your relationship is. I've never heard her mentioned before and you didn't introduce me..."

"You disappeared and my relationship with her is..." He lifted a shoulder and returned to the hinge. "Over."

She sucked in a little breath. "I thought I sensed something between you two."

His eyes shuttered, the smile still there. "Nothing to sense."

"But there was." She slipped back onto the stool. "How long did you date her?"

"A little while." He gave up on the door and straightened to look right her, a smile crinkling around his blue eyes. "You jealous, Beck?"

"Oh, please. Well, I wouldn't mind that beautiful head of dark hair." Or those legs. "I've always wanted to be a brunette."

He frowned and shook his head. "You're just right the way you are."

"Thanks." She sighed, smiling at him. "But, *should* I be jealous?"

Very slowly, he put down his hand tool, holding her gaze. "Only if you think I still have a thing with Gwendolyn Parker and that bothers you."

"Why would it bother me, Josh? We're friends. And, in case you forgot, I'm still married. And you're...Josh."

He laughed. "Okay, some of that makes sense. And, yes, Beck, we're friends and since you are married, that's what I know you want to be. But when you're not married?"

A little shiver danced over her. "Then, I don't know. I've never been *not* married, at least for thirty-four years. I wouldn't know where to start."

His mouth kicked up, like he would know where to

start. And wouldn't mind it a bit. "Well, there's a bachelor auction coming up." He winked. "You can get in line."

She laughed and slipped off the chair, waving him off. "Right behind Namastay Awhile, Coconut Key's very own Mother Teresa."

He cracked up as she grabbed her purse and slipped it on her arm.

"What? What's so funny?" she asked.

"You *are* jealous." He looked back down at the break-front door, grinning.

She didn't bother to deny it.

CHAPTER TWELVE

PEYTON

*F*or the first time, Peyton started to believe they could pull this cookbook off.

Jessie had let her take over half of the restaurant's management office and she made full use of the space to lay out *Cuisine of the Keys*, a project she believed in more than any of the boring non-fiction titles she'd helped usher through the publication process when she'd worked for Hudson Street Publishing.

"It's like you're everywhere now," Jessie said on a laugh as she came into her office. "If you're not in the kitchen learning to cook, you're in here, creating a book."

"It's true." Between this and being an apprentice in the kitchen, Peyton felt as excited about life as she had in ages. Oh, and Val. Yep. She was excited about him, too, knowing he would be showing up any moment.

Peyton smiled at Jessie, who was more than just a mentor or the author of Peyton's pet project. Jessie had truly become a friend. And as a friend, Peyton wanted to

know more about Tag Jadrien. But last night, after he left
the table, everything shifted to Ava and getting back to
Coconut Key, so the follow-up questions had to
happen now.

That was, if Jessie would answer.

"Come and see the whole first section on appetizers,"
Peyton said, waving Jessie closer to the laptop screen. "I'm
trying this very cool layout software we used at Hudson
Street Publishing. What do you think of having a map of
the Keys after the title page?"

"I think it's amazing." Jessie's brown eyes grew wide.
"And that's the title page? With my name like that?"

"Do you want your maiden name, too? I can add
Cross between Jessica and Donovan. Whatever you like."

"Wow." Jessie stared at the screen. "I think just Jessica
Donovan is fine. I guess I better start writing those
sections you need." She sighed. "If only I didn't have to
work my butt off to save a troubled business."

"This is going to save your troubled business," Peyton
promised her. "And there's actually very little writing
involved in a cookbook, although we could use a
powerful introduction. But I've made every recipe in this
book, so not a lot of new writing involved. And since I've
made them, a novice can, too, and they're awesome."

Jessie turned to her. "So, do you want to be a line
cook, a chef, or a publisher? Girl, the world is your
oyster."

Peyton lowered herself back into the seat as if the
weight of the decision was too much. "I like working on
this book, I'm not going to lie. I've wanted to be in
publishing since I fell in love with books as a child."

"Then that's your answer."

"Not so fast," Peyton said. "I love cooking. I mean, I *love* it. And now that I have a real mentor? It's one thing to watch cooking videos on YouTube, but when you take my hand and adjust my knife skills?" She reached over and touched Jessie. "Is it weird to find your passion at thirty-one?"

"Not at all! I wanted to run a business. That's what I studied in college, and I always figured I'd just work my way up some corporate ladder in a big city. But that's not how life happened. I fell in love with Chuck Donovan, who couldn't breathe anywhere but the Keys, and I stayed here and turned my hobby into a business. I never left because of Chuck."

"Did you want to?"

"I wanted to live somewhere else in my life, yeah, but now I'm here. Like Lovely, I'll probably never leave."

"But you went to cooking school," Peyton said, familiar with Jessie's resume.

"After we were married, yes. I commuted to Miami-Dade Community College and attended the Miami Culinary Institute, which was *not* where Tag Jadrien went."

Peyton let a smile pull. "Tag again."

Jessie tipped her head and gave Peyton an apologetic look. "I should probably have told you I knew him in high school. I haven't told anyone, but it was bound to come out. Coconut Key is a small town and there are still plenty of locals who know us both."

"So he opened this restaurant to come 'home' to Coconut Key?"

"I guess. He left after we graduated, and I don't think

any of his family still lives here. He had a younger sister, but to my knowledge, she moved away decades ago." She thought about it for a moment. "He went to CIA in New York—now *that's* a culinary school—and I guess he traveled and worked all over the world. But six or eight years ago, he opened Tropics in Key West and I never heard that much about the food, but, dang, it must be a massive success. I've heard he's rolling in money, driving a Tesla, lives in a big house in Key West, and he sunk a ton into the satellite location. So he's either killing it in the restaurant world, or investing wisely."

Peyton studied Jessie's face, still wanting to dig a little more. "Okay, so he's smart, successful, and seemed *very* happy to see you. The problem?"

She looked down. "We're just not on great terms."

"Really?" Peyton smiled. "'Cause he seemed zeroed in on you."

"He was, once. In high school." She pushed up. "I better get in the kitchen." But she didn't make it one inch because Peyton slammed a hand on her arm.

"Gory. Details." She narrowed her eyes, making Jessie laugh. "Now."

"It's not that fascinating, really. Two boys liked me. One was a little shy and awkward, uncomfortable in his own skin, and scared to look me in the eyes. The other melted panties by walking into a room."

"Aw, Chuck was shy?"

She snorted and slowly shook her head. "I married the panty-melter."

That made Peyton smile, but then she drew back. "Tag was shy and awkward? I'd have never guessed that."

"Tag was a track nerd I met in a cooking class, and I was only being nice to him. He mistook it for something more. I always had it bad for the football star who liked to fish." She moaned. "I wish you could have known my Chuck. I miss him every day."

"I know you do," Peyton said. "But I still don't understand the antagonism toward the guy who lost out on you all those years ago. Maybe he just wants another chance since he's changed so much. Is he single?"

"I heard he's divorced, and I don't know what he wants," she said, finally getting up. "But I'm not on the market. I really have to get in the kitchen, Peyton. We have actual customers coming in tonight, and I want to wow them. You're not on the schedule, are you?"

"No, did you need me? I have a date with Val."

"You go out with him and have a blast. How are things progressing, by the way?"

Peyton sighed. "Probably too fast for him and not fast enough for me." She rolled her eyes. "Story of my life, Jess."

"Well, why else do you date someone? You're either shopping with money and the intent to purchase or you're window shopping. Which are you doing?"

"I know what I'm doing, but Val and I just started seeing each other."

"He probably needs a little guidance in the right direction," Jessie said. "That is, if you're interested in him for the long term."

"I am, but..." Peyton gave a vehement shake of her head. "I gave an ultimatum to a man, and it blew up in my face."

"I get that." Jessie slipped a clean chef's apron off a hook and tied it around her.

"Hey, is Peyton back here?" Val's voice floated into the office.

"There's your man," Jessie teased with a wink. "Have fun tonight, whether you buy anything or not."

As Jessie left, Val walked in and, of course, Peyton's whole body reacted. She never got tired of looking at him, laughing with him, and getting to know him.

"I just delivered the day's catch," he said.

She looked up at him, brows raised, waiting for the rest of the joke.

"That's it," he said. "Wanted to say hi."

"I'm spoiled. I was expecting a fish joke."

He laughed. "I'll practice for tonight. We still on for dinner? I have some lobster you're going to love." When she didn't answer, he added, "Unless you don't feel like cooking."

"Can you save the lobster for tomorrow?" she asked. "I have an open invitation for a comped dinner at Coconut Tropics."

His jaw loosened. "You'd walk into the competition?"

Competition? Maybe. But the thing was, she'd seen how Tag Jadrien had looked at Jessie the night before. That wasn't a man trying to get vengeance for losing the girl forty years ago. He looked *interested*.

"Hey, free dinner and some competitive analysis."

He lifted both shoulders. "Sounds good to me. Actually, that's my next stop and I'll sell my gorgeous lobsters to that restaurant. We get to eat them either way."

"Perfect. I love lobster tails."

"Me too. Once upon a time, there were two lobsters."

At her look, he held up his hands. "What? It's a lobster tale."

She laughed and waved him out, already looking forward to the evening. No ultimatums, though. She'd never make that mistake again.

CHAPTER THIRTEEN

AVA

"Where have you all been?" Dad pushed out from underneath the kitchen sink when Ava walked into the Coquina House kitchen with Beck, Lovely, Savannah, and Peyton.

"Gallivanting," Savannah said, making Ava laugh. To be honest, everything her aunt said made her laugh. She'd done nothing for the past five hours *but* laugh. And shop. And eat, then laugh some more.

It reminded her of shopping with Mom and Adam when she was little, cracking up and having fun from one end of the mall to the other, getting ice cream, and riding that little train. But no trains today. After lunch at a place called Conchy Charlies—where she had more amazing fried fish called conch—they picked up Peyton at Chuck's and met up with Beck and Lovely. Then they went to an outdoor shopping center on another island. Not a lot of stores, but so much fun.

Dad wiped his hands on a rag and scanned the bags

Beck laid on the counter as she peered under the sink, interested in what Dad was doing.

"*Gallivanting* must be another word for buying out the store," he said, checking out the loot.

"The girl has no clothes, bro," Savannah replied, pointing to Ava.

"She shouldn't have run away without a suitcase," he countered, but Ava could see the smile he hid. "You bought all this, Ava?"

"*We* bought it," Beck clarified, holding up her hand as if to stop any argument before it started. "It's my holy and unassailable right as a grandmother to spoil her."

"They all bought me stuff," Ava admitted.

"I'm responsible for the lime green bra," Savannah said, getting a shocked look from Dad.

"A lime green..." It was like her father still couldn't think about her in bras.

"I believe if a woman's undies are bright and bold, then she will be, too." Savannah handed another bag to Ava. "Go change into that bathing suit Peyton picked for you?"

A bathing suit. The one thing Ava *didn't* want. "Why?" she asked.

"Grasshopper, we're going snorkeling, remember?"

She *so* wanted to forget that suggestion. Ava didn't answer but Dad took a step closer, concern on his face. He just thought she hated to go underwater in a swimming pool. He had no idea what the whole stupid ocean would do to her.

"You don't have to go in the water, A," he said. "She doesn't know how to swim."

"Snorkeling involves an actual breathing device," Savannah said. "She'll be fine. Trust me."

Could Savannah teach her to swim? Others had tried and failed miserably. Even Mom had given up trying to teach her to swim—and no one had tried harder—and finally let Ava wear floaties on her arms long after it was age-appropriate. And when she became a teenager? She just avoided pools and pool parties.

But here? It was kind of hard to avoid the stinking ocean. The place was surrounded by water.

"Kenny, what did you find with the plumbing and electrical?" Beck asked.

As the conversation shifted to things that didn't matter, Savannah poked Ava's back. "Chop, chop. I'll get the snorkeling gear. Pey, you coming?"

"I'm going to work on the cookbook some more," she said.

"Mom? Lovely?"

"I don't snorkel," Lovely said. "But I'll sit on the veranda and paint you as you snorkel by."

"I'm going to talk to Kenny about the kitchen," Beck replied.

Savannah looked at her, one hand on her hip. "I guess that just leaves us, little niece."

"'Kay." Ava headed upstairs to change, still gnawing on her lower lip when she got to the bathroom and slipped into the turquoise bikini and thigh-length cover-up Peyton had so sweetly bought for her. As she dressed, she waited for the first wave of pressure on her chest.

But nothing came.

Holding on to hope, she headed back downstairs

where she found her father leaning against the counter, his arms crossed as he chatted with Beck.

He turned to look at Ava, his expression sincere. "Are you sure you want to do this?"

Not really. "Absolutely." She forced a smile. "Savannah's the best, Dad. She's so cool and funny."

"You forgot gorgeous," Savannah called as she came into the kitchen wearing a baggy yellow T-shirt and carrying some masks and fins. "All right, let's find some colorful fish." She waved a little farewell to Dad, snagged Ava's arm, and dragged her toward the door. "Best day ever, right?"

Savannah chattered on, talking about nothing and everything as they walked down to the water, over the sand and seaweed and shells to water so shallow she could easily walk out about a half a mile and still be waist high.

She could totally do this.

"Not very many people on this beach," Ava noticed. "It's always so empty."

"They come by, I noticed, to pick up shells. But there are so few houses on this street, it's super private. I actually think Lovely owns the land between Coquina House and her cottage, so the real development has been on the other side, where the canals are. I really think that's why my mom's B&B is going to be a smash hit."

"Will you have to find another place to live, then? I mean she'll be renting out all the rooms."

"Yeah, hopefully I can stay until the tadpole is born. After that? I don't know. I'm not one for staying somewhere very long." Savannah stopped and bent over, picked up a pink shell and dropped it in her pocket.

"Although I guess my wanderlust days are coming to an end," she added quietly.

"You sound sad about that," Ava said. "Did you not want a baby?"

She didn't answer for a long time, looking out to the horizon and thinking. Ava waited, expecting some hilarious quip.

"I didn't think I did," she finally whispered. "But when I saw that pink line, something changed inside me." Savannah gave a sad smile. "Not that it's going to be easy. Going from a single woman who could, and did, pack up all her earthly belongings and fit them in the back of a Mazda hatchback to being solely responsible for a human life? Can you spell paralyzing?"

"Probably not, but I get the idea."

The answer made Savannah smile as they reached the beach in front of Lovely's cottage. The closest people were an older couple shelling their way down the beach, and the brightly colored house with the hammock looked deserted. Savannah threw the towels on the sand and handed the snorkeling gear to Ava. "But if she turns out like you, it won't be half bad."

The compliment warmed Ava more than the sun. "I can be a pain in the butt. Ask my dad."

"Yeah, I noticed with the whole 'take an Uber to the Keys to meet your biological grandmother with no adult supervision' trick. But is that the worst thing you've done?"

Ava shrugged. "I've had a few drinks but didn't really like it."

"Pot?"

"No, never. I get B's and the occasional C, but if I tried

harder, I could get an A." Would that count as a bad thing to Savannah?

"Sex?"

Her eyes widened and she shook her head.

"Smart kid." Savannah poked Ava's belly. "'Cause, I have to tell you, you are part of a long line of *way* too fertile women. That's not a chance I'd take in our gene pool."

"Good advice," Ava said, pulling off the cover-up and eyeing the water, trying to swallow. "Just for the record, I really can't swim. I mean, like, really."

She held up the rubber fins. "These will make you a fish." And the snorkel. "This will guarantee you don't drown." Then she offered the mask. "And you'll be able to see where you're going."

She took them all and gave a determined nod. "Okay, then. Let's do it."

As they walked toward the water, Savannah shot her a sideways look. "So, what happens when you get scared?"

"I...panic."

"Can't breathe? Pressure on your chest? Palms sweaty and head light? Pretty sure you're going to die?"

Ava slowed her step. "Yes. Exactly."

"I know the feeling," Savannah said. "For me, it's elevators or crowded rooms, anything super confining. I get the whole crazy shakes and can't breathe at all."

"How do you make it stop?" Ava asked.

Savannah thought about it for a minute. "I just think about what's the worst that could happen and then I realize that it's not that bad."

"If I drown it would be bad."

"I'm not going to let you drown, so what else could happen?"

"A shark could bite us," she said, laughing softly.

"Actually, that is more likely than you drowning."

"Really?" Ava almost tripped. "I saw a dolphin, but are there sharks out there?"

"You *think* you saw Flipper, but you may have seen Moby Dick." She smiled. "We'll be careful, don't worry."

Too late. Worry was crawling all over Ava's skin.

They reached the water's edge, about two inches deep and full of the wet, slimy grass stuff. "What is that stuff?" she asked. "It's gross."

"Hush, child. You'll get the environmentalists after you. That is seagrass or seaweed, sometimes called sargassum. Also known as algae, and some people think it's the heart and soul of the ecosystem here. Feeds the turtles, saves the sea, slides between your toes like wet floss. Eww." Savannah demonstrated by sliding her toes through a clump of the stuff. "Painless and fun. Come on, put that mask on."

She did, squeezing it over her hair and setting it on her nose, getting a lesson from Savannah on how to breathe.

"Ready?" Savannah asked when they were all set up.

"As I'll ever be."

"That's my girl!" Savannah threw her arms around Ava and squeezed.

Ava didn't hug back, but she didn't want to scream. So that was a huge victory.

"Let's go." Savannah started walking them out, the waves rolling over her feet, then up to her calves. And nothing inside Ava felt...panicked.

"It feels good," Ava said on a laugh, dancing a little bit. The water was warmer than she expected.

"It feels great!" Savannah bounded forward so that the water splashed up to their thighs, then the bottoms of their new bathing suits. "You okay?"

Ava nodded, still not feeling panicked.

"Good. Down we go!" Savannah stuck the snorkel into her mouth and lowered her head under the water, her dark blond hair floating like that seagrass around her head.

Ava did the same, sliding under and opening her eyes. The sun came through the water enough that she could see everything, including Savannah who waved at her, then pointed to a little fish going by.

She pushed through the water, hearing her breath hiss in her ears as she inhaled.

And then it started, fast and furious. Pressure and pounding, all focused on her chest. She wanted to stand and pop out of the water, but for one crazy second, she forgot how.

She started to scream, which was a huge mistake. Water slid into her mouth and some of the brown stuff wrapped around her feet and ankles, making the panic intensify. She slipped all the way under and heard a gurgle in her ear. In the snorkel. She was going to suck in water!

Oh, God. She was drowning.

No, no. She could swim. She knew how.

Stroke right, stroke left, kick, kick, kick.

Ava could hear her mother's voice as clear as if Elise Gallagher were standing in a pool next to her. She would put her hand on Ava's back, curling her fingers around the bathing suit so she could hold Ava up and say the same thing.

Stroke right, stroke left, kick, kick, kick.

And then...*You can swim, Ava Bear!*

But she couldn't. She flailed and kicked and rolled over, feeling Savannah's hands on her body but she couldn't breathe, which freaked her out. She pushed away and yanked the snorkel out of her mouth. Big mistake.

She could feel Savannah dragging her up as they stood and popped through the water.

"Whoa, there, grasshopper. You never—"

Ava choked. Coughed and spit and gagged until water came out.

"Oh, grass—"

Ava whipped her whole body away before it was touched again, her heart hammering so hard it felt like it could crack her ribs. She shook her head as the first flutter of dizziness rolled through her and then...then... the pressure nearly crushed her. Her chest squeezed. She tried to breathe but it felt like a hand was clamped on her throat.

She tried to walk, but her legs were wobbly.

"You okay, hun?" Savannah tried again to hold her. "Let's get back to the—"

She shook her head, pressed both hands on her chest, and tried to breathe. Nothing. Just tiny little sips of air that wouldn't keep her alive.

"C'mere, Ava." Savannah reached for her, but Ava shook her head violently, desperate to stand and run and breathe.

But she couldn't do any of that. Instead, her whole

body began to tremble. Hard. The blackness of a panic descended faster than that wave that nearly killed her. She was dying. And it wasn't good. There was nothing good.

"Ava!" Savannah's voice was so far away, she could hardly hear it. But she felt her arms and they were too tight. Way, way too tight. She tried to throw her off, but Savannah was strong and her arms were like steel bands.

"Stop!" Ava whipped left and right to free herself, finally succeeding, vaguely aware that Savannah was literally carrying her through the water to the sand, where she set her down.

Ava scrambled away, her whole body vibrating, and she still couldn't breathe. At all.

She managed to get up, to run away from the water, away from Savannah, tripping a few times until she fell on the sand next to the towels.

Savannah was next to her in an instant.

"Come on. Come on, let's get you up to Lovely's cottage."

"I...can't...breathe."

"It just feels that way, babe. You can breathe. Come on. Come on."

Ava just closed her eyes and let herself be taken away, shaking, panting, and lost in the worst panic she could ever remember.

CHAPTER FOURTEEN
KENNY

*K*enny turned the bedroom doorknob slowly, his whole being humming with worry, thrown back to the times he'd have to go to school to get her. After the first one they called a panic attack, the next two were deemed "mild breakdowns." From the way Savannah described what had happened on the beach, nothing about this was mild.

"Hey, A." He stepped inside the dimly lit room, aware that one of the little dogs had slipped in with him.

Ava's narrow frame was curled up on the bed, the sunshine blocked by drapes drawn over sliding glass doors. She held a small white dog, tucked against her belly. His heart hitched at the sight.

"Hi," she murmured. "Sorry for being such a butt pain."

"You're not a butt pain," he said, coming closer and perching on the edge of the bed. He tried to swallow, but his throat was tight. It always was when he had to have the kinds of conversation he was so bad at. This was

Elise's job, and he absolutely sucked at it. "You feeling better?"

She nodded and stroked the tiny dog's head.

"What do you think happened, Ava?"

"You know, one of my...things."

"Panic attacks?"

She curled her lip. "I guess. I'm okay now. I just couldn't breathe."

"Savannah said it was pretty serious."

She opened her eyes and looked up at him. "How'd she get to you? She never left my side. And, God knows, I tried to make her leave me alone."

"She texted Beck. And Peyton. And Jessie. Half of Coconut Key is out there." He pointed to the door behind him.

She made a face. "I might have been awful to Savannah."

"She's really worried about you, Ava. You scared her. All of us." His hand ached to touch her shoulder for comfort, but he knew from experience, she'd shake him off. "You said these incidents weren't happening anymore."

"It was better, but then Grandma Janet died." She bit her lip when her voice cracked. "I wanted to go in the water. I wanted to snorkel and have fun and be normal. I just...couldn't." She blinked back tears, her face ravaged with that pain that had etched onto her childish features after Elise and Adam died. "I have to go home. Today. We have to go home."

He inched back, startled. "Why? I mean, we do, but I thought you wanted to stay. I thought you loved it here."

"I do. I love this place. I love..." She worked to get the

words out. "I know this sounds stupid and it probably is, but I feel like I love...them. They feel like, you know..."

"Family," he whispered, knowing deep down in his soul it was the one thing he couldn't give her. And it was the thing she needed most.

"I can't let that happen," she said softly, her fingers digging into the dog's fur. "If I do, and something... changes." She closed her eyes and lowered her head, getting a lick on the cheek from the dog.

Even that didn't make her smile.

"What do you mean 'if something changes,' Ava?"

"You know."

"I don't." Maybe he did, but he had to be sure.

"Losing someone is...awful." Finally, she looked up. "I can't ever feel that way again. I still hurt every single day."

She was scared to love anyone. And that was no good. That was really, really bad.

Just the thought of that made him need to reach down and wrap his daughter in a hug. But that was the last thing that would make Ava feel better. "And you are worried that you're going to get attached to these people and then you're going to lose someone again? I don't think they'd ever let that happen. They seem very fond of you."

"Some things you can't control," she said softly. "And those are the things that make me...not be able to breathe. So, can we go home?"

He searched her face, trying to balance the one thing a parent constantly balanced: what the kid wanted versus what was best. And it always felt like he got it wrong with her.

Should he run from this place? Take her away from

these new, even scary, feelings that had her getting attached? What would that teach her? Run from fear? And what if they could help her? What if these generations of strong, smart women could be exactly what Ava needed in her life? Who was he to deny her that?

"Dad?"

"I'm not sure that's the right thing to do, Ava."

She stared at him, then pushed up on her elbows, brushing back some of her ridiculously colored hair. He'd lost that fight. But after a while, he forgot. He got used to her purple and pink strands.

"You said you wanted to go yesterday," she said.

"What if..." An idea took a slow shape in his head and as he considered it, wondering if it was right, wrong, stupid, or smart, he looked into her mesmerizing green gaze.

"What if...what, Dad? What are you thinking?" she asked.

"I was thinking about your eyes."

She flashed a look of disbelief. "Seriously?"

Yes, seriously. Her eyes were the answer...her eyes matched *theirs*.

"Have you noticed that Beck and Peyton and Lovely all have the same-colored eyes you have, Ava?"

She shrugged. "Yeah, kinda."

"Your mother and I used to talk about your eyes. How different they were. Hers were brown like mine."

"I remember."

"I always guessed..." He glanced over his shoulder to the closed door, knowing there were women gathered behind it, waiting for him. "It was because I was adopted, and those eyes were from my birth mother."

She nodded. "So, you were right. Dad, can we go home?"

He stared at her, petting the dog since he knew Ava would never accept him touching her hair or giving her a comforting hug. "I need to talk to Bill, but, honey. I think we need to stay here for a while."

"Really? What? How long?"

"A month? Six weeks? Maybe through the Fourth of July? Or August?"

She sat straight up. "Oh my God, are you for real right now?" There was just enough of a hitch in her voice for him to know that she loved the idea as much as it scared her. "Don't you have to work?"

He did, but he had to be a responsible, loving, present father first. "I'll call Bill. He can manage the houses we have without me. And the fire station can manage without me on the roster for a while."

She put her hand on her chest as if she expected it to hurt. "We'd stay here in Coconut Key for...like, the whole summer?"

"If I can swing it. But, Ava, I don't want you to feel like I pushed you into this. I'm going to make a phone call, while you think about it. Think hard. Don't be scared of getting feelings for someone. For anyone. I don't want you to live that way, honey. I don't want you to never...love."

She blinked at him, then nodded. "Okay."

He started to lean over to give her a kiss on the fore-head, then stopped himself. "I'll be back. You stay here with...who is this little guy?"

"It's Sugar. And that one staring at you like you might need to be barked at is Pepper."

He glanced at the little brown Cairn terrier. "Hi, Pepper. Keep an eye on my little girl for a minute, will ya?"

The dog barked in response, making Ava smile for the first time since he walked in the room. Holding that image in his head, he opened the door and practically walked right into Savannah, her eyes cloudy with concern.

"Is she okay?"

Maybe Ava shouldn't do that "thinking" alone. He angled his head toward the door. "Go talk to her, Savannah. I'm going to step outside and make a call."

He nodded to Beck and Lovely who sat on the sofa, yet another little terrier between them. They both smiled and looked expectantly at him for some news. He should have it momentarily.

"Would Ava like some lemonade?" Peyton asked from the other side of a small kitchen peninsula.

"I think she'd love that. I'll be right back."

He jogged down the front stairs to the shell-covered driveway, dropping down on the bottom step to call Bill Dobson.

A few minutes later, he'd given Bill the view from thirty-thousand feet and knew the other man was quiet because he was figuring out how the hell he'd get two houses finished without Kenny.

"So, what's she like?" Bill asked, making Kenny frown. Did he mean Ava or...oh. Beck. For a minute there, he forgot he was talking to his biological father while his biological mother was fifteen feet away in the house behind him.

What a tangled web.

"Beck? She's nice."

Bill chuckled. "Do better."

"She's charming and attractive and trying to renovate a huge house into a B&B. So I figure I can repay for my stay and her family's kindness by doing the kitchen. She's having a helluva time finding a contractor. You have any buddies licensed in Florida who might take that job?"

"I'm licensed in Florida."

"You are?"

"Of course. Alabama and Louisiana, too." He was quiet for a minute. Then he asked, "Has she mentioned me to you?"

"Not a word. I haven't asked, but, honestly, we haven't chatted a ton. Do you want me to—"

"No. No. I was just curious if the whole issue of who your father is ever came up."

"Not yet, but what if it does?"

He was quiet again. Then he said, "Don't lie, but I'd prefer to be kept out of it, if possible. I'm sure I broke some kind of adoption law by finding you and then, jeez, infiltrating your whole life. I mean, we haven't told Ava, why would we tell your birth mother?"

Tangled, tangled. "I get that." Did he? Kind of. But his loyalties lay with Bill, now and forever.

Bill let out a noisy sigh and Kenny could practically picture the man running his hand through his thick silver hair. "Look, I got stuff going on here anyway, so..."

Stuff usually meant family problems, mostly with his ex-wife who was a handful and a half.

"You gotta do what's right for Ava," Bill said quickly, before Kenny could ask. "That's all that matters. In the whole world, Ava is all that matters."

Spoken like a true grandfather, even if no one — including Ava— knew that. "I know."

"Stay there, let her get to know her family, and, whoa, see if she can get over these attacks. That's scary as hell."

"It was. Thanks, Bill. I have some of your tools in my truck. Sorry. I never expected—"

"Keep 'em. Use 'em. Do a good Dobson Contracting-level job on that kitchen and I'll see you when you guys get back to Atlanta."

Kenny closed his eyes, a little overwhelmed by the reaction. Man, he'd been not only given the best adopted parents who ever lived, he might also have two of the best biological ones.

"Thanks, man." He tapped the phone and sat very still for a moment, until he heard footsteps behind him.

"Everything okay?" Beck asked.

He turned and looked up at her, feeling more than a little guilty for not saying, *Yeah, you'll never guess who I was just talking to.*

But Bill wanted to stay in the background, and he had to respect that. "It is," he said, pushing up. "I actually have a, well, a proposal of sorts."

Her eyes flickered with interest. "What's that?"

He took a step up, coming eye to eye with her. With those green eyes so much like Ava's. For some reason, just looking into them made what he was about to say so much easier. So much...righter.

"How'd you like to have your kitchen finished in the next month or six weeks? I'll do it," he added quickly. "But only because Ava and I would be your current boarders. I'll do the kitchen for the cost of the materials if you'll let us stay."

Her mouth opened into an 'o' of shock. "Are you serious?"

Funny, she sounded exactly like Ava, with the same intonation and hope that he was, indeed, serious. And that made everything feel good. They needed each other, this kind woman and her somewhat lost granddaughter.

"I just talked to my boss." He swallowed, knowing he'd have to be careful not to say the guy's name if he was to keep Bill's identity on the down low. "He can spare me. My station has a long roster of replacements for me if I want to take a leave. I can stay and work. If Ava can..."

"Heal?" she suggested.

"Learn to love a family without panicking over it. That's kind of what she needs right now. But..." He looked beyond her at the open front door. "I gave the final decision to her. She's a little freaked out."

"Panicking over family? I thought she was just afraid of the water."

"It's more than that. It's fear of losing control, I guess. And the fear of losing *someone* again," he said, feeling a little awkward discussing this, but it was that awkwardness that made him quiet all these years. And that wasn't helping his daughter. "I'm sure it doesn't surprise you to know she was really wrecked when her mom and brother died. And she's lost both grandparents, now. It's been rough."

She nodded, listening. "I guess these attacks happen when anything makes her feel closed in or vulnerable or out of control," she said. "And what can make you feel more out of control than losing someone you love? Many someones."

Exactly. How awesome that she understood. "She

asked me if we could go home," he told her. "I think she's scared of how attached she could get to you."

"That could happen," Beck said. "I'm already attached to her and she's only been here two days."

He smiled. "But I think she has to learn that attachment is good. I've done a crappy job of teaching her that. I've been in mourning for years and trying to hide my head in a hole and hope she manages to grow up." He let out a quick sigh. "What I'm saying is I need your help."

"And we are more than willing to give it."

"That is, if she wants to stay."

"C'mere, Kenny." She gestured for him to follow her into the house. He did, continuing to follow her to the open bedroom door.

From there, he heard Savannah's voice, followed by Ava's laugh. It felt so good to hear that.

Beck just smiled as if to say, "Doesn't that answer your question?"

But he had to know. He walked into the room, where three dogs, one grandmother, and two aunts surrounded his little girl. She looked up at him, bringing Sugar up to her mouth to kiss the dog's head.

"Well?" he asked, unable to hide his smile.

Her eyes glimmered and despite their color, she suddenly looked so much like Elise that it nearly gutted him. "Let's stay, Daddy."

He couldn't remember the last time she'd called him Daddy. Probably the day of the fire. He knew that instant that this was the best decision he'd ever made.

"Sounds like a plan, A."

CHAPTER FIFTEEN
BECK

*I*t didn't take long to settle into a new normal at Coquina House. Not that anything in the house felt remotely *normal* to Beck. For one thing, a mere ten days after Kenny and Ava decided to stay for the summer, and there was essentially no kitchen—just the hot plate and fridge they'd moved into the dining room, using the sink in the laundry, and somehow managing to "make do" with five people living in the house.

There were a lot of meals at Lovely's cottage, and they'd had "private dinners" at Chuck's on the nights that Jessie kept it closed. With takeout and Kenny working the grill outside, Beck had to admit that not having a kitchen somehow became a great family adventure, and she loved that.

They even made the bedrooms work, proving that once Beck worked out how she'd renovate and add at least one more room in the third-floor attic, she'd have plenty of space for guests. With Kenny in one of the second-floor bedrooms, Savannah and Ava were sharing the oversized third floor in twin beds.

That left Peyton in one of the second-floor bedrooms, while Beck had made the downstairs suite her home. She'd already decided that's where she'd sleep when Coquina House was a working B&B, a dream that was little by little starting to feel like it might really come true.

A Christmas opening? Maybe. That would be the height of the tourist season down here. It was June now, so surely she'd secure a contractor soon and could make the holidays. That was, as long as it was a light and easy hurricane season.

Hurricanes. She shook off the thought as she finished dressing for the day and headed through the main living area, following the sound of a drill and a slightly raised voice.

That wasn't Savannah or Peyton talking to Kenny, was it?

Oh, it was Maggie! She'd totally forgotten the designer was coming over to get some final measurements on the counters now that the kitchen was essentially empty.

"You absolutely cannot do that," Maggie said, her voice a little sterner than Beck could remember hearing it. And she heard it a lot. In fact, it seemed the designer found a multitude of reasons to stop by the house since Kenny started the demolition work. Many things, Beck mused, that could have been handled by a text or phone call.

But when she was there, there was usually a lot of laughter, and some teasing, when Kenny and Maggie discussed kitchen remodeling details. He was far enough along that he could usually deal with whatever Maggie needed, so Beck had actually missed her last few visits. The two of them seemed to work well together, which Beck figured was great since Maggie handled the design ideas and Kenny made them come to life.

In fact, the very first weekend Kenny was here, when Maggie had come to get her samples, Beck couldn't help noticing the young woman brightened considerably. And Kenny seemed more than a little amused and interested in Maggie, too. There weren't exactly sparks flying, but Beck couldn't help wondering if there could be.

"I can and I will and that's that, sorry." Kenny's voice was low, calm, and sounded a lot like when he was disciplining Ava.

So, from the sound of things, there were sparks flying plenty right now—and not the romantic kind.

"Hey there," Beck called as she bypassed the coffee maker they'd set up in the dining room and headed right to the kitchen. "What's happening, you guys?"

The two of them froze, each looking at the other with a challenge in their eyes.

"I woke up in the middle of the night and thought of a plan change," Kenny said. "And the designer is not happy with me."

"Change them how?" Beck asked.

"Look, Beck, if the sink is here..." He stood about four feet from the plumbing that remained from the old sink. "And not where it is now, you have all that extra prep space, it's better situated under the window, and you can put in a second dishwasher. When you have guests and twenty coffee cups a morning, you're going to want that."

"Oh, I like that—"

"I like it, too," Maggie said. "It was in my original design."

"Then what's the problem?" Beck asked.

"You can't make that change without a permit," Maggie said, crossing her arms. "Anything that moves plumbing or changes electrical wiring in the county requires a permit."

"Then let's get one," Beck said.

Maggie lifted her brow, hands on hips. "He isn't licensed to do work in Florida. Our county will never give him a permit."

"We don't need a permit for this," Kenny countered. "You don't have original plans because the house was built a hundred years ago and updated many times. None of those updates are on file, and I know that because I did a search. When you have a building inspection after you do the contracted work in the rest of the house, there will be no evidence that we moved plumbing."

"But we *will* have moved the plumbing," Maggie said.

"Who would look? Why would they?" Kenny countered. "And you know as well as I do that the plumbing permit for something like this is a joke, just a way to charge a hundred and fifty bucks and line the county's pockets."

Maggie lifted a shoulder and turned to Beck as if she were judge and jury.

"I don't want anything to be illegal," Beck said.

"It's not illegal—"

"It's not permitted." Maggie cut off Kenny's argument.

"Well, what can I do?" Beck asked. "How can we get a permit? How long will it take? Do I have to have a contractor?"

"You have to have a tradesman licensed in Florida and you, as the homeowner, have to go in person to the county building office and apply. Pay the fee. Wait for inspection, which could take weeks, and finally get the permit."

Beck sighed at that. "Wow, that's a delay we weren't expecting. Not to mention that Lovely is technically the homeowner, so she'd have to go to the office with me. And you..."

"Would need to get a Florida license."

"Is it hard or expensive?"

"It's time consuming, like everything else," Kenny said. "I have to apply, pay the fee, prove I have insurance, get fingerprinted, show a credit score." He shook his head. "I can do all that and we can get the permit, Beck, but this kitchen won't be done until September."

"Then maybe we leave the sink where it is," Beck said on a sigh. "Which is a shame because I love the idea."

"My back-up plan is just as good," Maggie said, shooting him a victorious look. "Now can we work on the measurements for the countertops?"

He shook his head slowly. "They're just going to change when we move the plumbing."

Maggie took a few steps closer, looking up at him, silently fuming.

Kenny held his ground, staring down, a smile threatening.

Their argument was not helping Beck get her kitchen remodeled.

"Give me a week," Kenny finally said. "I'll fix the problem by then."

"If you move that plumbing without a proper

permit..." Maggie didn't take her gaze off his. "I'll quit the job."

"You're stubborn," he said, half under his breath and with a hint of dismay.

"I do things the right way," she lobbed back.

Beck opened her mouth to argue, but didn't say a word as Kenny dipped his head a little lower. "Well, don't quit the job," he said softly. "I wouldn't like that at all."

Whoa. Beck drew back, suddenly feeling like she'd stepped into a very private moment. Sparks weren't just flying, they were frying up her unremodeled, unpermitted, unfinished kitchen. Half of her wanted to go full client here and snap her fingers to break the tension crackling between the two of them. But the other half?

She was enjoying the heck out of this new wrinkle.

"Fine." Maggie backed down first, her cheeks flushed, her dark eyes fiery when she finally looked away from him and turned to Beck. "I'll be back in a few days or a week to measure. Oh, and I have that wallpaper book in my car, Beck. Can you come with me and I'll give it to you?"

She had a feeling her designer wanted to give her more than a wallpaper book, but Beck simply agreed and walked outside and down the stairs with Maggie.

"Sorry it got so hot in there," Maggie said as they reached her car. "The man makes me a little crazy."

"Is he cutting corners? Not doing a good job?" Beck searched Maggie's features, looking for clues to the truth, but seeing only a gorgeous woman who was probably captivating to Kenny.

"He's doing a great job," she said on a sigh. "And it

pains me to admit it, but the sink move is the absolute right thing to do."

"But it will cost us weeks and weeks."

"It might. I could pull some strings down at the department and speed things up, so that will help. I just didn't want to tell him and have him start the work before I finalized that."

"So then, what's the problem?" Beck asked, frowning.

"The problem is with me, and I'm sorry." She gave a tight smile. "He just drives me crazy, and all my Greek comes out. I'm sorry."

"Crazy...in what kind of way?"

She puffed out a breath that fluttered her nearly-black bangs. "In a not so professional way, I'm afraid. I know he's working for you, so it's not cool. Plus, he's your *son*."

"Not...technically," Beck corrected. "I mean, yes, I gave birth to him, but another woman raised him."

"I know," Maggie said. "Are you telling people that?"

"Well, we're not hiding it, but it's not something you announce to the world. He's spending a good part of the summer here and we're getting to know each other, and really enjoying it," she added. "He is a great guy."

"A little too great."

"Ahh. I thought I sensed a little...attraction. Mutual, if I know anything about people."

Maggie smiled. "Yeah, there's definitely a little some-thin' somethin' goin' on," she joked.

"Well..." Beck gave her a jab with her elbow. "Give him a reason to stay or live closer. I certainly wouldn't mind."

She looked past Beck, up at the house. "He's a serious guy, though. I doubt he's just looking for a good time."

"Are you?"

"I'm a workaholic and very independent," she said. "I'm not looking for forever, just, you know...good company."

"Well, he's a single father so I guess he has to be somewhat serious, but would it hurt to date him?"

"Hurt?" She winked. "I think it would feel pretty damn good."

"Then why don't you ask him out, Maggie?"

Her eyes flashed, then she turned to reach into the back seat of her car. "I'd rather he did the asking, as old fashioned as that sounds. I guess it's the Greek in me."

"Want me to help things along?"

She shook her head. "That'd be weird."

"Then how about you help him get that permit, Maggie," Beck said. "It's the first step."

She gave Beck a warm smile. "Thanks for being so understanding, Beck. You have every reason to tell me to back off, do my job, and stop ogling the trades, especially when this one is your son."

"I also have every reason to want him to stick around," she admitted, taking the wallpaper book. "So this is for the accent wall?"

"One wall, opposite the island. You can go crazy." She laughed. "Obviously, I already have."

Beck laughed at that and said goodbye to Maggie. A few minutes later, she wrapped her arms around the book as she headed back up to the house, thinking about the conversation. Was Kenny open to a new woman in his life? To the possibility of love? He sure seemed closed off, which was probably why he could flirt a little with a young woman as attractive as Maggie, but not make a move.

This time, she did stop and get coffee in the dining room, flipping through the wallpaper book when her phone buzzed with a text from an unknown number.

Hi this is Gwendolyn Parker! I heard you're opening a hospitality business in Coconut Key!

She certainly was trying to. She skimmed the text with interest. It wasn't too surprising that Gwen, the yogi with a heart of gold, was hitting up Beck, a soon-to-be business owner in Coconut Key, for help with the next big Habitat for Humanity fundraiser. She wanted to know if Beck could help with any of the upcoming events —a 5K race, a spaghetti dinner, or the bachelor auction. All of them could build awareness for Coquina House B&B, plus help a good cause.

A slow smile pulled as she walked into the kitchen with a cup of coffee for herself and one for him, ready to get him to help more than one cause.

CHAPTER SIXTEEN
AVA

"*And* that, my friends, is a wrap on the author portrait," Savannah announced, lowering her camera. "And it's not even eight in the morning."

"Thank God." Jessie pushed up from what looked like a totally unnatural and uncomfortable position, standing over a table on the Chuck's patio with the sun coming up over the Atlantic behind her.

Ava sipped her second cup of coffee. It had been the bribe that Savannah had to give her to get her up and at 'em at the ungodly hour of...whatever time sunrise was. Savannah had made them all come out with her because the light was "insane" at this hour. Poor Jessie had to put on makeup and do her hair and dress like a chef for her picture that would be in the cookbook.

But Ava didn't really mind. Whatever she did with her aunts, especially Savannah, was fun.

"We could do one more on that bench," Savannah said.

"Please no more," Jessie pleaded. "You've taken six hundred pictures of me."

"But only one will be perfect. Pey, you're the boss here." Savannah walked over to her and let her sister click through the images on the camera screen. "More, or are we done?"

After a minute, Peyton smiled. "Look at that shot," she said, turning the camera so Ava could see it. "You were right about the light, Sav."

The picture was beautiful with a golden glow around Jessie and the food on the table almost looked three dimensional. "Wow, pretty."

"Look at this one, Jessie." Peyton carried the camera over to Jessie to show her.

"You know what that means?" Savannah grinned at Ava. "We are up with the sun and a whole day with no work in front of us. Want to do something fun and exciting?"

Ava beamed at her, that now familiar warm feeling shooting through her. "I'm down," she said, lifting the coffee. "At least I'm awake."

"It's a nice day for a swim."

Ava drew back, her eyes wide. "You're kidding, right?"

"You promised you'd try again," Savannah reminded her.

She had promised the day after Dad said they could stay for the summer, but Ava had been so high on the news that she might have promised anything. "I was in a weakened condition."

Savannah laughed and leaned in. "Have you had a panic since the first one?"

She loved that Savannah used her word of "a panic"

for the incidents, knowing that was her way of letting Ava know she understood the whole thing.

"Nope, not one," Ava said.

"Do you think they're over?"

"I don't know," Ava said.

"There's only one way to find out."

Her heart dropped in an already tight chest. "I'm not ready to go swimming, Savannah," she said softly. "Please don't make me."

"I would never," she assured Ava. "If you want to before the end of the summer, it will be your decision completely. But what I want is for you to beat the panics. What's a completely safe thing that might make you feel a little stressed? How about a little ride on the skiff? It's just a glorified canoe with an engine. On the water, not *in* it?"

Part of Ava wanted to shake her head and stop this right now. But another part—the part that wanted to be cured and over with these episodes—was keenly interested in having Savannah help her. Still, the boat on the water was a little too...scary.

"I don't think so, Savannah."

"Your call, kiddo." Savannah dropped the subject when Peyton and Jessie came back, chatting about the photos and discussing all their options. While they talked, Ava walked out to the railing of the patio, looking out over the water.

Could she do it again? No. Not a chance. In fact, she had to turn away from the surf, looking to the right back down the beach. Her gaze fell on the mesh hammock just outside of Lovely's cottage. And it gave her an idea. A silly, crazy idea, but if she knew anything about

Savannah Foster, it was that she respected the silly and crazy.

After they put everything away, packed up Savannah's gear, and headed outside, Ava tugged on her aunt's arm.

"Okay. I have an idea for something that might be safe but a little out of control."

Savannah's brows lifted. "I'm listening."

"Let's go down to Lovely's hammock."

"Always game for that. What's the plan?"

Ava took a deep breath as they walked. "You're going to swing me in it. Hard and fast. And I'll close my eyes. It's the kind of thing that just might stress me out, but be manageable enough that I won't have a panic. But if it starts, you can help me."

Savannah looked at her for a long time, a slow smile forming. "Not a bad plan, grasshopper. But you need to have a safe word. You have to be able to say a word that isn't stop or wait but means you don't like the feeling, and I will instantly stop and help you."

She smiled. "You don't think this idea is dumb?"

Savannah put her arm around Ava's shoulders and she stiffened, but forced herself not to slip out of the touch. It was one step closer to...normal. And the only thing Ava wanted when she left this island was to be normal.

"I think that it's brilliant. Safe word? Something weird and out there that you would never say so I know you are having a moment."

Ava thought about that. "Like...hamburger?"

"What if you're hungry and thinking about food? No. More out there."

"Olive oil?"

"Do you need breakfast, Ava?"

She laughed. "Too much restaurant stuff. Okay. I got one. How about..." She pointed to one of the big pink flowers in bushes that lined the street. "Whatever that is."

"Hibiscus, I think. Okay. That's your word. *Hi-bis-cus*. If you say that, I stop everything and help. Cool?"

"Cool." Ava ran toward the beach, gesturing for Savannah to follow.

"Hold up, youngster. I'm running for two here."

Still laughing, Ava reached the hammock and slid into it, letting it sway easily the way it did that very first day when she got here.

"All right, close your eyes," Savannah said as she reached her. "And don't hold on. You're going to swing. Ready?"

"Ready?"

She felt the pull as Savannah dragged the hammock to one side, and suddenly, Ava was transported back in time to a playground...a swing...the feel of being pulled back before getting let go.

Her mother was there. Laughing and clucking at baby Adam while she swung Ava.

Oh, no. Here it comes.

When Savannah let go, Ava braced for the tightness in her chest, the first squeeze of breathlessness.

But all that came out of her was a sudden laugh when Savannah snagged the hammock, pulled it further and asked, "Again, grasshopper?"

"Yes!" And this time she was ready for the thrill and the memory. Best of all, there was no panic. "Again and again!"

Savannah played along, swinging her higher and

faster until she darn near flipped, but Ava never felt a single thing except...elation. Freedom. Joy.

When the hammock started to slow down, she was almost happy enough to hug the woman who'd helped her. Almost, but not quite.

"How do you feel?" Savannah asked, plopping in next to her and making the swing sag a little.

"Great." She put her hand on her chest, feeling her heart beat in a way that was perfectly natural for this situation. Perfectly...normal. "It worked!"

Savannah fist pumped. "Any other great ideas? I'm game. As long as we take it slow and safe."

Ava looked at her, letting her gaze slide all over Savannah's face, emotion welling up until it nearly choked her. "Let's try that skip thing."

"You mean the skiff? Which is another word for a truly lowbrow boat that anyone can steer?"

Ava laughed. "Yeah. I want to try it." *On* the water, not *in* it. How bad could that be?

Not bad at all. In fact, not an hour later, they were skimming over the water, a good half mile offshore, with Ava holding the stick connected to the motor, steering them straight, left, and right. And they even saw dolphins.

"You doin' okay?" Savannah asked, lifting her face to the sun and rubbing her belly with one hand.

"I'm doing great," Ava said. "This is easier than driving a car."

"Which you hate, I'm guessing."

Ava laughed. "Just left turns across a highway with no light." She grunted. "My personal hell."

Savannah straightened and looked across the little

boat at Ava. "Here's the good news. You don't really outgrow the attacks, but you learn how to avoid and mitigate them."

Ava didn't know what "mitigate" meant, but she got the idea. "Is that what happened to you?"

"Yeah. I'd say around college they simmered down a bit. I could, you know, climb into an elevator and not freak out. You want to go get some lunch?" She patted that belly. "Pink Line is starving."

"In this boat?"

"There's a dock behind the Coconut Key market. I am craving chicken salad on potato chips. Don't make a face. You have no idea what it's like to be pregnant." Savannah pointed to the right. "Follow the shore until you see the blue awnings of Conchy Charlies. It's the dock right past that."

Taking a deep breath of what felt like raw confidence, Ava followed her instructions, feeling incredibly in control and calm. She loved this. She loved...Savannah.

"Great idea, the skiff," Savannah said, leaning all the way back. "I'm mellow and joyous. You could ask me for anything and I'd say yes. Don't tell Pink Line." She patted her belly. "I don't want her to be spoiled."

"You sure it's a girl?"

"No idea. Don't want to know."

"Does the father want to know?"

Savannah's body tensed and she stayed silent for a long time. "He doesn't know I'm pregnant," she finally said, so softly Ava almost didn't hear the words over the engine.

"Really?" Her eyes popped as she asked the first question that came to her head. "Is that legal?"

Savannah sat up. "I don't know. Isn't it my body, my choice?"

"Isn't it half his baby?"

She swore—something she rarely did—and dropped her head back down. "You're gonna give *me* a panic attack, grassy."

"I'm sorry," Ava said, and meant it. "We can talk about something else."

"There isn't anything else," Savannah muttered. "I just hate the topic of telling him."

Ava nodded, trying to think of something else to talk about, but of course, now she was laser focused on the baby daddy. But she had to try because Savannah's smile was completely gone.

"What's it like being pregnant?" she asked, grabbing at conversation straws.

"Mostly it's fine, punctuated by moments of terror, starvation, and self-loathing. Sometimes it's actually exciting to think about being a mother, but then I think about being a mother and..." She grunted. "I'm gonna suck."

"No you aren't! You're going to be the best mother ever." Well, since Elise Gallagher, but she didn't add that because knowing Savannah, she'd shift the whole conversation and they'd be talking about Ava's mom. Which she loved to do, but something told her that Savannah was the one who needed to unload right then.

"Please," Savannah said, sitting up to make her point. "I have no idea what I'm doing. I'm pretty much the most selfish person you want to meet. And I've never lived anywhere as an adult for more than a year. I..." She shook her head, at a loss for words. "I don't know what the hell

I'm doing, but here I am, six months pregnant, and Pink Line is going to be a real person and I..."

"She's the luckiest kid in the world, Savannah," Ava said. "You're so much fun. And you're kind. And real and present and..." She swallowed some tears she did not want to shed. "You remind me of my mom, who always made me laugh and feel safe."

"Aww." Savannah reached out and squeezed Ava's hand. "That's so sweet. Thank you, Ava. I'm touched."

"So don't be scared," Ava said. "You'll do fine."

Savannah gave a tight smile and turned to see where they were. "Oh, just aim for the turquoise coconut," she said, snorting a laugh. "Words you only hear in Coconut Key. That's the back of the market. Follow the sound of chicken salad and potato chips calling my name."

Ava giggled at that, steering them that way.

Savannah stayed turned even as they reached the dock, giving instructions over her shoulder until Ava slid the boat next to the wooden pilings where a rope hung down. Ava stood, spreading her legs so she didn't fall, and it was only then that Ava saw that Savannah had been crying.

"What's wrong?" she asked, almost losing her balance when she looked at Savannah's tear-streaked face.

Savannah answered by pressing her hand to her chest and Ava slowly dropped down to sit next to her on the tiny bench that crossed the middle of the boat.

"Are you okay, Savannah? Are you having a panic?"

She managed a smile. "Of sorts. I know what I should do. I know what I'm supposed to do. I know what the right thing to do is." She looked down at her belly and gave the bump a slow stroke. "I don't want to face...him.

Or feel like I have to go back to California. Or share my Pink Line with anyone. Is that wrong?"

She was seriously asking a fifteen-year-old? The very idea of it gave Ava a boost of confidence and happiness that she couldn't describe. And the urgent need to give the right advice to this woman who had become so dear to her.

"I don't know." Dang. It was the best she could do.

"I do," Savannah said. "But I really like living in this bubble."

"Really?" Ava asked. "'Cause I would think a claustro-phobic person would hate a bubble."

Very slowly, Savannah smiled. "Touché, grasshopper. You are wise beyond your years."

Ava let the compliment warm her. "So what are you going to do?"

"Eat chicken salad. And hug you, whether you like it or not." Savannah reached out and folded Ava into a hug, squeezing her so she couldn't pull out of the tight grip. "Hibiscus?" Savannah asked on a whisper. "Let me know if anything has to stop."

Ava shook her head and let herself be hugged. "I'm okay."

Really, it was the most amazing thing ever.

CHAPTER SEVENTEEN
KENNY

*C*rap. Big fat crap. Was he really doing this? Elise would howl. A bachelor auction? Seriously?

Kenny leaned back from the bathroom mirror, rubbing a hand on his freshly shaven face and letting his gaze drop over the dress shirt and slacks he let Ava and her sidekick, Savannah, pick for him. A smile pulled as he thought of that afternoon spent with his daughter and his sister.

He had a sister. Two of them—well, three, counting the one he'd never met—and he couldn't deny the fact that he liked them. All of them, Beck included. And Lovely, who'd volunteered to stay home from the "adult" fundraiser and hang out with Ava, which he thought was very cool.

He'd been here almost a month. He'd driven down and planned to get his daughter, turn around, and go home, but here they were, three and a half weeks later... attending a Habitat for Humanity fundraiser. How many times had Bill tried to drag him to some overdressed event like this for the company?

Many. And he'd always failed because who wanted to do anything "fun" without Elise? Not him. He couldn't remember the last time he'd gotten dressed up, other than his mother's funeral. And this could only end up one way: with a date. A *date*.

Well, he sure hoped Maggie Karras was in a spending mood.

Smiling at that, he turned and opened the bathroom door and almost walked right into Peyton, coming out of her room across the hall.

"Oh, hello, there," she said, her smile just as bright as Beck's, whom she so clearly took after. "Whoa, look at you. Snazzy."

He laughed and nodded toward the black cocktail dress she wore. "And you look lovely."

"Thank you, but it's not about the women tonight. All that matters is my checkbook."

He gestured for her to go ahead of him down the stairs to where he could already hear laughter and glasses clinking as family and friends gathered in the living room.

"Hey, Pey-pey." Savannah showed up at the bottom of the steps, wearing a fire engine red dress that actually showed off her growing bump. "Val just pulled up. And you didn't even buy him yet."

"He said he wanted to go with us." Peyton walked by her sister and tapped her chin. "You buy the date, not the man."

"I'm not buying anyone," Savannah muttered as Peyton walked toward the front door, then she smiled up at Kenny, a few steps behind. "But, if I were and you weren't my brother, I'd drop a Benjie on you, handsome."

He laughed, which was actually the only thing he could do around this woman. And try to show her how deeply grateful he was that she'd taken a shine to Ava and was helping her so very much.

"But then I'd have to wrestle Maggie Karras and she surely has more money than I do." Savannah beamed at him. "Am I right, big bro?"

He tried for a "get real" look instead of answering.

"What, you think we're all blind and stupid?"

"I think you're..." Absolutely right. "Imagining things."

"I guess we'll see tonight. Here." She handed him an open beer. "I'm the DD tonight and always."

"Thanks. And thanks for all you're doing with Ava. She told me that you said you'd take her driving next? She has a permit, but every time I try to teach her, we get into an argument or she has some kind of meltdown."

She narrowed her eyes, looking like she was considering just how honest to be. "I think you should call them panic attacks, Dad. She's not melting. She's trying to cope."

"Sorry," he said, feeling a little ashamed that he'd belittled his daughter's issues. "And she told me yesterday she hasn't had one since the day in the water. Credit to you, Aunt Savannah." He lifted the bottle in a toast, hoping he sounded as genuine as he felt.

She smiled and tapped her nail on the bottle. "She's a good kid. Actually, a great kid."

"I know that." He looked past her in case Ava came zipping around the corner and caught them talking about her. "She seems really steady here, too. That much I can see."

"A lot of women," she said, stepping back so he could come down the last step. "It's a supportive and nurturing atmosphere."

He let out a sigh, knowing how much that would change when he left. "I guess my mother really knew what she was doing when she told Ava to find Beck," he mused.

"It seems to have meant a lot to her to find family. And we like her." She winked. "You're okay, too. You know, for the pesky big brother I never had."

"I'm going to bet if anyone was pesky in this family, it was you."

"Oh, yeah. Cornered the market on peskiness." She laughed but didn't move toward the living room, searching his face as if she had more to say.

He paused for a second, waiting and not wanting to be rude by walking away.

"Ever wonder about your dad?" she asked suddenly.

Oh, yes. More to say. "Not...much."

"Have you asked my mother?"

He shook his head. "Pretty sure that's ancient history and she has never mentioned it to me. I respect her too much to press her on it."

"But don't you wonder?" she asked. "I mean, now you've met us and we're awesome. Aren't you just a little curious who he is? My mother steadfastly refuses to say a name but it's not our business. However, if I were in your shoes, I'd want to know. If for no other reasons than, you know, health and DNA."

He just stared at her, not at all sure how to answer that.

"You see..." She bit her lip and kept him well back from the crowd. "It's starting to keep me awake at night. Tell him, not tell him? Tell the kid, not tell the kid?"

"You haven't told the father?"

She shrugged. "I doubt he cares, honestly."

Ouch.

"Still want me hangin' with your baby girl?"

"You're a wonderful influence on her, Savannah, so the answer is yes." She looked relieved, which he appreciated. "But as far as your other question?" He thought for a moment, about Bill Dobson, specifically.

The man who fathered him was his closest friend, but they only knew each other because of dumb luck and the swiftly changing world of DNA testing. He could have lived his whole life without knowing Bill, and that would have been a damn shame. He probably wouldn't have cared too much because he had a great father in James Gallagher, who taught him that a man isn't measured by his DNA but by how he used whatever gifts God gave him.

That said, his life was better because Bill Dobson was in it. So he couldn't answer her

question without taking that into consideration.

"Yes?" she prodded.

"I don't mean to make you lose any more sleep, but you might not really have the right to keep that from him. He should probably make the choice of whether or not he wants to be part of your child's life."

She winced. "I know."

"Savannah!" Ava called from the living room.

"C'mere! Tell Beck about how I handled the skiff yesterday!"

They let the conversation drop and headed into the living room where the pre-auction party was in full swing. The center of attention, for once, were the guys in the group.

Josh looked as "out of uniform" as Kenny felt, wearing dress clothes instead of his usual T-shirt and cargo shorts. Kenny high-fived him when they shared a smile and mutual "bachelors up for auction" eye-roll.

Val Sanchez didn't seem quite as bothered by the whole thing, but obviously, with his arm around Peyton and his gaze on her, he already knew how this event would end up for him.

"Dad!" Ava fairly floated over to him, looking like that happy little ten-year-old he remembered so well, laughing like her mother, teasing her little brother, goofing around like a kid should. Only she didn't look ten. Not at all. Ava was well on her way to becoming a woman and the very thought of it terrified him.

"You're on the auction block." She made a chopping action and a funny face.

"Hope I don't get my head cut off," he joked.

Beck joined them, smiling at him. "You look very handsome, Kenny. You're a good sport and I appreciate this."

"I'm going to represent Coquina House B&B as best I can, and hope that it gets some people excited about your business when it opens."

"If it opens," she sighed. "Maggie still hasn't been able to reach her friend about getting you that license sped up."

"I have a few more days of work before you have to give up on the sink move. But who knows, Beck?" He lifted the beer bottle. "Maybe a licensed contractor will be up for auction tonight and you can buy him."

She laughed at that, but Josh gave her a look. "So, you're shopping tonight, Ms. Foster?" he asked with a tease in his voice.

"I have a limited budget," she fired back. "Way less than Gwendolyn Parker."

"Isn't she the one organizing this whole thing?" Kenny asked.

Savannah joined them. "Organizing and, from what I hear..." She elbowed Josh. "Shopping for her next good time."

Josh threw a look at Beck. "What did you tell her?"

Beck tried to look innocent, but Savannah just laughed, and Kenny was sure he was missing something, but he had no idea what. It didn't matter. The whole vibe was fun and, dang, he hadn't had much of that lately.

As they gathered up to head for two cars to leave for the hotel, Kenny walked over to the sofa to say goodbye to Ava, sitting with Lovely and three dogs.

"You two going to watch a movie or something?" he asked.

The two of them shared a look and a secret smile, and Kenny was struck again by how strong the green-eye gene was, even separated by, what? Three generations?

"Something," Ava answered with a devilish look in those eyes.

He lifted a brow and gave Lovely a questioning look.

"Something fun," Lovely said. "You just go have a good time and raise lots of money for a good cause."

"Yeah, Dad. I hope you get a really pretty date."

"And *not* Germaine Branthauser," Lovely added.

"Germaine..." He frowned. "Who's that?"

"The owner of the Coconut Café."

His eyes widened as he thought of the much older woman who frequently waited on him when he had lunch there. She was...friendly. Very friendly. Like touch-his-arm-every-time-she-served-him-coffee   friendly. "You're kidding, right?"

Lovely shrugged. "She's in my book club. Couldn't stop talking about you last week."

He felt the color drain as Ava threw her head back and laughed like he hadn't heard her laugh in five years. And that right there might be worth a date with Germaine Branthauser. But he really hoped not.

KENNY WAS PLEASANTLY surprised to see the turnout in the banquet room of the Marriott on Little Torch Key. This was much more than the local crowd, from what he could tell, drawing people from all of the Lower Keys.

Looking around, he could see Bill enjoying himself at a shindig like this. He took a sip of beer at the thought of Bill. He had a lot of nerve telling Savannah to be honest with her unborn child when he hadn't breathed a word to Beck that he knew his biological father.

Would it change things? Would it matter?

He didn't know and, honestly, wasn't ready to rock this boat. Ava was happy and he was—

"I have good news and I have bad news. Which do you want first?"

He turned to look right into the bottomless brown eyes of Maggie Karras and finished his thought. He was happy, he finished mentally. Happier now, anyway.

"Bad first," he said. "Always the bad first."

"Really? I like good first," she said, those dark eyes dancing playfully, and a little brighter with sparkly makeup. He could never tell if she was flirting with him or just really friendly.

"Nah. Get the bad over with," he said, letting his gaze take a quick trip over her to appreciate the white silk top that accentuated her tanned skin and the thick black hair tumbling over her shoulders.

"Wrong! If the good is good enough, then the bad won't matter." She smiled up at him, the tip of her tongue just visible behind perfect white teeth. Yeah, flirting. And he was not hating it.

"All right," he conceded. "We'll do it your way. What's the good news?"

She reached into a little handbag and pulled out a paper. "Congratulations. You officially have a temporary trade license for a limited amount of work, including a plumbing move."

"Seriously?"

She handed him the paper. "You may move your sink, Mr. Gallagher."

He tapped the license against her arm. "Well done, Ms. Karras. And thanks. I owe you one."

"And that's the bad news."

He lifted his brow. "What do you mean?"

Back into the bag, this time to pull out a checkbook. "I'm buying...you."

A kick of something he hadn't felt in a long, long time

hit him right in the solar plexus. "Can't say I see that as bad news at all," he said softly.

"You say that now." She winked and walked away, leaving him with an open jaw.

"Shut it, bro." Savannah walked right up to him and tapped his chin. "She's just a beautiful woman with a checkbook. Oh, look, they're starting the auction."

His sister kept him entertained through the first five guys, with each one making him feel a little better about doing this. No one was taking it too seriously, the bidding was reasonable and fun, and it should be over in no time. And then he could concentrate on that woman who'd gotten under his skin.

"Come on," Savannah said, tugging his arm. "Josh is up next and Mom's in prime position for bidding. Let's join them."

As he walked to the small group that included Val and Peyton, as well as Jessie and Beck, he threw a look at Savannah. "Beck's bidding?" he asked.

"On Josh? Of course."

"I thought that Gwen woman wanted him."

"They both do," Savannah said. "Which is why this should be fun."

"All right, ladies," the emcee, a young man who had a future in stand-up, bellowed to the crowd. "Our next bachelor is a master woodworker from Coconut Key." He waited a beat. "The wood jokes are going to write themselves. Let's get your checkbooks out for Joshua Cross."

Savannah hooted like a nine-year-old at a sporting event, earning a quick look from her mother and laughs from Josh's sister, Jessie.

"I'll open at twenty-five dollars!" A woman a few feet away said, raising her hand.

He glanced over and saw dark hair and his heart hitched for a moment, but then he realized that it wasn't Maggie.

"There goes Gwen," Savannah whispered.

In front of him, Beck sighed. "I'm going to have to do this, aren't I?" she said under her breath to Peyton.

"If you want him, you do."

Did she want him, Kenny wondered? Based on the bidding, which reached a solid one-fifty before it was called in Beck's favor, she did. He clapped with everyone else as the next bachelor was introduced and Peyton turned to him and pointed at the stage.

"You're up after this guy," she said.

With one more sip and a high-five from the women around him, he rounded the perimeter of the room and took his place. Scanning the crowd, he spotted Maggie, who'd joined Beck and the others.

"Brand new to our community, when this next bachelor isn't nailing someone—er, some*thing*—to the wall, he's saving lives as a paramedic. This handsome hero is from Atlanta, Georgia, currently on loan in Coconut Key. Ladies, let's get the bidding started for Kenny Gallagher, here representing what will surely be a very exciting addition to Coconut Key, the Coquina House Bed and Breakfast, opening soon!"

Following what the other men did, he crossed the stage, gave a smile to the crowd—which turned into a chuckle at Savannah's noisy whistle—and found Maggie. He held her gaze and enjoyed the rush of that eye contact, barely aware that someone else had just bid twenty-five bucks.

And then it went to thirty. And thirty-five. And forty. And it kept going higher.

But Maggie hadn't said a word. Was she kidding before? Just jerking his chain? Knowing full well he was into her and—

"Let's make it a hundred!"

He tore his gaze from Maggie just in time to see Gwen Parker wave her hand as she made that last bid. Seriously? Not what he wanted or expected.

And then someone else he couldn't see knocked it up to one-twenty-five. It went once, but Gwen took it to one-fifty. This brought a significant amount of hollering but not one single word from Maggie Karras.

Guess she lied.

"Do I hear one-seventy-five?" The auctioneer asked a quiet room. "All right then, going once, going twice, and it is..."

"Two hundred." Maggie's voice cut through the silence like a sweet little song that sent the cheers up again.

Gwen gave a noisy grunt of defeat.

"Going once, going twice...and Kenny Gallagher is sold for two hundred dollars!"

Words he never thought he'd be so glad to hear. With a nod to the applauding audience, he hustled off the stage, passing Val Sanchez on his way to the stage.

"Get your bait out ladies, this is one of the best-looking fishermen in the Keys."

The rowdy response confirmed that this group couldn't agree more.

Smiling at Maggie, he joined the group, high-fived and tapped knuckles, but sidled right up to Maggie. "You had me a little worried there," he said softly.

"No need to worry." Her eyes sparked with humor. "And Beck's right, you are a good sport to help out like this."

"You're the one who donated to the cause." He took a chance and put a hand on her shoulder. "Can I buy you a celebratory drink?"

"Me?" She stepped out of his touch. "I didn't donate a thing."

He wasn't sure he'd heard that right over the out-of-control bidding going on for Val behind him. "Two hundred dollars?"

"I was authorized to go up to three hundred."

Now he was sure he didn't hear her properly. "Authorized?"

She smiled and slipped out her phone. "Germaine couldn't make it tonight, but I promised to text her the minute I finished bidding on her behalf."

"Germ..." He couldn't even finish.

"Germain Branthauser. At the Coconut Café. She adores you and it's for such a good cause." Cool as a cucumber, she started tapping her phone, then lifted it. "Here, let me send her a picture so she knows her dreams have come true."

"Maggie?"

She took the picture and returned to the text. "Yes?" she asked after a second.

"You didn't bid for yourself?" He still couldn't believe it.

Finally, she hit send with a flourish and looked up at him. "No, Kenny, I didn't. Are you disappointed?"

Crushed. "Just...surprised."

"Don't be. If you want to go out with me, it's not going to happen by me asking or buying. You're going to have to do both." She added a sweet smile, then inched to the side to see what was going on.

A frenzy of cheering, that's what.

"...And Valentino Sanchez has been sold for two-fifty to Gwen Parker!"

Peyton's eyes widened in shock, while Savannah used a word Kenny hoped she didn't say around Ava. And as they all buzzed at the loss, he turned, just in time to see Maggie stepping away.

No, not so fast.

"Maggie," he called after her.

She stopped and turned, giving him an expectant look.

"Maggie," he repeated, his throat closing just a little bit. Did she have any idea that it had been *decades* since he'd officially asked a woman on a date? The last one was Elise Winthrop, his high school sweetheart and most beloved wife.

"Yes?"

He wasn't even sure how to do this anymore. "Is Maggie short for something?"

She blinked, obviously not expecting that question. "Actually, yes. Magdalena."

"Pretty," he said. "That's very pretty. And so are you."

"Thanks, Kenny." Her smile faltered as a few more seconds ticked by.

"So, I'd love to take you out to dinner sometime. Sometime soon," he added. "Like tomorrow."

She laughed softly at the sudden enthusiasm. "I guess if it's okay with Germaine..."

"I'll take her out separately," he said.

That really made her smile. "How sweet. My answer is yes. I'd love to have dinner with you."

Funny, his first thought was that he wanted to tell Ava. And that's how he knew this woman was someone special.

CHAPTER EIGHTEEN
PEYTON

"*E*asy, girl." Using her fingernail, Savannah tapped Peyton's just refilled wine glass and gave a warning look, sending irritation skittering up Peyton's spine.

"Please, don't go holy on me, Sav. I'm not pregnant." She took a healthy swig and hoped she didn't sound too pathetic. "Heck, I can't even buy a date."

Savannah followed Peyton's gaze to where Val stood laughing with Gwendolyn Parker, who had him by a good ten years or more. Didn't stop the woman from flirting like the cheerleader with her eyes on the quarterback.

Savannah made a soft growling sound. "Cougar on the loose."

Peyton snorted. "He can't be interested in her."

"Yeah, 'cause she's ugly. Not in amazing shape or anything. I heard she's a yoga instructor, which means God only knows how she can bend."

Peyton narrowed her eyes. "You're enjoying this, aren't you?"

"I'm amused, but, hey, when you're this pregnant and stone cold sober, you take the humor where you can get it." She took one more look and came closer. "You're not really worried, are you?"

"I don't know what I am," she said glumly, putting the glass to her lips. "But whatever it is, wine makes it better."

"Wine makes your cheeks rosy," Savannah said. "So if you're going for the Rudolph look, by all means, down the hatch."

Peyton lowered the glass, then set it on the table. "God, I hate when you're right."

"Fortunately, it only happens about once a decade." Savannah grinned.

Peyton studied her for a moment, noticing how much Savannah was changing right before their eyes. Pregnancy made her skin glow and the extra weight really put some softness in her normally hollow cheeks.

"What?" Suddenly self-conscious, Savannah wiped her nose. "Do I have a booger or something?"

Peyton laughed softly. "A booger? You've been spending too much time with the under-sixteen set."

"Because my sister is too busy somehow managing two actual jobs when I don't even have one." She rolled her eyes. "You're glued to Jessie and doing the typical 'if one job is good then two is better' Peyton Foster thing."

Peyton heard the old familiar edge in Savannah's voice. Not jealousy, exactly. But there was always an undercurrent of tension between them. "You could work at Chuck's if you want, but..." Her gaze dropped.

"In this century, pregnant women work."

"I don't mean that," Peyton replied. "But do you get tired?"

"Not this trimester. I feel amazing."

Peyton searched her sister's face, trying to figure her out. Would she, though? Ever? "What about your photography business?"

"I tried to get the gig to cover this, but Lady Gwendolyn already had someone doing it gratis."

"And that wedding you called about?"

She shrugged. "They never called me back."

"Your work is so good, Savannah."

"Don't patronize me."

Peyton drew back. "I'm not. I'm trying to help. You never could tell the difference." She reached for the glass, then changed her mind. Instead, she watched Gwen clasp Val's arm and whisper something in his ear that must have been hilarious based on the way he laughed.

Were they trading fish puns?

Savannah stepped to her left to block Peyton's view and force all attention on her. "If you lose him that easily, you never had him."

"Says the woman pregnant by a...is he a married man?" The minute she said the words, Peyton regretted them. "I assume that's what you mean by a professional liar."

"Ouch, Pey. Low blow. Below the big baby bump low."

"I'm sorry, Savannah. That *was* low. I'm sorry."

She gave her head a quick shake, swallowing hard enough that Peyton knew the comment really had hurt. She reached for Savannah's arm. "Please, I didn't mean that."

"Well, you did, but you don't usually say things like that. Especially since we've been here." She patted Peyton's hand.

"Don't sweat it, big sister. You're not *that* far off the mark regarding my kid's dad. Which makes me a wreck while you are working two jobs, and just as close as ever to Mom, and even managed to snag the hottest guy on the island." She wrinkled her nose. "Perfect Peyton never changes."

"Oh, please." Now it was Peyton who felt her throat tighten. "Perfect Peyton who's on her third glass of house merlot."

Savannah waved it off.

"And who never made it in publishing. Couldn't get the Master of the Universe to marry her. And probably will only ever be an aunt and not a mom." The words came tumbling out, her tongue loosened by the wine and self-pity because...jeez. Would that woman *never* stop talking to Val?

She tore her gaze from him to see Savannah's quizzical look, then heard her sigh. "You've always set such high goals, Pey, and, of course, you meet them."

"Not always. Callie's the goal-setter."

"Oh, Callie's in a different league," Savannah said. "She's all Foster. You and me? We got a mix of Dad's ambition and Mom's ambivalence. You more on the ambition side. Me? God, I have nothing."

"Nothing? You have the one thing I want most in the whole world." Peyton's gaze dropped to the baby bump. "And you're so much like Lovely, too, which is amazing."

"Well, we come from a long line of women who've made a few mistakes but didn't stop trying and usually figured out a way to make it work." Savannah gave a sad smile. "And getting pregnant doesn't seem to be a problem for any of us, if that's all you want. I can tell you how it's done. I've heard it goes in easier than it comes out."

Peyton laughed softly. "But I want the whole thing. The husband, the home, the family round the table. I want what Mom and Dad had."

Savannah just shot one brow north.

"Before Mari Cummings wrecked everything," Peyton added.

"Mari *and* Dad," Savannah added. "He's not blameless. So I'm glad he's not happy."

Peyton drew back. "He's not? Have you talked to him?"

"No. I've been talking to Callie."

Some guilt threaded through Peyton. "I haven't had much more than a few texts with her. How is she doing? Working at Dad's firm for the summer, right?"

Savannah nodded. "Where she has a front row seat to the drama."

"There's drama?" Peyton leaned in. "Please tell me there's trouble in paradise."

"I don't know, but from what I get in the subtext, Mari liked being the other woman a little more than she likes being the soon-to-be-wife."

Peyton made a face. "Who would prefer to be a mistress than a wife?"

"Don't ask me." She rubbed her belly and closed her eyes, probably because that was the most she'd revealed yet about her baby's father. "I have to tell him, Pey."

And that was even more. "Yes," Peyton agreed. "You do. What are you waiting for?"

"The nerve."

"What do you think he's going to say or do?" Peyton

sucked in a breath as a thought occurred to her. "Do you think he'll want to take your baby?"

"I don't think so," she said. "I'm ashamed to admit I don't know him that well. But he's rich and fa..." She caught herself and stopped.

Famous? Was that what Savannah was going to say?

"He might throw money at me," Savannah finished.

"Then take it."

Savannah shook her head. "I might take a page from the Used to Be Grandie but Now She's Auntie Olivia Handbook and make him sign something. Callie said she'd ask Dad if he could draw something up."

"Why don't you ask Dad yourself?"

She shrugged. "'Cause he'll make me feel like the loser I am."

"Savannah, you are not a loser!"

Savannah turned and looked behind her, catching Val just as he walked away from Gwen and set his gaze on Peyton.

"Neither are you, big sister, despite what happened in the bachelor auction. Are you desperate enough to take some unsolicited advice from *moi*?"

Peyton sighed and nodded.

"Lay it on the line, girl. Tell Val what you want. Make sure he understands that you are in this for the house, picket fence, and a few hungry little mouths to feed. Don't waste another minute on a man who doesn't put you on a pedestal and dance around you like you are a goddess."

Peyton laughed. "I'm just looking for a good guy to be my partner and father of my children. No worshipping necessary."

"Then tell him that. Here he comes. Spell it out, sister. Make sure he knows. Give him a timeline. This is your life and you know what you want. You always have and that's what I hate and admire most about you."

Peyton stared at her, the words sinking in and hitting her heart.

"Hey, gorgeous." Val wrapped his arms around her waist and pressed his mouth to her hair, planting a kiss. "Couldn't seem to get her to clam up. Har har."

She almost smiled, but even his bad jokes weren't funny. With a quick look at Savannah that she hoped conveyed her gratitude for the pep talk, Peyton turned in his arms and looked up into eyes so dark she could see her own reflection. "We need to talk."

He drew back. "You sound serious."

"I am," she whispered.

Searching her face, he nodded slowly. "Come on, let's take a walk on the beach."

As they stepped away, she shared one more look with Savannah who gave her a secret smile, reminding Peyton that no matter how much they argued, her sister always had her back.

Or she'd just played a bad joke on Peyton, who was about to wreck everything with Val.

🌴

THE MOON WAS NEARLY FULL, big enough to bathe the sand in soft white light, so Peyton and Val didn't step on shells after they kicked their shoes off to walk on the beach. She slid a look at Val, who'd loosened his tie and unbuttoned the top of his shirt, which just made him look sexier in the moonlight.

But it wasn't about sex appeal, which obviously he had in spades. What mattered to Peyton was the man on the inside and if he was even capable of being what she needed. These last few months had been fun—exciting and easy and a perfect escape after the hurt of her breakup with Greg. She fell into Val's arms without a fight...or even a parameter of what she wanted.

And it was time to make sure that what happened with Greg didn't happen again.

"Still can't believe I was outbid," she said on a laugh. "What's her date plan? A yoga class and out to sea in your trawler?"

"We didn't really talk about the date. But I think I agreed to donate half my haul to the food bank for a Fourth of July event she's planning."

"Really?" Well, that made Peyton feel a little better. "She really does seem to care about people in need."

"She does," he agreed. "I like that."

And her heart dropped. "And her?" she asked softly. "Do you like her?"

He just smiled. "I like when you get jealous. It makes me feel..."

"Oh, here comes the fish joke. Hooked? Like *any fin* is possible?" She leaned into him with a tease, wanting to make the conversation a little easier.

"It makes me feel good," he said simply, turning to her with no humor but plenty of warmth in his eyes. "Like I have the best girl."

Her heart lifted right back up again as she slowed her step. "So, I'm your girl, huh?"

"You want to make it official? We can use titles. You're my girlfriend." He scanned her face, looking uncertain. "Am I supposed to ask that? I'm not sure of the protocol anymore."

Why would he not know that? It wasn't the first time he'd referenced not dating much, but it didn't make sense for a guy as good-looking and flirtatious as Val.

"I'd be delighted to be your girlfriend," she said. "Does that mean you'll take me to Miami to meet that big Cuban family now?"

He slowed his step. "You met my brother and his wife."

Briefly, in passing one day when she had stopped by the docks to surprise him. "It felt like you didn't really want me to talk to them, though." She'd tried not to let it bother her at the time, but the rushed introductions had given her pause.

He blew out a breath and guided her closer to the water to let it splash on their feet. There were quite a few more people on this beach than in Coconut Key, mostly tourists from the hotels, with the echo of laughter and steel drums playing from the restaurant bars.

But all that faded away as she waited for his answer.

"Bringing a girl home is kind of a serious move in my family," he finally said. "I'm not sure."

And, once again, her heart tumbled.

"We've been seeing each other for a few months and meeting my parents, at least in my family and culture, is tantamount to..." He just lifted a shoulder. "You know what I mean."

She knew. She also knew if he couldn't say the words

or even find a euphemism for "this is the real deal" then they weren't as close as she thought.

A ribbon of fear wrapped around her chest. She didn't want to face the rejection she got the last time she essentially gave a man an ultimatum. She hadn't exactly done that with Greg, but he cheated and then admitted he was suffocating from how much she wanted marriage and family—and he had wanted neither one.

Peyton couldn't go through that again. She couldn't. She dug deep for the fortitude she'd found during her conversation with Savannah.

"I do know what you mean," she finally said. "And that's what I wanted to talk to you about."

His brows rose with interest, but he didn't say a word.

"I do want to be your girlfriend," she said softly, letting her fingers curl into his bigger, callused ones. "But that's not my...end game."

"It's a game?"

"No, Val. It's not a game to me." She brought them to a halt, turning to look up at him. "It's very serious. And you know why I broke up with my last boyfriend."

"He cheated on you." He shook his head. "Peyton, I would never—"

"I'm not worried about that. But there was more to the breakup. More...problems."

He held her gaze, looking hard at her, waiting for what she would say next.

"I wanted to marry him," she whispered.

"Thank God you didn't," he fired back. "The guy was a cheater, and you deserve better than that, Pey."

"I know I do. I also deserve...forever."

He gave the softest, quickest laugh. "Well, sure."

She stared at him. "I'm not joking."

"I...can tell. What are you asking for, Peyton?" He sounded just scared enough that her heart had to buckle up for the next freefall. She could be sending him away with this conversation. She could be blowing everything right now.

"I just want to be completely honest about why I'm in this relationship," she said. "It's fun and easy and wonderful, yes. I really like you. A lot. I love spending time with you and laughing with you and cooking with you." She had to smile. "I *really* love cooking with you."

"And dessert's not bad, either," he joked.

Always a joke with him. Suddenly, it bothered her. "I'm serious," she said. "This isn't funny to me."

His eyes closed as the words seemed to really hit him, but she refused to stop until she was sure he understood exactly what she was saying. What did she have to lose? Well, besides *him*.

"I want to know that this is leading to long-term," she finally said. "I need to know that you're dating me with the possibility that there's a future. Otherwise..."

Even in the moonlight, he paled. Yep, she could certainly lose him. Well, then she never really had him, did she?

"I know that, Peyton," he said, his words barely a whisper and bathed in pain. But why? What hurt him? Was he *that* afraid of a real commitment?

"And you?" she asked.

He touched her face with his knuckle, grazing her chin, holding her gaze, quiet for long enough that she suspected he was very carefully planning what he'd say next.

For one terrible, ugly moment, she was looking up at Greg in the kitchen the day he admitted cheating, the day he said he felt the walls closing in on him, the very last day she ever saw him. And once again, her heart dropped like it might hit the ground.

Did she just make that same mistake again? Better to know now than in two years.

"I need some time," Val whispered. "I am still figuring out my life, my business, and my...my life."

She swallowed and nodded, still not sure why he'd sound hurt and confused by this.

"I just don't want to settle," she said quietly, the words coming out without giving this truth too much thought. "I don't want to be someone's backup plan. I don't want to be a sometime in the future thing. I don't want to be a maybe."

"All right," he said. "Then brace yourself."

"For what?"

Silent for a few minutes, he stroked her hair, wrapping a strand around his finger as he studied her. "I was engaged before."

Her eyes widened at this news. "You were? I'm...surprised."

"I don't talk about it." For the first time in as long as she'd known him, his voice sounded humorless and numb.

"So...what happened?"

He took a slow, deep breath. "She died."

"Oh." She put her hand over her mouth. "I had no... oh, wow. I'm so sorry, Val. When was this?"

"Two years...well, not quite two years. Twenty-two months and...three days? No, four."

And he was still counting days.

"Val, I'm so..." She shook her head, reeling. "I had no idea. I never heard this."

"No one in the Keys knows. It's why I moved here. I wanted a fresh start without our families around. And our relationship was as close to an arranged marriage as you can get in this day and age. We grew up next door to each other, were friends since we were in diapers, and were high school sweethearts, together all through college, and graduate school. We were saving money for a house, planning our wedding when..." He stopped for a moment to gather himself. "She was diagnosed with leukemia."

"Oh, Val."

He nodded. "It wrecked us all. Her family, obviously. Mine, too, since she was just like an extension of ours. I wanted to get married immediately, to give her hope and give us a miracle story, but..."

"You didn't?"

"She wouldn't. She was sick for two years, but refused to get married until she was in remission. That never happened. The whole time I wanted to get married, but she said it was just me being romantic and if I married her, I'd take away that honor from the woman I would eventually marry." His voice cracked. "And I told her there never would be anyone else."

She pressed her fingers to her lips, trying to reconcile this tragedy with the funny, lighthearted man she'd come to know.

"I left Miami a few days after the funeral. I moved out of my apartment and quit my job, threw everything in my truck and headed south. Stopped at Coconut Key and

decided to do the only thing that gave me comfort
—fish."

She frowned, something he'd said finally rising to the
surface. He'd gone to graduate school? He never told her
that. "What job did you have?"

He smiled for the first time, a wistful "you're not going
to believe this" kind of smile. "I was a financial analyst. I
have an MBA from the University of Miami and worked
for a huge accounting firm."

"And you gave that up?"

He lifted a shoulder. "The money and work meant
nothing to me. I didn't need them. Didn't need a steady
future without..." He shook his head. "I started a whole
new life here. It was that or end the one I had. Like,
literally."

On a soft groan of pain, she wrapped her arms
around his waist, pulling him closer, needing to comfort
him. "I'm so sorry I made you talk about it. So sorry I
even mentioned—"

"No." He drew back and looked hard at her. "Don't
apologize for saying what you want. If anyone should
apologize, it's me for not telling you. But it's very, very
difficult for me, and see how it changes everything?"

She didn't quite see, but she suspected she would
when she had time to process this.

"But I will tell you this, Peyton. Life is freaking short,
so you keep your eyes on the prize. You should do and get
and be exactly what you want." His voice vibrated with
the urgency and emotion behind his words. "With...or
without me."

In other words, he was so not ready to try love again.
And she completely understood.

"Now, if you don't mind, I'm going to walk you back to the fundraiser and head home."

She nodded and walked silently over the sand with him. At least her heart wasn't falling anymore. Now, it was just...shattered.

CHAPTER NINETEEN
BECK

*T*he bachelor auction was winding down when the group who'd arrived together re-gathered to head home.

"Where's Peyton?" Beck asked, looking around at the few stragglers as the lights came up in the banquet room and the staff started clearing tables.

"She left a while ago," Savannah said. "She texted me that she was taking an Uber back to Coquina House."

Beck frowned. "And Val?"

"I guess they're together? She went for a walk with him, then I got the text."

That was odd. "Did she get home okay?"

Savannah rolled her eyes. "She's thirty-one and with her man, Mom. Chill. Whoever is driving with me, I'm ready to roll." She shook her keys. "Pregnant woman needs her sleep."

"I'll take you back to Coquina House," Josh said, lowering his head to whisper to Beck. "After all, you bought me."

She smiled up at him and nodded, liking the idea of unwinding alone in his truck on the way back to Coconut Key.

A few minutes later, they were rumbling down US 1, following the moonbeams on the Gulf of Mexico to their right.

"I hope Peyton's okay."

He shot her a look. "You heard Savannah. Grown woman, let go."

"But does one ever stop being a parent?" she mused.

"Maybe not, but you do dial back on breathing down their necks."

She waited for him to elaborate, to talk about the three grown children he'd had with Lily, his ex-wife. But he looked straight ahead, quiet as always. Calm and steady. Which was exactly what she liked about Josh and why she chose the less "dramatic" ride home with Savannah at the wheel, doing the post-mortem on the bachelor auction.

"Do I breathe down my girls' necks?" She let out a small laugh. "Okay, maybe sometimes. But Peyton's tender. And you-know-who bought Val. That had to hurt."

"I don't think Gwen Parker is a threat to Peyton. And if she's not home when we get there, you can relax. She's thirty-one and Val's a good guy."

Beck tipped her head in agreement and studied the moonlight some more. "Did you have fun?" she asked.

"I'm still having it." He threw her a smile. "And I like who bought me."

"I didn't *buy* you," she said on a chuckle. "But I guess I

should ask what you want to do for our 'date.' Can I make you dinner?"

"In the kitchen you don't have?" he joked. "Don't feel compelled to do anything, Beck. You donated money to a great cause and Gwen wrestled some free furniture for a Habitat house out of me. We did our good deeds."

She studied him for a moment, aware of how close they were to Coconut Key and how much she didn't want this interlude to end. It was nice to be driving home from a night out with a man again. Nice to be chatting about kids and life, relaxed from a glass of wine, shoes kicked off.

It reminded her of the things she missed about being married.

"What if I said I wanted to make good on that date?" she asked softly.

He smiled but kept his eyes on the road. "I'd say...is tomorrow night too soon?"

She laughed. "We'll see."

"And she backs out."

"I'm not backing out."

He slid her a look. "Don't worry, Beck. I know your situation." He reached over the console and found her hand, closing his strong fingers around hers. "I'm a very patient man."

"Patient and kind and steady and strong." She sighed. "You're pretty much perfect, Joshua Cross."

"Hardly," he snorted, but threaded their fingers and guided her hand to his lap, holding it tight. "But you are, you know?"

"I am not." But the compliment sent a sweet flutter through her. "Starting with the fact that I'm married. And distracted by a new business. And still licking the wounds of my husband's infidelity." She sighed. "And based on that bidding, you really are one of Coconut Key's more eligible bachelors."

"In the silver set," he joked. "Look, you're not going to be married for much longer, right? And the new business is keeping you here, which is great. And your husband's infidelity?" He lifted a shoulder. "All the more reason to show you what a loyal man is like."

She looked at his profile for a long moment, letting the words sink in. He'd shown his interest before, either by his very kind and caring actions or by some comments that made it clear he was attracted to her. But this was more than anything else she'd ever heard from him, and she had to process the feelings it brought up in her.

Confusion. Fear. Longing. Hope.

"And...dead silence." He laughed. "Too much, Beck?"

She rubbed his knuckles with her thumb, feeling safe and close in the dark truck, knowing she didn't have to respond with this man. Didn't have to make assurances and promises or be coy or flirtatious.

"Not too much," she finally said. "If I were single and free, I think you know what could happen."

He turned on to Coquina Court, his truck beams highlighting the white shell-covered road and the thick foliage on either side of the street that dead-ended with Coquina House.

"You will be single and free soon," he said, slowing the car to about ten miles an hour. "So, maybe that date should wait until then."

"See? Sweet, kind, and patient." She gave his hand a

squeeze. "I appreciate that you would say that, Josh. You know it would make me feel better."

"Hey, you're giving me too much credit," he said as he came to a stop in front of Coquina House. "I figure once that paper is signed, our date can be real." He turned to her, bringing their joined hands to his lips. "And that means I can get a kiss."

"Josh." She breathed his name and felt her whole body inch a little closer. "We did kiss once."

"On the beach," he said, his voice warm enough to know he held the memory dear, as she did. "After you got the good news that your soon-to-be-ex was going to make your B&B dreams a possibility."

She smiled, remembering the day that Dan had told her that he and Mari had decided to give Beck the entire profit from the sale of the house in Alpharetta. It had been a magnanimous gesture on Dan's part, and a life-saver for Beck, giving her the money she needed for the renovation. "That was a nice moment."

"That was a nice kiss."

She smiled, a centimeter closer, wanting to experience that feeling again. Wanting to show him just how much his friendship and support had meant these months since she'd moved to Coconut Key. Wanting to... kiss him. Slowly, this time. Just for the pure pleasure of it.

"Like I said, I can wait." He planted another kiss on her knuckles, torturing her just a little bit because if it felt good on her hand...what would it feel like on her mouth?

"I expect papers any day now," she said, hoping she didn't sound as breathless as she felt.

"Any day?" His brows lifted. "Really?"

She laughed because, honestly? He sounded just a

little bit breathless, too. "That's the first step. The divorce won't be finalized for another six weeks or so after that, for filing and court stuff."

"Will you have to go back to Atlanta?"

She shook her head. "My attorney says it can all be done on paper and virtually. I'm not going anywhere."

His whole expression, golden in the porch light someone had kindly left on, softened as he gazed at her. "That was all I wanted when you first came here. I just wanted you to stay. Lovely was happier and healthier. My sister was overjoyed to have her best friend back. And I..." He took a slow, deep breath. "I saw a woman with the kind of heart that appeals to me."

"Josh." She breathed his name, her whole being aching for that kiss.

"I can wait six weeks, Beck," he said. "I can wait six months if I have to because I don't expect you to be ready to jump into anything the second the ink's dry on a divorce decree. You've been hurt. Bad. And I like being your friend. I like it a lot."

She let a little whimper escape her throat. "I like it, too."

"I want to give us a chance," he said. "A fair chance. When you're ready, and not a minute before."

She sighed as he did, his breath warm and inviting. "You'll be the first to know," she promised him.

With one more kiss on her knuckles, his gaze shifted behind her. "Is that Peyton's room with the lights on?"

She turned and looked, nodding. "Yes. Looks like she's home."

"Alone?"

"I don't see Val's truck," she said, a niggling feeling

tugging at her mother's heart. "I think I better go see what's going on with her."

When she turned back to him, he was looking at her again. "You're a great mom, you know that?"

"Aww. Thank you. I have great girls." She glanced over her shoulder again, not able to shake her worry about Peyton.

"Because of you." He tapped her nose. "And I can see you need to go. Which is fine, because two more minutes and all my patience is going to disappear."

She laughed, inching away and reaching for the door handle. "Good night, Josh."

"Night, Beck."

She climbed out and blew him a kiss which earned her one more smile, one that she'd remember as she fell asleep and started counting days until she could go on a date with the bachelor she'd bought that night.

🌴

ALL THAT SWEET humming inside Beck slowly disappeared as Peyton, awake and drinking tea in bed, shared Val's story, fighting tears as she did.

"Oh, Peyton," Beck whispered, letting this all sink in. "That poor man. What a tragedy."

She nodded, swallowing hard. "I can't imagine going through that," she said. "And not telling anyone here. No one knows, except me."

"Are you sure it's okay that I know?" Beck asked.

"He's not hiding it, he just doesn't want to talk about it. After she died, he left Miami, like literally after the funeral. He was a CPA, Mom. My fisherman who always smells like shrimp." She managed a smile. "Except he's not mine."

"Give it time," Beck said, the echo of Josh's words still in her head. "Anything worth having is worth waiting for."

Peyton bit her lip and shook her head. "Except, I kind of gave him an ultimatum tonight. That's how the story came out. I told him I was in this for the long haul, that I wanted to be married and have kids, and if that wasn't his end game, then...we shouldn't be dating."

Beck considered that, nodding. "That couldn't have been easy for you, but I think you did the right thing."

"Really?"

"Well, first of all, you didn't know his backstory and, to be perfectly fair, he should have told you. That's pretty major, don't you think? I mean, he knew about Greg cheating on you and that breakup. I'm a little disappointed he didn't tell you sooner."

"I guess. It was very hard for him to talk about it. And I get the impression he was just waiting for the right moment."

But was he? Sometimes Peyton could be blind with a guy when she wanted him to be perfect. And as awesome as Val was, not telling Peyton that she was competing with the memory of a fiancée who'd passed in her twenties? Not really fair.

"So, what are you going to do?" Beck asked.

On a deep sigh, she finished her tea and reached over to put the cup on the nightstand. "Sleep."

"Always good. Then what?"

"Cook." She gave a sly smile. "I really love cooking in a restaurant kitchen, Mom. Is that weird?"

"That you found your passion? Not weird at all. I'm sorry I wasn't the mother who brought you into the kitchen and taught you all the family secrets. Recipes, I mean."

She laughed softly. "God knows we have enough secrets of the other kind."

"But what's going to happen with Val?" Beck asked.

"I don't know, but..." She gave a tight smile. "I didn't come here for Val. I didn't even come here to be with my momma, although it's been wonderful." She took Beck's hands and looked into her eyes. "I like it here. With or without Val, even with or without a job at Jessie's restaurant, I really love the Keys. I'm not going anywhere. In fact, I'm thinking about getting an apartment. You know those cute little townhouses right across US 1? Vista Pointe?"

Beck nodded. "The white one with all the blue shutters? Really nice."

"I could rent in there. Maybe Savannah and I could get a three-bedroom and raise Pink Line together."

Beck's jaw dropped. "That would be amazing. You think she'll stay?"

"Where the heck else is she going to go?"

"Ahem, she's right here." Savannah walked into the dimly lit bedroom, one hand on her belly, the other holding up a mess of hair. "Uninvited to the slumber party."

"C'mere." Beck patted the bed. "We've got lots to tell you."

"'kay. Let me get tea. I've got something to tell you, too."

"What?"

"Callie'll be here in the morning. She just texted. She's bringing papers for you to sign and some gossip." As she walked out and headed to the stairs, Beck and Peyton stared at each other.

"You okay, Mom?" Peyton whispered.

"Divorce papers."

"You know what that means?"

Beck bit her lip. "Yeah." She was going to get that date and kiss and chance with Josh. "In six weeks, I'll be a free woman."

"Welcome to the club." Peyton leaned forward and planted a kiss on her cheek. "I love you, Mom."

Beck just held one daughter, smiled at the one returning with tea and sass, and braced for the arrival of the youngest one. She loved them all and would be lost without them.

"*M*other of God, what did you do, Lovely Ames?"

Beck's eyes grew to giant saucers, making Ava, currently sipping coffee at Lovely's kitchen counter, crack up. "Told you we'd be in trouble," she muttered.

"No trouble, since last I checked, I'm the boss of me." Lovely reached up to stroke her long hair, currently three fabulous shades of pink with one dynamite strand of purple in the front. "I admired Ava's hair, so she suggested I try some myself. Come in and tell us about the bachelor auction. Who won and who lost and how much money did it cost? And, is it true that Germaine Branthauser really bought Kenny? It's all over the book club group chat."

Beck blinked, still in shock. "It's...pink."

"It's called Raspberry..." She turned to Ava. "Rebellion?"

"Rebel. Raspberry Rebel on the length and Wild Orchid on the streak," Ava supplied, slipping off the counter stool to stand with Lovely in solidarity. "It washes out pretty fast. I gave her the temporary kind."

Beck looked from Ava to Lovely and back to Ava again, then burst out laughing. "God, I'm so happy you're here, Ava."

Ava lifted her cup in a toast. "Happy to be here, Grandma Beck."

"Oh!" Beck put her hand on her chest, biting her lip. "Grandma Beck! Still not used to it!"

Ava didn't mean to make her so emotional, but it was sweet that she liked the name.

"Are the girls on the way over?" Lovely asked, bringing Beck into the house. "Jessie left scones last night and we're ready to dive in, but wanted to wait for you."

"The girls are in Key West."

"What?" Ava gasped without thinking. Wouldn't Savannah want her to go?

"They're picking up a new arrival." Beck looked at her mother with a weird twinkle in her eye. "Callie's coming."

"Callie? I get to meet Callie?" Lovely exclaimed. "Oh... with pink hair." She gave a look to Ava. "That'll make a grand first impression."

It would, and Ava was only a little put out by the fact that Lovely seemed a little ashamed of the fun hair she'd been so excited about last night. "I keep forgetting you guys hardly know each other," Ava said.

"We forget, too," Lovely said, reaching for Beck to give a hug that always seemed so natural with this family. "I'm very excited. I've been aching to meet my last granddaughter."

"Well, don't worry, Lovely," Ava said. "If we wash it a whole lot today, most of the color will come out."

"Oh, sweet child." Lovely shifted her hug from Beck to Ava, who braced for the affection she was starting to get used to. "I love my hair and will be proud to show it off to my granddaughter. I think I'll wear something pink to make it all match. Want to help me pick it out?"

Ava smiled. "Sure. Oh, Beck. Did someone bid on my dad?"

Beck laughed. "Lovely was right. Germaine Branthauser, but Maggie Karras did the bidding and I'm pretty sure she managed to get your father to ask her out. Haven't confirmed that yet because he was working in the kitchen and men don't like to be pounced on for details first thing in the morning."

Dad and Maggie? Interesting. Not a total surprise, either.

"And did you do a little shopping?" Lovely asked.

"I purchased a nice date with Joshua Cross, to be collected after my divorce is final."

"Wow," Ava said. "People were busy last night."

"Gwen Parker bought Val, which did not make Peyton happy."

Lovely and Ava gasped in unison. "So much gossip," Ava said. "Did Savannah buy anyone?"

"Not a soul, but she's thrilled that Callie's coming, as we all are. So why don't you two get dressed and come on over to wait for them? They should be back from the airport soon. Bring the scones!"

Lovely was crazy excited about meeting this granddaughter, and especially thrilled when Ava offered to French braid her newly colored hair and put a pink ribbon in.

"She's going to love her grandmother," Ava said as

they walked out, carrying the scones. "I always adored my Grandma Janet."

"From all you shared last night, she sounds like a wonderful woman."

"It's funny," Ava said. "I think she would have fit right in here. You'd have liked her, especially if you'd gone to church with her. That woman loved her Sunday service," she added with a bittersweet laugh. "Sometimes when I would spend the night with her on Saturdays, I'd go to her church instead of ours, and she always took me to the little donut and coffee thing at the end to show me off like I was her prize."

Tears welled up, the sudden grief surprising Ava. She hadn't cried for Grandma Janet since...well, since she got here.

"We have a nice church here," Lovely said as they reached Coquina House. "And I would love nothing more than to take you. You can get all the credit for my fabulous hair when I show off to the choir ladies."

"Credit or blame?" Ava asked on a laugh.

Lovely put her arm around her and squeezed, but just for a second. "I guarantee you at least six sopranos with gray hair will be your next customers."

As they started up the stairs to the house, Savannah's car came screaming down the street, horn honking. Instantly, the front door of the house opened and Beck came out, with Dad not far behind her, a hammer in his hand.

"Morning, A," he called over the noise. Then he grinned at Lovely's hair. "Nice."

"Isn't it?" she quipped, turning to watch the arrival.

"I'll take the scones into the dining room," Ava said,

not really wanting to be one of the first to greet the long-lost Callie.

Dad gave her a smile and stepped back in with her. "So, you and Lovely had fun last night."

"We did. I heard gossip about the designer chick." She lifted her brows. "Magpie?"

He choked a laugh. "You have definitely been hanging out with Savannah too much."

She glanced over her shoulder, catching a glimpse of the car doors opening, then turned to head into the house. "Well, her sister's here now, so that might change." She put the scones on the sideboard they were using as a quasi-kitchen next to the coffee maker.

"Don't worry about that, Ava."

"Do I seem worried?" she snapped, and instantly regretted it. "Sorry, Dad. That was rude."

"That was...old Ava," he said. "You haven't talked back to me in ages."

She took the plastic wrap off the scones and thought about that, looking at him after a moment. "I really like it here, Dad."

"It's a good place to spend some time."

Her heart slipped a little. "Some time?"

He gave her a quizzical look. "The kitchen'll be finished soon, so..."

"We have to go home."

"That's kind of how it works, kiddo."

Suddenly, there was an outburst of noise and laughter from the living room, so Ava took a deep breath and headed in, not really sure why she was dreading meeting this third aunt but recognizing that she was.

"Oh, there you are, Ava." Beck beamed at her. "Come and meet Callie. *Aunt* Callie," she added.

Which seemed ridiculous when Ava looked at her. She was so young! She knew she was ten years younger than Savannah, yet somehow she expected another woman in her twenties. Callie was like a teenager...also like an Instagram model. Savannah and Peyton were both pretty, but this girl? She was the kind of beautiful that takes your breath away and doesn't exist in real life.

Her hair was coal black and pulled back into a ponytail that reached more than halfway down her back. Her eyes were giant, dark, and perfectly made up. Even her brows were stunning, and Ava didn't even want to look at the rest of her.

"Hello, Ava." Callie used that tone that adults saved for kids under five, adding a smile that might be as gorgeous as the rest of her but was just a tiny bit condescending. *Come on, girl. We're literally like four years apart. Maybe less.*

"Hey, nice to meet you."

"It must be pink hair day," she said on a laugh, looking from Lovely to Ava and back again. "Whoops. Didn't get the memo."

Ava just gave a tight smile, crossing her arms and inching back from the group.

"How about something to eat, Callie?" Beck asked brightly, covering up the millisecond of discomfort.

"We had food in Key West," she said, turning to Savannah with a gleam in her dark eyes. "And I've been promised a swim in the ocean while you look over the papers, Mom."

Beck flinched a little, either from the way her

daughter just brushed her off or the idea of her divorce papers. Ava didn't know, but something defensive rose up in her.

"I'll have a scone with you, Beck," Ava said quickly. "I've been dying for one all morning, but..." She shot a look at Callie. "We were waiting for you."

She saw Savannah's eyes flash at the quick exchange. "Let's get you up to Peyton's room to change. You guys can share a room."

"I want to share with you, Sav." Callie scooped up a handbag and slid it on her shoulder. An expensive Gucci bag, Ava couldn't help noticing.

"Well, our room is full," Savannah said, tugging the strap. "Dad must be paying his interns well."

"You can have my bed," Ava said quickly, not even giving herself a chance to think.

Beck shook her head. "Callie can bunk with Peyton. It wouldn't be the first time."

Callie grimaced. "I told you I can stay through the Fourth of July. Which means I'll be here for my birthday for anyone who's shopping or planning parties. It also means I'll be here for, like, ten days. I cannot share a bed that long." She turned to Savannah. "Plus, hello. The Do-Over Game? We haven't played in years."

Savannah laughed at whatever the Do-Over Game was, giving her little sister a squeeze. "I'm so going to beat you."

Their connection was strong and real and...didn't include Ava.

"I was super comfortable last night on Lovely's couch," Ava said, turning to Lovely. "If it's okay with you, I can sleep there."

"Of course." Lovely smiled. "As long as you like, sweet girl."

"Perfect," Callie said with that smug look of a girl who always got her way. "Show me our room, Savvie." She slipped an arm around Savannah and put her head on her shoulder. "I want to hear all about this niece I'm going to have! I can't believe I'm going to be an *aunt!*"

As they headed around the corner and up the stairs, Ava could actually feel the jealousy rise up and threaten to choke her.

But before she took her next breath, Beck was at one side, and Lovely at the other. Neither one wrapped their arms around her, but that was because they knew she would slip out of their touch. But they looked at her with gazes that were just as loving as any embrace.

"She means her other niece," Lovely said.

"Callie's always adored Savannah," Beck explained with a smile.

Peyton came right up behind them. "And don't forget, Callie plays for the other team," she added into Ava's ear. "*Dad's* team."

For a moment, Ava just stood there, then she smiled, weirdly comforted by the support of these women.

"I like the team I'm on," Ava replied as they headed to the scones.

CHAPTER TWENTY-ONE
PEYTON

*N*ow those were some crab cakes. Perfectly round, gorgeous texture, and they would fry up like a dream.

The back door of Chuck's kitchen opened, and Peyton immediately forgot her latest creation, her heart ratcheting as she waited for a certain set of dark and dreamy eyes to meet hers when Val came around the corner.

But the eyes she met weren't dark brown, but more of a golden brown, set in an older man's face, at least her mother's age.

She frowned at him, trying to place the man, and then she remembered he was the competition.

"Mr. Jadrien?" she asked, trying to hide her shock at the sight of the renowned chef. "Can I help you?"

"I'm looking for Jessica. Is she here?"

Jessie was in her office and Peyton had a feeling she would not be happy about this new arrival. "Um...she might be on a call."

His mouth kicked up in a half smile as he crossed his

arms and cocked his head. "Why don't you tell her I'm here?"

Arrogant thing, wasn't he? She flicked a look at him, then picked up a dishtowel to wipe her hands. "Hang on a second."

He glanced around with a judgy look. "Doesn't anyone else work here?"

"We're closed today."

"Mmm. That's right." He leaned against the prep bar. "Uh, Jessica?" he reminded her. "You were going to get her?"

"Excuse me." Tamping down some more irritation, she slipped back to the office and tapped on the door.

"Come on in," Jessie said, the sigh in her voice evident. And the look on her face matched that frustration when Peyton opened the door. "Don't tell me, someone wants money."

"Actually, it might be worse than that."

"Based on this spreadsheet, I'm not sure it could be," Jessie said. "What's up?"

Peyton came into the office and perched on the guest chair, just sensing that Jessie wasn't going to like this news. "You've got a visitor," she said. "Tag Jadrien is in the kitchen."

"Wait...*what*?"

Peyton nodded. "He just walked right in and asked to see you."

"Because I refuse to call him back." She shook her head. "Why won't he leave me alone?"

"Maybe he wants to mend fences, Jessie." Although his arrogance made that seem doubtful. "When we saw him in Key West that night, he was nice to you. Didn't want to be the competition, right? Didn't he say something about friendly businesses that co-exist? I can't remember but—"

She huffed out a breath and stood up. "I'll see him."

"Better idea," Peyton said. "Let me bring him back here. You're in power behind a desk. My old boss in publishing taught me that. Jane always said never go to neutral territory with an enemy, stay in the home court."

The first hint of a smile showed on Jessie's face. "All right, then. Send him in to my home court. But one question."

"Anything."

"How do I look?" Jessie asked.

Peyton smiled. "Like you own the place, and don't let Taggert Lipshitz forget it." With a thumbs-up, she headed back to the kitchen, slowing her step when she heard two men laughing. Good God, that was Val out there with him.

Taking a breath for composure, she came around the corner to find the two of them shooting the breeze like a couple of old friends. Didn't Val know he was the enemy? Didn't Val ever not look stunning?

"Hey." Val turned and gave her a tight smile. "I was looking for you."

"Here I am." And why didn't he have his fishing clothes on, she wondered. He was dressed in a button down and khakis, like he dressed for their dates. "Mr. Jadrien, Jessie can see you now. Come on, I'll walk you back."

"Good to see you, Val," Tag said, holding up knuckles for a tap. "And good luck to you, kid."

Good luck...for what?

With a tendril of worry spinning through her, she escorted Tag to the office and opened the door for him. She heard Jessie's cool greeting, but she slipped away, anxious to know what was going on with Val...because something was.

"You look...dressy," she said as she came back into the kitchen. "Got a date or a fancy lunch today?"

He took a slow breath and let it out, clearly nervous. "Can you walk outside with me?"

Oh, boy. Her heart crawled up her chest and settled into her throat. "Of course." She set the towel she'd been squeezing on the counter and came around the prep area. "Everything okay?"

He nodded, then ushered her toward the door, out to a rare dreary and rainy sky over Coconut Key. They stepped into the lot behind the kitchen, where her car was parked, along with Jessie's, and a shiny black Tesla. Right at the door was Val's truck ...with a whole lot of stuff in the back.

"What's going on, Val?"

"Peyton." He stabbed his hands in his hair and pulled it back, his features drawn and tired. "That night, at the auction? It really changed things for me."

She felt her eyes close. "I shouldn't have said anything."

"Of course you should. I told you never to hold back on what's important to you. But the conversation..." He puffed out a breath. "It broke a dam in me, Pey. It made me realize how bottled up I've kept everything. How messed up I still am. How much work I need to do."

She searched his face, trying to empathize but

knowing she'd never experienced any pain like he had. "I want to help you," she whispered. "I really do."

"I know, but the thing is, you can't. No one can do this for me. I have to go home."

"What?"

He nodded. "I'm going back to Miami."

Disappointment curled through her. "For...good?"

"For my own good," he said with a sad smile. "I need to face my demons, Peyton. I ditched my family, and Marisa's."

Marisa. He'd never told Peyton her name. "What are you going to do?"

"Tell them I'm sorry for disappearing. Sit down with my parents and talk to them. Spend time with Marisa's parents and cry with them. Think. Heal. Pray. Mourn. I don't know." He reached out and took her hand. "But I have to thank you."

"Thank me?" She closed her fingers around his, trying to not believe this would be the last time she'd hold his hand. The realization almost strangled her. More than when she broke up with Greg, which made no sense since she'd dated Greg for three years and Val for three months.

"You opened my eyes, Peyton. You made me realize how much I'd stuffed inside me and refused to face. You made me want..." He swallowed. "You made me want to try to feel...things again. I can't, yet. But you made me want to."

"Oh." It came out like a little whimper, pathetic enough that he pulled her into a gentle hug.

"I'm gonna miss you," he whispered.

But not enough to stay. Not enough to do his healing

at her side. "Me, too."

"You're a great woman." He drew back and looked at her, shocking her with tears in his eyes. "You're beautiful and smart and sweet and nurturing. And you should get what you want.

You should be married and have kids and get...everything."

Yes, she should. Just...not with him. "Thanks," she managed. "That means a lot." Hurts like hell, but means a lot.

"I may get my old job back."

She felt a smile pull. "As a CPA?"

"Don't laugh." He tapped her nose. "I was a damn good accountant."

"You're a damn good fisherman."

His gave into a wistful smile. "I'll miss getting crabs with you."

"I'll miss your dumb fish jokes." *And your sweet kisses. And your good heart. And everything else.* "Let's just say I'm shell-shocked." Her joke fell flat, but he gave her one more squeeze.

She swallowed against the lump in her throat and willed herself not to cry. "Goodbye, Valentino Sanchez."

With one more sad smile, he planted a kiss on her forehead and stepped away, rounding his truck and climbing behind the wheel. She turned, unwilling to have the image of him driving away burned in her memory, walking to the back door just as it swung open and Tag Jadrien walked out.

"Oh," she said, sidestepping so he didn't run her over. "Are you leaving?" It was a dumb question, but she was dumbstruck, so too bad.

"For the moment." He slid into a surprisingly warm smile. "Do me a favor, eh, kid?"

Kid? Was everyone a *kid* to him? She managed not to curl her lip. Actually managed not to punch his face because, wow, she felt like punching something. "What's that, Tag?"

"Tell your boss to be smart."

Something about it sounded threatening, enough for her to step away. "I don't have to," she said. "Jessica Donovan is a genius."

"We'll see." With a nod, he jogged away and got into the Tesla with the grace of someone who felt like he owned the world.

On a sigh, she headed back in, looking for Jessie, but not seeing her in the kitchen or the office. She pushed open the door to the dining area and squinted into the room, finally seeing that Jessie had gone out to the patio. She was leaning against the railing, looking out to the ocean.

Not sure what to do, but needing support herself, Peyton walked out and stood next to Jessie, silently putting her arm around the woman who'd become a dear friend and mentor.

"Val's going back to Miami," she whispered. "For good, I think. He just came to say goodbye."

Under her touch, she felt Jessie's shoulders slump in silent solidarity.

"Tag wants to buy my business."

"What?" Peyton inched back. "This business? The restaurant? Chuck's?"

"Yep." She brushed back some curls and turned to Peyton, her eyes as moist and pained as Peyton imagined her own were right then. "He wants this location for Coconut Tropics."

Seriously? "Well, he can drop dead."

She swallowed and one of those tears escaped. "Chuck already did that."

"And left you the money to build your dream, Jessie. You wouldn't..." Her voice trailed off as she searched Jessie's face and tried to interpret her expression. "Would you?"

"I'm running out of options," she said on a whisper. "We are functioning in the red. Barely. I'm not even sure I like this restaurant anymore."

"But we'll get that cookbook out and—"

Jessie swiped her hand to stop Peyton. "He offered a lot of money. A lot. A metric butt load, actually."

"For the building?"

"And the business. He said he'd keep the name."

"Jessie, no." She took Jessie's hands, her miserable broken heart forgotten. "This is your dream. Chuck's legacy and gift to you. And it's Lovely's property, isn't it?"

"I bought it from her for a song. Less than a song. Not even a chorus." She gave a dry laugh. "Selling to him would allow me to...stop fretting about how I'm going to pay my vendors."

"Well, you have one less vendor as of today," Peyton said sadly.

"And my staff is next to nothing, and he said he'd hire everyone, so I'm not putting people out of work."

"Not me. I won't work for that...that..." Peyton shuddered. "Dreamwrecker."

"Oh, and he wants me to run the kitchen."

Peyton gasped. "Would you do that?"

"I don't know," Jessie admitted. "I don't know what I'd do. I came out here to talk to Chuck and see what he thinks." She notched her chin toward the water. "They never found his body, so I like to look out to sea and talk to him."

Peyton grunted at the bone-deep pain of that, turning to the blue horizon, suddenly longing to be on a boat out there, away from everything. "What does Chuck say?"

"Chuck says...be happy."

"Would selling the restaurant to the man who has nearly put you out of business make you happy?"

She shrugged. "What's happy, Peyton? After Chuck died, I knew I'd never be happy again. Not really, not in my deepest soul. And this is why I always wanted a child. No one wants to face this life alone."

"You have me." She reached around and hugged her hard, covering for how the words hit her heart. Peyton didn't want to face this life alone, either, but sometimes fate had different plans. "I love you so much. I hate that you're miserable. I hate that you have to make this decision."

She hugged Peyton back. "I hate that your sweet man left town. I had a feeling there was more going on with him than just fishing. I'm sure he'll be back."

"I'm not." Peyton huffed a breath. "Oh, Jessie, what are we going to do?"

"Cook. Eat. Laugh. Survive." Jessie planted a kiss on her cheek. "That's what strong women do."

Peyton smiled. She didn't feel so strong, not yet. She felt cheated out of the kind of love that Jessie had, but that might just be the plan for her. It might just be.

CHAPTER TWENTY-TWO

KENNY

*H*oly cow. This was the best kitchen he'd ever done. The best. Kenny took one last picture of the farm sink, making sure to get the full length of the quartz countertop and the jaw-dropping view of the massive window behind him. He hit send and didn't even caption the photo he sent to Bill. Let the old guy drool.

"Is it official?" Beck came into the kitchen with a wide smile. "Are you done?"

He lowered the phone and smiled at the woman he might never think of as his mother, but was proud to call a friend. "We are done. Welcome to your kitchen."

She pressed her hands to her mouth. "It's beyond my wildest dreams." She looked around as if it were the first time seeing her new kitchen, even though she'd been in here every single day since he'd started and when the cabinet and counter guys were installing. "You, my friend, are an artist."

"I don't know about that..." He ran a hand over the island edge. "I'm pretty happy with the way this came out.

I was just sending pictures to my boss, Bill Do..." He caught himself. "...*Does* like to see a new kitchen."

Dang. That was close.

"I bet he's missed you," she said. "Although we've loved having you and Ava so much. She's such a dear girl."

He smiled, trying to remember the last time someone called Ava "dear." Probably his *other* mother, his adopted mother, on her deathbed.

"Yeah, it's been great for her." He looked out that magnificent window to the water, catching a glimpse of Ava, Savannah, Callie, and Peyton, all hanging on the beach in the sunshine. There she was, surrounded by family. Something she didn't have at home. "She loves your daughters," he said to Beck.

"Two of them." She took a few steps closer, following his gaze out the window, smiling at the sight of the four of them lined up on towels. "I think she's still finding her way with Callie, but then, so am I."

"She's attached to Savannah, that's why. And I get the impression Callie and Savannah are close, so Ava senses a rival."

She turned and smiled at him. "How astute of you to figure that out, Kenny. No wonder you're a great dad."

"Great?" He snorted. "That's only because we've been here. Most of the time we're at each other's throats. I..." He shook his head. "That girl mystifies me most of the time. Elise, her mother? God, she knew exactly what to say to Ava. They had this mysterious bond and didn't even have to talk, and Ava was only a little kid. I can't imagine what they'd be like now."

"They'd be like Peyton and me," she said, leaning into

the farm sink to study the girls. "We have that sort of secret, silent language. And you know what?" She glanced at him. "Given enough time, I think Ava could form that bond with Savannah. I can't thank you enough for that."

"For...what?"

"For letting her get so close to Savannah this past month or so. It's been wonderful to see that my middle girl has a nurturing side, which obviously she's going to need soon. I always knew Peyton had it. She was putting baby dolls to bed from the minute she could hold one. But Savannah wanted to climb trees and drive cars and kiss boys." She gave a dry laugh. "Probably how she got herself into the single mother situation."

He laughed, too, an emotion he didn't quite understand welling up. Fondness? Gratitude? Just flat-out respect? Beck tapped all of them. "You know, I gotta say something to you."

"Uh oh." She laughed. "Should I be worried?"

"You should be proud," he replied. "Ava blew into your life and family, uninvited and possibly unwelcome, without any regard to how much her very existence could have wreaked havoc on your life. And you didn't flinch."

"I flinched. I think I stared in stunned shock. I might have been knocked over with a feather."

"I bet. But you took her. You accepted her and, well, loved her. So did your daughters and mother and friends." He blew out a breath and looked out to see two of the girls running to the water. Savannah stayed with Ava, which just kicked him in the solar plexus. "I wish I could do something like that for you."

She choked a laugh. "Are you kidding? What more

could I want? You've given me time with my granddaughter. A chance to get to know a son I...I didn't know I missed but certainly have. Not to mention a showcase of a kitchen." She put her hand on his arm. "I'm the one overcome with gratitude, Kenny. Thank you for staying. Thank you for sharing her. For the kitchen. For everything."

Not everything, he thought with a twinge of guilt that was starting to bother him more every day. When he got here, he was loyal to Bill, who hadn't asked him to lie, but requested to stay in the background. But did Beck have a right to know that Kenny knew his biological father like, well, like a father? Would it change anything? Affect her life?

She'd want to tell Ava, of course. She might insist on it, he wasn't sure. And that would tilt his daughter's world again to find out her "Uncle Bill" was really her grandfather.

Damn these tangled webs of lies.

"Are you okay?" Beck searched his face. "You look troubled."

In fact, he was. "I'm just...thinking about Ava." True...*ish*.

"It's going to be hard to let her go," she said. "You're still thinking about leaving on the fifth? The day after our Fourth of July New Kitchen party?"

He nodded. "Two more days, Beck, and we'll be out of your hair."

"Please. I'll miss you both every day. We all will." She pressed her hand on his arm. "Is there any chance in heaven or hell you'd stay longer? Or, you know..." She gave a nervous laugh. "Forever?"

He didn't laugh. He just stared at her, letting the idea sink in. It wasn't the first time he'd thought about moving here, that was for sure. He thought about it every time he heard the ring of Ava's laughter. He thought about it every time he woke up and looked at that beautiful sea. He thought about it when he saw that "temporary" license and realized how easy it would be for him to get certified and work down here.

Then he thought about Bill Dobson.

Not only would he be bailing on a great job and boss and friend, he'd be taking Ava away from her grandfather, whether Ava knew who he was or not.

"Oh my word, you're thinking about it." Beck gasped. "You are, aren't you?"

He let out a soft laugh, knowing his expression was giving his thoughts away. "I admit, it's tempting. But...complicated."

"Of course, your job. Well, jobs, since you are an EMT. I'm sure there's plenty of part-time work here for those skills," she added. "And I'd be willing to wait for you to get a contractor's license and you could singlehandedly renovate this whole B&B. And Ava could go to Coconut Key High School..." Her voice rose with each idea, along with her color. "Feel free to stop this old lady from fantasizing."

But he didn't. He was fantasizing right along with her. What would stop him? This was his chance to start over, to escape the constant memories of Elise, to bring Ava to a place where she was surrounded by family who clearly loved her instead of alone in Atlanta, missing her mother and grandmother.

What would stop him? Bill Dobson, who doted on that girl and would be bereft to say goodbye.

"It'd be much easier said than done," he finally replied, a little gruffly.

"Yeah, because what would be here for you?" She did a fake cough. "Maggie Karras." And another fake cough, making him laugh.

"We had one date, Beck."

"And you whistled all the next day while you worked."

"I did?" He chuckled. "I do whistle when I'm happy."

"Then your whistling was music to my ears, because I've heard it before—just not with as much, well, vigor, as the day after you went out to dinner with Maggie."

Still smiling, he stepped away from the sink. "I better start gathering up my tools. I feel like there are pieces of my stuff everywhere, all over this house."

"I sure wish you'd leave them that way," she said wistfully. "I mean, now that the idea is planted..."

He looked back out the window, wondering if now would be the perfect time to tell Beck Foster about Bill Dobson. Clear the air, get rid of secrets, and pay the price for keeping them. But his gaze landed on Ava, in her bright blue bathing suit that Savannah had bought her, walking...toward the water.

He wanted to. He owed her honesty after all she'd done, but he had to tell Bill first. That was still where his loyalty was. "You look around, Beck. Make sure there's not one single thing on the punch list we missed. I have to make a quick call."

He didn't give himself any time to second-guess the decision, but walked out to the front, down the steps, and tapped the phone to Bill Dobson's contact before his feet touched the broken coquina shells on the driveway.

Bill answered instantly, with a low laugh in his voice. "Kenny! You better get your ass back up here and make the Wilsons' kitchen remodel look exactly like that one. Nice work, my boy!"

Kenny took a deep breath. "I gotta talk to you, man. It's important."

"Sure, what's up?" All the humor left his voice and Kenny could picture Bill's expression turning serious, maybe running one of his big, callused hands through his mop of silver hair as he stepped away from a job site to give Kenny his full attention.

"Listen, man, I have to..." He cleared his throat. "I feel like I owe Beck the truth and she should know that you and I...know each other."

He was quiet for a long moment. "Has the subject of your biological father ever come up?"

"Not once."

"Then why tell her?"

"Why not?" Kenny countered. "I'm so damn sick of lies. I'm sick of Ava not knowing who you are. Why not tell her, Bill?"

"Because she had a grandfather and she loved him. And she just lost her grandmother less than two months ago. She's a tender one, Kenny, despite the pink hair and whatever jewelry she sticks in her nose or ear. She's soft and scared. I don't want to be the one to upset her little apple cart." His voice grew gruff. "I love the hell out of that kid, and I don't care if she knows we share DNA. I just want her to be steady and strong."

Once again, gratitude and an emotion he didn't

understand bubbled up and he tried to control it by walking between the stilts under the house, toward the beach. As he stepped up a slight rise, he could see Ava waist-high in the water, Savannah next to her.

"She's getting steadier and stronger every day," Kenny said, smiling at how Ava not only let someone hug her, she did it in water. "It's remarkable, really. And finding out Beck was my biological mother didn't throw her at all. It grounded her, I think. The only thing she's going to be pissed about where you're concerned is that we didn't tell her sooner."

"You said tell Beck, not Ava."

"I want to tell them both. At the right time, but..."

"No," he said emphatically. "Don't muddy up the waters."

Irritation punched. "Bill, Ava tells these people everything. It's just a matter of time until she mentions 'my dad's boss, Bill Dobson' or her 'Uncle Bill' and Beck asks about him. I hate this deceit."

"This isn't your truth to tell, son," Bill said sternly. "Gimme some time to think about how to handle this and I'll tell you what to say. I might need some, I don't know, legal counsel."

Legal counsel? "Bill, I've met Beck. No one is talking about you or the fact that my sealed adoption was opened. Anyway, it wasn't. You found me through DNA. Ava found Beck because some nurse told my mother her name the day I was born. No law has been broken."

"Don't tell her yet," he said. "Look, I'm up to my armpits in alligators, son. I can't add this to my plate. Not now. Now when are you coming back?"

He didn't answer but instead watched Ava and

Savannah doing some kind of dance, the sounds of their voices and laughter floating up over the sand. Ava bent over and spoke directly to Savannah's belly, then pressed her ear against the bump, and whatever that exchange was, it had them letting out gales of laughter. The other two, Peyton and Callie, joined them, and suddenly, they all hugged. Hugged. Arms around Ava and she hugged them back.

"Kenny?"

"Yeah, about coming back." And he knew what else he had to do. He just knew. "Bill, listen..."

On the other end, he heard Bill groan. "You're staying there, aren't you?"

Kenny just let out a quick laugh. "You always do read my mind."

"Not reading your mind, looking at my phone, son. You've been sending more than pictures of a kitchen, Ken. Ava looks...happy."

"She's like a different girl, Bill. I didn't even know it could be like this."

The other man sighed. "How long? The rest of the summer?"

I'd be willing to wait for you to get a contractor's license and you could singlehandedly renovate this whole B&B. And Ava could go to Coconut Key High School...

He could hear Beck's words echo in his head. Wise, tempting words that spelled out a whole new start for Kenny and Ava.

Bill swore softly. "You're not." It wasn't a question.

"Look, I'll have to disentangle myself from life in Atlanta, break the lease on my house, and talk to the chief. We'd have to find a place to live and get Ava enrolled in school, but..." He squeezed his eyes shut. "I hate to take Ava away from you, Bill. I hate it. But I haven't seen her this happy since...you know."

"The kid deserves to be happy," he said. "More than I do."

God, he loved this man.

"I'll help you up on this end," Bill added. "We'll get you moved down there."

"Thank you, man."

"Just...give me some time on that other stuff," he said. "When I'm ready for you to tell Beck and Ava, I'll let you know. Okay?"

"Sure, that's fair. And thanks, Bill."

"Any other surprises?" Bill asked on a dry laugh.

Just then, Kenny heard a car door slam from in front of the house, pulling his attention. He turned and took a few steps back, catching sight of dark hair blowing in the breeze.

Maggie Karras. Now that was a surprise.

He felt a smile pull. "Yeah," he said softly. "I met a woman."

"Holy hell. I don't stand a chance."

He looked from Maggie back to Ava, then to Maggie again, getting a kick in his chest when she spotted him and waved. "No," he said to Bill. "You really don't."

CHAPTER TWENTY-THREE
AVA

"Are those...fireworks?" Ava stepped out to the veranda and blinked at the pile of brightly colored boxes stacked on the dining table.

Josh grinned as he pulled a few more boxes from a pile. "We do them on the beach tonight."

"Does my dad know?" Her paramedic father who steadfastly refused to let her near a sparkler?

"He'll be our safety consultant," Josh assured her.

She laughed. "My dad's idea of firework safety is watching them on TV."

"Maybe I've changed, A." Her father stepped outside, a cup of coffee in his hand, a smile on his face. He'd been wearing that smile for a few days now and Ava had to admit, it was sure great to see it. She suspected it had something to do with Maggie, but it could be more than that. He didn't seem like Dad these days. Well, like the Dad she'd known for the last five years. Could he have changed?

"Nobody changes *that* much," she said with a secret smile of her own.

"Says the girl I saw swimming."

Her smile grew to a grin over her own personal victory. "The same one who made a left turn during my driving lesson yesterday."

Dad put his hand on her shoulder and she didn't flinch. Another victory. "In a compact car. Could you do it in a truck?"

With a soft laugh, she inched back. "Not that behemoth you drive."

"Then you can't take your driver's test the day you turn sixteen in August."

Her jaw loosened. "I can't?"

"You have to be able to drive the truck." He angled his head and held out his keys. "And I just told Beck I'd do a run to the store for ice. Wanna drive?"

Oh, God. That truck. It was so stinking big. But she longed to show her father what Savannah had taught her. And what did Sav say? *What was the worst that could happen?*

She snagged the keys. "Let me get my bag so I have my permit."

Dad held her gaze for a moment, his look just pure... old Dad. Happy Dad. The man she remembered from when she was little, running around the backyard throwing a baseball with Adam or grilling burgers and dogs while Mom set the picnic table.

Was he back? Was that possible?

The smile that seemed permanently planted on her face disappeared the minute she climbed up into Dad's big, fat bus of a Ford truck. Did a truck have to be that high? Was that even legal?

Ava suddenly felt small and inconsequential and like this thing would drive her...and kill her.

"You can adjust the seat," Dad said as he got in next to her. "Bring it higher and closer. Use that little button on the left."

Taking a breath, she reached down and pressed, moving closer and higher. "Where's the confidence button?" she joked. "I need a big boost of that."

"You're fine. We can take the backroads and stay off US 1 except for the very end."

She closed her eyes and pictured the route to the market, knowing every turn, stop sign, and landmark. And that last left turn with no light. Ava's record was currently four and a half minutes—that's how long she sat there until there were no oncoming cars in sight. And that was a Thursday night. This was the Fourth of July with tourists flying like crazy on the way to Key West.

"Hope you have a lot of time," she said. "Because I simply won't make that left turn until it's clear."

"Make it when you're ready," he replied.

Silent, she latched her seat belt, checked all the mirrors, and finally pressed the fancy ignition button. Very slowly, she shifted into drive and touched the accelerator with the lightest tap.

And they jerked forward.

"Oh!" She bit her lip. "I'm used to a car."

"Relax, A."

She breathed in through her nose, then out through her mouth, like the way she'd read years ago. It kind of helped her chill, almost as much as when Dad pushed his seat back to get comfortable and opened his window so warm, salty air blew into the car.

"You always hear about how miserable Florida is in the summer," he said, taking a breath of his own. "But it's not that bad."

"Ocean breeze," she said, happy that she could keep the conversation going and concentrate on the road. Savannah said that was the sign of a real driver.

"I like it here."

Her father's simple statement threw her almost enough to slide him a look, but she didn't dare. Instead, she got the feel of the gas pedal and squeezed the leather-covered steering wheel with damp palms.

"You do, too," he said. It wasn't a question.

"Well, duh." She managed a quick laugh, vaguely aware that she was passing Lovely's cottage where she'd had so many hours of fun.

"Don't you miss your friends?"

She thought about that and the fact that there was a stop sign coming up in exactly five seconds, so she lifted her foot. "I text Ashley and Gabrielle every day. Liza, once in a while, too. But, other than that, no."

"You miss Grandma Janet." Again, not a question.

"I'll miss her forever, Dad," she said, sliding to the brake and bringing the monster truck wheels to a stop. "But a lot less when I'm with Lovely and Beck. They do the grandma thing pretty good, I think."

Fully stopped, she finally gave him a glance, a little surprised to see he still wore that happy expression. Wow, talk about things she'd missed. That expression was high on the list.

Her own smile wavered a little when she got closer to

the first intersection and had to make an easy right turn. She leaned out, looked to her left, made sure everything was clear, and tapped the accelerator, doing a mental fist pump when she didn't jerk them forward.

"You're doing great, Ava."

"Thanks."

"And not just driving."

She almost stole a look but there was a car ahead and it needed her unwavering attention. "What do you mean?" she asked, keeping her four car lengths.

"I mean you seem stable and secure. No...incidents?"

She let out a soft laugh, knowing that's what he called her panics. "Not for a long time. Savannah's helped me a lot."

"Savannah's been awesome with you."

A teeny-tiny less awesome since Callie came, but, to her credit, Savannah made an extra effort to include Ava no matter what they did. That helped smooth out the rough edges of being around a girl who was everything— and she did mean everything—Ava would never be. Brilliant, driven, confident, and witty, Callie was the most intimidating girl Ava had ever met. She also had a bit of a mean streak whether she meant to or not.

"Savannah taught me how to drive a boat *and* a car."

"I remember how much you hate left turns," Dad said. "Are you over that?"

"We're about to find out," she said on a laugh.

He chuckled, too, shifting in his seat. "So, what do you want for your sixteenth birthday next month?"

"My license," she answered without a second's hesitation.

"Is that all?"

"Money, I guess." She shrugged. "I honestly don't want to think about it."

"Why not?"

She couldn't help it. She took her eyes off the road long enough to give him an "are you serious" look and notice that he was still smiling. A little silly grin, if she had to be completely honest.

"Why do you think?" she asked.

"Because it means you're a few weeks from school and you're dreading your junior year?" he guessed.

She *was* kind of dreading her junior year, but only because she didn't want to go back to Hawthorne High.

"Dad," she said, forcing herself to think because a serious intersection was coming up. A right turn, but it was onto US 1. The last turn before *the* turn. "You know."

"I know," he agreed. "You really don't want to leave Coconut Key."

The truth, stated as plainly as that, nearly took her breath away. "I'm having the best summer of my life," she admitted, looking down the road to count at least a dozen cars whipping by. "I never had so much...family." She sighed on the last word. "Even when we actually had one, it was never like this."

He leaned forward, looking past her at the traffic. "You could go after that Prius."

"Rule of the road?" she asked.

"Don't tell the driver what to do?" he guessed. "But I'm teaching so I'm allowed."

"No, the rule is don't use car names. I wouldn't know a Prius if it drove over me, which I don't want it to. So, say the 'little red car' or 'that blue truck.' But don't tell me the make, model, and year, because it's meaningless to me."

He dropped back on the seat. "Huh. I never thought of that."

"Savannah taught me." The little red car passed, and Ava stepped lightly on the gas, easing into the turn with confidence. Holding on to it, Ava peered ahead, the first tap of pressure dancing on her chest. There was a butt-ton of traffic today and that turn was gonna suck.

Two more lights, then the intersection without a light that led to the side street where the market was. Thank goodness.

"Everyone has really enjoyed you, Ava."

The first light was green and she eased through it, looking into the rearview mirror because she had to get out of the right lane and into the Lane of Death, as Savannah called it with nothing but a bucket of irony.

"Mmmh. Yeah." Lane of Death ten feet ahead.

"So, let me just be one hundred percent clear. Everyone here loves you."

She slid to the left with ease. *Huzzah.* "Yeah. Great." One more light and then...the turn.

"Which is why I think you're going to be really happy with my news."

And the light was green, too, which meant no more delays. She gauged the oncoming traffic, seeing just enough breaks to make her feel stupid for not turning, but terrified if she did.

Another deep breath, and she put her signal on again and just the sound kicked her heart rate up. She had to do this. She had to show Dad that she'd conquered this fear.

"Don't you want to know what it is?" he asked.

She had no idea what he was talking about as she

watched what had to be four thousand cars screaming down US 1 in the opposite direction, spread out just enough to make this hellacious.

"What I want to know," she said, forcing herself to be calm, "is when I can safely make this turn." She looked again. "Other than, you know, tonight at ten."

He laughed. "Maybe after the Maz...uh, white compact car."

"You think? Okay. Maybe." She wiped her wet palms on the leather cover again. "Is he going a little fast?"

"You tell me."

She squinted into the sunshine. She could do this. Right after that white car, there was a good long section of nothing followed by a big fat deadly truck.

"My news, Ava?"

"Yeah. Yeah." She could do this. She leaned forward, took a breath and watched that white car whiz by. Refusing to give into the urge to squeeze her eyes shut and scream like she was falling down a rollercoaster, she hit the gas—maybe a little harder than necessary—and zoomed across two lanes.

She reached the other side of the intersection and looked in the rearview mirror, five full seconds before the truck barreled by. "I did it!" she exclaimed as relief dumped over her. "Did you see that?"

"I did." He gestured toward the market entrance. "But you still don't know my news."

She rumbled into the parking lot, spotting three empty spaces together, already planning on taking the middle one. It was the only safe way to dock this boat.

"Yeah, sorry, Dad." She laughed a little, adrenaline still pumping through her as she eased into the spot.

"What is it, other than I can totally get my license on my sixteenth birthday?"

"If you know where the DMV is."

She frowned, shoving the massive gear into park. "For my license? The same place I got my learner's permit. The one past Rock Hill Road is the closest."

"I think you have to go to Marathon."

What? She unlatched her seat belt so she could turn to him, finally focused on what he was saying. He was running in a marathon? "Don't you remember where we went when I turned fifteen? Grandma Janet couldn't go and..." Why was he still smiling like a total goofball? "Dad?"

"I looked it up," he said. "There's no DMV in Coconut Key. But there is a good high school. It's not too far from this little house I found that we could rent for our first year."

"Rent...high school...first year." Nothing made sense because her head was buzzing. Humming. Screaming, actually. "Dad." And that word actually sounded like a frog.

"I think it's time for a fresh start, A. You and me and... our family. Here, in Coconut Key."

"Dad." This time she choked on a sob. "Are you serious? Please tell me you're serious. Oh, please tell me this is real!"

"It's real, honey. We're not going anywhere."

"Oh, Daddy!" She threw her arms around him, practically crawling over the console to hug her father with every ounce of strength she had. "I love you! I love you so much."

When they finally parted, Dad's smile was replaced

by a few tears of happiness, just like the ones on her cheeks.

❦

NOTHING COULD WRECK Ava's mood that day, not the heavy clouds and occasional burst of rain spitting from a summer stormy sky, and certainly not her brutal loss in the last cutthroat round of Old Maid she was currently playing with Savannah and Peyton on the veranda during a break in the rain.

But something had affected Lovely's mood, Ava noticed, when the woman stepped outside and slipped into the empty seat next to Peyton.

"What's wrong?" Ava asked.

"I need help," she whispered.

"Well, I need a seven." Savannah plucked a card from Ava's hand and grunted when she looked at it. "Thanks for nothin', 'hopper."

"What do you need, Lovely?" Ava asked, lowering her cards.

"Help," she repeated in a serious voice, getting all of them to ignore their hands and look at her. She leaned in, beckoning them closer, to whisper, "The dogs ate the dogs. And the burgers. Some cheese is missing, too."

"What?" They all asked in unison.

"It might have been Sugar. Definitely not Basil. Pepper? Yeah, a real weakness for hot dogs. Anyway, they're gone, and we are going to have some disappointed people when Kenny comes up and asks for the food for the grill and finds out..." She closed her eyes. "I left every-thing on the table, forgetting that they can get up on that new bench and..." She squeezed her hands. "So, I need someone to go the store, fast. Really fast, because the market closes at five today, which is in thirty-five minutes."

"I'll go." Peyton threw her cards down. "Just the name of this game is depressing me. Old Maid. *Please*."

"Beats Pregnant Old Maid," Savannah joked, putting down her hand. "Pey, you stay here and guard the dogs before they eye the flag cake Jessie made. If they eat that buttercream dressing and strawberries, Pink Line and I will cry. Let's go, Ava."

"Driving won't work," Lovely said. "That's the problem. Beck already went out and turned right around. US 1 is a parking lot today. When the rain stopped, every single person came out to go to the beach. You won't make it to the market before it closes."

"We can take the skiff there," Ava suggested. "It takes fifteen minutes from here, straight to the turquoise coconut."

Savannah eyed the skies. "It's cloudy, but it doesn't look like it'll rain for an hour or so. Let's go, but we'll have to kick that sucker up to its full speed of thirty-one." Savannah reached over and pulled Peyton's cards down to look at her hand. "Do you have my seven?"

"No."

Ava laughed. "Right here at the very end of my hand, Sav."

"You monster!" They pushed the chairs out just as Callie stepped out in a bathing suit, looking at the sky.

"Where is the sun today? I can't go home tomorrow without a tan."

Savannah grabbed her arm. "Come with us, Cal.

We're taking the skiff to the market for a secret errand to save Lovely's behind."

"Well, Pepper's," Lovely corrected. "I didn't eat the raw hot dogs."

Ava watched Callie consider the invitation and felt her heart drop, wishing she didn't mind the extra passenger, but she totally did. In all honesty, Ava was perfectly happy that this intimidating young woman was leaving the next day.

Callie looked like she might say yes, but then shook her head. "I can't deal with that little motorized raft."

"Okay, princess, next time we'll fire up the yacht." Savannah rolled her eyes and tugged Ava's arm.

A few minutes later, Ava was in her usual seat at the back of the boat—the stern, as she now knew it was called—holding the till and heading out to open water, bypassing the "riff and raff" as Savannah referred to the tourists. While Ava drove, Savannah leaned back on her bow bench, her face to the cloudy sky.

"You know, I never noticed that Callie can truly be a bitch until this visit," she mused. "I think she's jealous of you."

"Of me?" Ava choked. "A girl who is pre-law at Emory, drop dead beautiful, and will probably be president someday? I'll be lucky to get into a community college and work at Starbucks." She caught herself the minute the word came out, remembering that was exactly where Savannah worked when she lived in L.A. "Or, you know, somewhere."

But Savannah just smiled, eyes closed. "Maybe you, too, can meet your baby daddy when he comes in for a Cold Brew Reserve with cinnamon oatmilk foam." She choked softly. "I should have known then he was a butt pain. I like a man who drinks coffee. Black. Hot. And with no *foam*."

Ava felt her brows raise in surprise. Savannah *never* talked about Pink Line's father.

But she stayed very quiet and Ava didn't know if she should ask more or not.

"You know what terrifies me a little?" Savannah asked, eyes still closed Then she shifted in her seat and blocked Ava's view of the blue awnings of Conchy Charlies guiding her course, which was the first landmark before the Coconut Key Market.

"What?" Ava asked.

"You living here."

"Me?" Ava blinked, forgetting the shoreline and navigation. "What? Why?"

"Because..." Savannah lifted her hair and kept her face to the sky as if there were actual sun shining down on her. "It's one more thing that could keep me here."

There was a compliment—a good one—buried in there, but Ava was fixated on the possibility of her leaving. The thought of it made her heart pound.

"Are you thinking about moving away?"

"I'm always thinking about moving away," she said, absently rubbing her belly. "I'm a leaver. Hasn't everyone told you that, yet?"

"So, you're leaving Coconut Key?" She didn't even want to think about that. Couldn't, actually, think about it. Not on the same day she learned she was staying here.

"Someday." Savannah eased back again on a noisy sigh like she couldn't find a place to get comfortable. That must be what her whole life was like. "I get itchy, you know? I like to start over a lot."

"Why?"

The question made Savannah chuckle. "You know, I don't think anyone's ever asked me that before. I just do, I guess. Contrary to most rumors, I've never been in therapy to figure it out. I just get anxious to go somewhere else."

"I'd miss you," Ava admitted, the words a little trapped in throat, making it thick. "I honestly don't know if I'd want to live here without you."

She held up her hand as if to stay stop. "Don't do that, Ava. Don't tighten the ropes when they are strangling me."

Seriously? Ava tried to swallow, but the only thing that was strangling in this conversation was the idea that Savannah could just up and leave. "It would be like losing my mom and my grandmother all over again," she murmured.

Very slowly, Savannah pushed up and stared hard at Ava. "No pressure or anything, huh?"

"I'm sorry. I just..." She dug for the right words. "I love you." They were right, weren't they? They were honest. "And I get really scared of losing someone I love."

Savannah stared at her, then reached her hand over to put it on Ava's knee. "You know what, grasshopper?"

Ava smiled at the nickname she'd come to love. "What?"

"You've taught me more about being a mother than my own mother, and she was a darn good one. I love you, too."

"You'll be a fantastic mother, Savannah. And I'll

babysit Pink Line...I'll do anything for you to stay."

Savannah opened her mouth to answer, but suddenly she froze. "Oh, God," she said, suddenly whipping around to see where they were, making Ava realize how far away from those blue awnings she'd veered. Far.

Then Savannah looked over Ava's shoulder again, her eyes wide with horror. "What you need to do is haul ass!"

Ava spun around, letting out a shriek as she saw a funnel shooting up from the water like a skinny, swirling, menacing tornado. "What is that?" she screamed.

"I think it's a waterspout." Savannah shot across the skiff's small space, slamming down next to Ava to take over the till. "I'll steer us to shore. You...watch that thing."

Ava turned, sucking in a breath as she watched the spout spin and dance over the water, with no idea how far it was or how fast it was moving or where it was going. But it was definitely getting closer, and for the first time ever in this little boat, the water was churned up, making whitecaps and rocking the tiny vessel back and forth.

"Can it hurt us?" she asked.

"I don't think it's gonna lift us to Oz, but I don't want to find out the hard way."

The first few splats of rain hit Ava's face as another wave crested under them. "I've never seen anything like that."

"I heard they're super common down here, but I haven't seen one, either." Savannah twisted the handgrip, her whole face screwed up by the effort of trying to get more speed out of the tiny engine. "Come on! Go faster, you stupid little piece of crap!"

It was the fear in her voice that gut-punched Ava. No, that wasn't a punch to her gut, it was her chest, which constricted like a full-blown panic was bearing down. Not now. Not *now*.

She clung to the bench as they pounded up and down on the waves. Each time they

crashed against the water, Savannah cringed in pain.

She swore viciously, almost standing as if that would give her some more strength to make the engine she controlled with her hand go faster, but she nearly toppled, making Ava scream again.

"Savannah! Don't stand up!" She grabbed Savannah's hand and pulled her closer. "We'll make it. We'll make it!" They had to. Unless that thing followed them onto the land.

Ava turned to look at the beast bearing down on them, moaning when she realized how much closer it was. "It's following us," she cried.

"It feels that way. Hold on, big wave coming."

Just as she said it, the skiff went high, balancing precariously on a wave, then slammed down with a brain-rattling thud. Before Ava could react, buckets of water splashed into the hull.

Savannah threw her head back and let out a howl.

"What's the matter?"

She didn't speak, shaking her head, letting go of the till to put both hands on her stomach and double over.

"Savannah!"

"Steer! Fast. Oh my God, it hurts so bad."

Waves of panic rose up and threatened to choke Ava, but she forced them down, refusing to give in. She just kept her eyes on the shore, holding the till, scanning for that stupid blue coconut.

"Go left or right," Savannah sputtered, looking over

Ava's shoulder. "Change the course, now!"

Ava yanked the till and turned the boat sharply, glancing back to see the waterspout barreling down, not twenty feet away. Forget the shoreline, she had to get away from this *thing*.

Gritting her teeth, she headed south, rain and saltwater spraying into her eyes, blinding her.

"Something's wrong," Savannah cried, sliding off the bench into the puddle of seawater in the bottom of the boat, rubbing her stomach. "Something happened to the baby. Something's wrong, I can feel it. Hurry!"

They shot up on another wave and even more water dumped into the boat and Ava's mouth, making her sputter and gag. Suddenly, the little craft spun around and rain drenched them, as the whole world seemed to turn white and wet and wild.

"It's got us!" Savannah hollered, gripping Ava.

Before she could think or react, she felt the entire boat slide up on the next wave and it seemed to just stay there, suspended, and then they twisted, flipped, and flew through the air.

Then everything was black. Wet. Churning and whipping Ava's body through the water.

She was underwater! She kicked like crazy, flailing and throwing her arms in a rage of horror and fear, hitting something hard. Wooden. The boat! She had the boat.

Holding on, Ava used the edge of the boat to pull herself up, popping up for air that she sucked in noisily.

But everything was still black. Why? She was above water.

"Savannah!" Her voice echoed, louder than the

churning water. What was going on?

Suddenly there was a splash and the sound of Savannah's voice, and her hands reaching for Ava.

"We're under the boat!" Savannah rasped as she gasped for air. "We're under the damn boat!"

"What?"

"Reach up. And hold on!"

Kicking hard to stay above the water, Ava stuck her hand up and hit wood again. She was right. The skiff had flipped, and they were stuck *under* the boat. Automatically, her hand closed over one of the benches, which she could hold onto and not slip underwater. Rain pounded overhead but the noise of the waterspout was less...it was going away.

"We have to flip it over," Ava said. "Somehow."

"We can't. We'll never do that. We're not strong enough." Each word was painful for Savannah, Ava could tell.

"Are you okay?" Ava asked.

"I'm not dead," she said. "But I can't the same for my baby." Her voice folded with a sob. "And I really don't like it under here." Another sob, and this one tore Ava's heart out.

"Can you swim?" Ava asked.

"Not in this much pain."

What could she do? How could she...

Ava managed a breath and reached out with one hand for Savannah. "I'm going to swim to shore."

"You can't do—"

"Yes I can, Savannah. I can get there. I can get help. And you just have to stay under this boat, hold on, and wait for me to come back."

"Ava..." She could barely speak.

"We can do this," Ava said with far more conviction than she felt. "I'm going. Now."

Her answer was a moan in the darkness.

"Don't be scared, Savannah," Ava said, squeezing her arm. "I can do this for you. For Pink Line. I can do this."

Savannah moaned again, then added, "Hibiscus."

The safe word. The secret word. The word that meant she seriously needed help.

It was all Ava needed to hear. She sucked in a giant breath, closed her eyes, and shoved her whole body underwater, instinctively swimming away from the sound of the motor. As soon as she was out from under the boat, she popped up again, kicking wildly and blinking into the soft rain.

The water had calmed down a little, and shore was in sight. And Savannah needed her.

Stroke right, stroke left, kick, kick, kick.

Ava's whole body moved as if someone else was in charge, someone holding off the panic that had to be ready to explode in her head and chest. She couldn't stop. She couldn't give up. She had to swim, moving her arms and kicking her legs the way her mother had tried so hard to teach her.

Stroke right, stroke left, kick, kick, kick.

She sliced through the water like someone was literally pulling her to the shore. Probably because someone was.

You can swim, Ava Bear!

She could hear her mother's voice in her head all the way to the turquoise coconut.

CHAPTER TWENTY-FOUR
SAVANNAH

"Bed rest." Savannah groaned, the very sound still hurting her throat that had been abused by saltwater, choking, and way too much crying. "Are there two uglier words in the English language?"

"I could think of a few." Mom managed a smile as she fussed with the comforter around Savannah's bed.

"I know, I know. This could have been worse."

"So much worse." Her mother perched on the edge of the bed, the shadows under her eyes as deep and dark as Savannah could remember them. "We almost lost Pink Line," Mom whispered. "And Pinkie's mom."

"Should we call him Blue Line, now that we know?" Savannah smiled, happy that she'd given in and let the doctors at the hospital tell her the baby she'd nearly lost was a boy. She'd needed to know; it had helped her fight through the darkest hours.

A boy. A baby boy.

His father has a right to know.

The thought that had echoed in her head during

most of those dark hours had only gotten louder since Savannah had been released and brought home to Coquina House, tucked into her mother's first floor bedroom.

Mom put her hand lightly on Savannah's belly, a sizeable rise in the comforter. "We can call him whatever you like, as long as you follow the orders and stay on your back for three months until he's born, fat, happy, and healthy on October 2."

Savannah swallowed, finally clearheaded enough to let the reality of what happened to her sink in. It had been three days since that little grasshopper swam her ever-lovin' butt off in an act so heroic, it defied logic. Three days since the Coast Guard dove under that skiff, pulled her out, and got her to the hospital. Three days since she learned that one of those waves hit so hard, she suffered from what the doctors called a partial placental abruption, which meant there was a small separation of the placenta from her uterus.

She barely remembered anything but the suspended time while she was in the water with the sharpest, most searing pain she'd ever felt, hanging on to an upside-down boat for dear life.

The dear life inside of her.

She barely remembered the time under the hull, as the pain had been so bad. But she'd clung to the board, slowly kicking, breathing, and imagining her niece doing what no mere mortal could do.

But they'd all survived. Somehow, miraculously, they made it. "Where is everyone?"

"You want company?"

"I want everyone I love in this room right now," she

said. "And they better get used to it because bed rest doesn't mean solitary confinement."

Her mother laughed and leaned over to kiss her forehead. "Clearly your brush with death hasn't hurt your sense of humor."

"Some things can't die." She patted her belly. "That means you, Baby Boy."

When Mom left, she nestled deeper under the covers, the gratitude that had gripped her since the moment she woke up and realized the baby was still alive and kicking taking hold of her heart again.

She would never take life for granted. Ever, ever.

And that life deserved to know who his father was... and his father deserved to know this child existed. She let out a soft grunt, hating the thought.

"Knock knock," Peyton called. "Can we come in?"

"With chocolate, an iPad, and your own chair."

She heard the different laughs that she'd come to know this summer. Callie muscled in first, of course, followed by Peyton and Lovely. Jessie and Josh were here, with Mom between them as they all circled the bed. Way in the back, Kenny stood with his arm around Ava.

"You stayed?" Savannah pointed to Callie.

"Of course I stayed. You think I'd leave you in your hour of need?" Callie tipped her head. "But I'm leaving this afternoon."

"We'll miss you," Savannah said.

"I'll be back in August with the final..." She glanced at their mother. "Papers for signing."

"We'll have a divorce party," Savannah said with a wry smile as she turned to Peyton. "You knew I'd figure out a way to get the best room in the house, huh?"

"Mom and I are fine sharing, but..." Peyton smiled. "I may snuggle in here, so don't get comfy."

"I may let you, big sis." She pursed her lips and blew a kiss, turning to Jessie. "Now you can pay me back and take pictures of me until Pink, er, Baby Boy is born."

"I would love that," Jessie said, perching on the end of the bed and patting the covers where Savannah's foot was. "We saved you some of the flag cake."

"What exactly happened over here that day?" she asked.

"After Ava swam right up to Conchy Charlies, they called the Coast Guard and then us." Kenny stepped forward with this bit of news. "We all left and went straight to the dock where they were bringing you in to the ambulance."

"Wow." She sighed. "Way to wreck the holiday."

"You didn't wreck anything," Lovely said. "Except our hearts. It was terrifying."

Savannah pushed up and inched to the side, pinning her gaze on Ava. "Get over here, grasshopper."

"Maybe you should call her goldfish now," Lovely said. "Because she swims like one."

With a sly smile, Ava stepped forward, sliding her arm around Lovely to join her at the bottom of the bed. "I like grasshopper," she said. "It's the best nickname I ever had."

Savannah looked at the teenage girl for a long time, not caring that her eyes got misty as she did. They'd talked very briefly at the hospital, a few words, nothing that could possibly convey all Savannah wanted to say. And she wanted to say it in front of everyone.

"You..." She pointed at Ava. "Are the strongest,

bravest, most incredible human I've ever known. Fearless and fierce, the way a woman needs to be."

Ava managed her shy smile. "It was no big deal," she said, making them all react. Everyone in that room knew what Ava had done—swimming almost half a mile to shore—was a *very* big deal.

"And since you are fierce and fearless, I would like you to be godmother to my son because neither of us would be alive if not for you."

Ava gasped softly, along with a few others in the room. "Really?"

"Absolutely without a doubt," Savannah said. "I couldn't love you more, Ava Gallagher."

"Oh." She put her knuckles to her mouth and blinked, leaning into Lovely who gave her a squeeze. "It wasn't me, though."

Savannah snorted. "Don't ever sell yourself short, Ava. It was all you."

"Actually, it didn't feel that way." She glanced around, as every eye in the room settled on her. "I felt like I had help."

"An angel?" Lovely suggested.

"It was my mom," she admitted on a soft whisper. "She taught me to swim—or tried—and I could hear her voice the whole time."

Behind her, Savannah saw Kenny's eyes shutter closed when Ava said that.

"Is that crazy?" Ava asked.

"Not a bit," Lovely assured her. "Take it from a woman who has literally been to heaven and back. Your mother was certainly with you that day."

"And maybe your Grandma Janet," Beck added, stepping closer. "Because that woman had your best interests in mind when she insisted you deliver her letter in person. I read the letter again last night, and I had a little bit of a shock."

"Why?" a few of them asked, looking at her expectantly.

"Hang on a second." Mom stepped out and came back a minute later, holding papers. "Grandma Janet wrote this to me: 'My concern is Ava, who is at a difficult and delicate age, and so desperately needs a good woman to help her navigate the whitewater of life. And what could be better than a woman who is already part of her family? Could that woman be you?'" Mom lowered the letter and looked at Savannah, while not a person in the room breathed. "I think that woman was you, Savannah."

Savannah managed a smile despite the lump in her throat. "Well, we had plenty of whitewater, grasshopper."

Ava's eyes filled. "You're going to be an amazing mom, Savannah."

Kenny came up behind her and put his hands on her shoulders. "She knew that Ava needed to be around strong women," he said, looking over her at Savannah. "And, for the record, my wife would have loved you. All of you."

"Big brother." Savannah slipped into a smile, looking up at him. "I've always wanted one of those. Happy you're here."

There was some oohing, awwing, and group hugging, but after a bit, Savannah's jokes turned into long yawns.

"All right, our patient is sleepy." Mom stepped forward. "There will be plenty of time to visit with her."

"Almost three endless months of bed rest," Savannah added with a groan.

"They'll go fast," Mom said. "But now you need sleep. Say your goodbyes." She ushered the crowd out the door, but Ava stayed after everyone else left, her green eyes pinned to Savannah.

"What's a godmother do, exactly?" she asked.

"Back-up mother," Savannah said. "God knows I'll need help."

"But you have Grandma Beck and Lovely and two sisters."

"But I only have one grasshopper," she said, reaching out her hand. "And Baby Boy is going to love you so much."

She came closer, holding Savannah's hand. "Are you staying here, then?"

Oh, boy. Was she? She'd had a lot of time to think the last few days, in and out of consciousness, and she'd made two decisions. It was time to announce the first.

"I am staying," she said, the words kind of catching in her throat. "My son needs stability, family, and a home. This is going to be it."

"Oh, Savannah!" She nearly fell onto the bed, wrapping her arms around Savannah. "I'm so happy to hear that."

Savannah patted her niece's long pink and purple hair. "I'm happy to say it," she said. "Now can you get my mom? I need to talk to her before I make..." *Decision number two.* "A phone call."

"Sure!" She bounded to the door, then stopped and turned. "If you get tired of grasshopper, I can be fairy godmother."

Savannah laughed. "You catch on quick, kiddo."

A minute later, her mother came in the room, ready to fuss with blankets and blinds, but Savannah patted the bed, inviting her to sit down. "Need some advice, Mrs. Foster."

Her mother's eyes flicked in interest as she settled on the edge of the bed, reaching up to smooth Savannah's hair. "What is it, honey?"

"I need to tell him."

Her mother stared at her for a moment, then nodded in agreement. "Yes, you do."

"It could change...everything," Savannah said. "It means this baby isn't just mine. He has a say. He has rights. He has opinions and...a life in L.A. He has money, Mom, and lawyers and power and...fame."

"You always say he's a professional liar."

"Because he's an actor. A famous one. Like, you'll know his name when I say it."

"Really?" Her eyes widened. "Are you going to tell me who?"

"First, put yourself in my shoes and use your imagination. Pretend it's, oh, 1980...something. It's Christmas night. You're working the cash register at your dead-end job, feeling woefully sorry for yourself. And...Brad Pitt walks in."

"Brad Pitt?" She made a face.

"Not old Brad Pitt when he got weird. This is like *Legends of the Fall* Brad Pitt. *Thelma and Louise* Brad Pitt. But he's wearing a hat and you don't follow celebrities and have no idea. He flirts with you. Hounds you. Waits for you to get off work. Then takes you to the fancy hotel not far away for a drink. A second drink. More flirting. And...you don't figure out who he is until...after."

"But it's not Brad Pitt?"

She snorted. "No, Mom. It's not. But it was a one-night stand with a celebrity."

Mom stared at her, a little horrified. Probably disappointed, too.

Savannah closed her eyes so she didn't have to see that look, but then she felt her mother's hand on her arm. "I have one thing to say, Savannah."

"How proud you are of me?" she asked dryly, looking up at her.

She shook her head. "If I have learned anything from living in Coconut Key, it's that a real mother never judges."

Relief washed through her, making Savannah realize how much she'd dreaded that confession.

"The other thing I've learned is that secrets—especially those kept in shame—lead to a lifetime of unfair separations. I could have had Lovely as a mother but for secrets and shame. I could have known Kenny and Ava their whole lives but for secrets and shame. And this man, no matter what his sins or your reasons or his name, could know his son unless *you* keep this pregnancy a secret out of shame."

"Okay," she sighed out the word, stunned by how totally right her mother was. "Give me my phone over there and I'll call him. Maybe he'll say congrats, hon, here's a million for college...have a good life."

"Is that want you want?"

She inhaled and let it out slowly. "I don't know what I want except..." She patted her belly. "The best for this boy. Like, that's all that matters. You understand, don't you?"

"Better than anyone." With a smile and one more kiss, Mom handed her the phone and left, closing the door behind her.

Savannah tapped the screen and zipped through the contacts, finding his name and the number she'd blocked months ago. She had no idea if he'd ever called her or tried to reach her, and she didn't want to know.

But God willing, he would answer his phone now and not have one of his assistants call her back.

It rang twice, then stopped, and whoever answered was silent for a second.

"Well what do you know? Savannah Foster? What did I do to deserve this honor?" His rich baritone was somehow comforting and terrifying at the same time. She could picture him with that flop of sandy blond hair, achingly blue eyes, and the face the camera, and women, adored. Men, too. Hell, everyone adored Nicky Frye.

"Hey, Nick."

"You okay, Savannah? You sound...weak."

Not anymore. She might have to fight for this baby and that would take a strong, strong woman.

"I'm not the least bit weak," she assured him. "I am, however, flat on my back, six and a half months pregnant."

Once again, nothing, not a sound. Just dead silence for two, three, nearly five heartbeats. And then he started laughing.

"I'm not joking," she said coolly.

"I know," he responded. "I'm just so freaking happy."

Oh, no. That was *not* the response she expected.

CHAPTER TWENTY-FIVE
BECK

*H*er hand shook, which was a little bit aggravating to Beck. Shouldn't she hold this pen with confidence, ready to scribble her name on the line at the bottom of the page and finalize her divorce? Dan had rushed the paperwork, greased the legal skids, and managed to get them to the point of dissolution in record time.

"He must really be dying to tie the knot with Mari Cummings," Beck muttered.

"But it doesn't exactly go both ways."

Beck looked up at Callie, who sat across the dining table from her, wearing her serious "I'm going to be the best lawyer in the world someday" face. She'd actually dressed up for the divorce-paper signing, in a stiff-looking blouse and skirt despite the brutal August heat in the Keys.

Beck glanced down at her white shorts and tank top, which seemed appropriate, especially with the veranda full of family and friends ready to toast to her new life.

All she had to do was slide this pen over this paper and her thirty-four years of marriage to Daniel Foster came to a calm and quiet end.

And then her daughter's words hit her heart. "Wait, Callie. What do you mean it doesn't go both ways? Mari isn't dying to be the next Mrs. Foster?"

Callie just lifted one perfectly shaped brow, a barely readable expression crossing her beautiful features.

"What aren't you telling me?" Beck demanded.

"Mom, you know I have to honor attorney-client privilege here."

Irritation scampered up Beck's spine, a not-uncommon reaction with her youngest, and most puzzling, daughter.

Callie had been saying that since this whole thing started, when her only real claim was being a daddy's girl. She was and always would be the apple of Dan's eye. Which was fine and wonderful, but now that the divorce was final and Callie worked in Dan's office on school breaks, would Beck's already tenuous relationship with Callie get even worse?

Didn't matter. She was real with her other two daughters, so she wasn't going to beat around the bush with this one. "First of all, honey, you're not actually the attorney here. They did all the work virtually and got paid handsomely. You're the messenger with the papers." Beck leaned forward. "And you're the daughter of both parties. Is there something about Dad's life I should know?"

She searched Beck's face, her cool exterior almost warming. Almost. "Well, I see things because I'm in that office ten hours a day. Sometimes twelve."

Beck flinched. "They do that to their summer college

interns? I dread to think what will happen when you're a first-year associate."

"Two thousand billable hours is what will happen," she said matter-of-factly. "But, yeah, I'm in Dad and Mari's faces a lot, and..." She lifted a shoulder. "I don't think they are getting married, at least not instantly."

Beck felt her jaw loosen with surprise, remembering that morning when her husband and the fifty-something woman sat at the kitchen table and explained that they were in love and wanted to spend the rest of their lives together as more than law partners. It certainly seemed... like they didn't want to wait an extra minute.

"I thought they'd be at City Hall this afternoon."

Callie gave a soft snort. "Mari's in DC trying a case this week and I think she's going to London after that."

"Without Dad?"

"He's running the firm."

Beck shook her head. "Dan's problems aren't my problems anymore," she said to herself as much as to Callie. "He chose Mari, and divorce. And I chose a new life in Coconut Key."

"Then..." Callie tapped the legal page. "Sign it, Mom."

She put the pen to the line, stared at it, then lowered it again. Dear God, was she having second thoughts? Considering reconciliation? Or just plain scared?

"Is he happy?" Beck asked on a whisper.

Callie gave a tight smile. "Firm billings are up thirty-seven percent over last year."

"Callie."

Even she had to acknowledge what a lame answer that was with a sigh and a shrug. "I don't know, Mom. He bought an expensive car. He's sleeping with his partner.

He walked away from you. Don't they call this a mid-life crisis?"

"In the movies."

"And how do they usually end?"

"Happily, I hope."

Callie put her hand on the page again. "You're getting a great settlement, Mom, including all the money on the sale of the house and fifty percent of your investment income. You have a new business, great friends, and a gorgeous place to live. And, come on, we can all see Josh is ready to swoop in and build a handmade pedestal to place you on. Let Dad go. He made his choice."

Let Dad go. Easy to say, but...*thirty-four years.*

Beck let out a long, slow exhale. "You sure got brains, Cal. And that's some good advice for a twenty-year-old."

Callie winked. "Wait until I can charge five hundred an hour."

"I pity the opposing counsel." Beck picked up the pen and signed Rebecca Mitchell Foster with a flourish, then initialed all the other pages as Callie flipped them for her.

"I know there's a celebration about to happen," Callie said. "And that's why I rented a car at the airport. I'm getting on the next flight to Atlanta."

"I would have picked you up and taken you to the airport, Callie."

She waved her hand. "You just relax, Mom. I got this. I'll be out to say my goodbyes to the crew as soon as I put these papers in order."

"All right." Beck stood, not shaking at all anymore. But she was glad for the airport reprieve because, boy, she could use a mimosa right now.

As she stepped onto the patio, Jessie popped the champagne. Everyone looked at Beck—most of them around Savannah who rested on the chaise, but held up her phone.

"All done, Beckerella?" Jessie asked.

"Signed, sealed, and...initialed." She gestured toward the phone. "What's so captivating?"

"Well, we're in the middle of storm season in the Keys," Josh said, pointing to the phone. "Get used to watching those red blobs in the ocean. Most of the time, they sail right up the coast and leave us alone."

"Most of the time," Savannah said.

Josh straightened and met Beck's gaze with one as warm and blue as the sky behind him. "Mimosa?"

She smiled at him, feeling so grateful for their friendship. Grateful...friendship. Not exactly swoony and romantic, but she was a fifty-six-year-old divorcee now. The swoony and romantic days were behind her.

What she needed was a solid and steady friend, like the man coming toward her with one of Jessie's freshly poured mimosas. As solid and steady as a man could be.

"Eighty percent champagne," he said with a wink. "Seriously, you feel okay, Beck?"

"I'm good, thank you." She took the glass and stepped closer to where her mother and Ava sat at the table. "I'm also divorced." She raised her glass on a light laugh. "So, there's that."

As she passed the chaise longue, Savannah lifted a bottle of Pellegrino from her prone position. "To new beginnings, Mom." Ever since Savannah had told Nick Frye he was going to be a father, she seemed more at peace with having a baby. They'd been talking, a lot, but no decisions had been made yet.

Beck tapped her glass to the bottle, but didn't take a drink. "And new lives, Sav."

Lovely rose from the table and came closer, sliding a supportive arm around Beck's waist. "And to my new business partner."

Beck lifted the glass again. "To Coquina House, the best Bed and Breakfast in the Keys...if we ever get a contractor."

"Hey, hey," Kenny said, holding up a beer bottle. "I don't have a contractor's license yet, but I'm working on it. If we get a contractor, we'll be done by Christmas. If not, then we'll be done...eventually. To the reno."

She smiled at her son, the baby she reluctantly gave up, the boy she never knew, and the man she never dreamed she'd meet. Once again, she raised the glass to him, but Jessie sidled up to Beck's other side, preventing that much needed sip.

She held a lemonade that might be laced with something stronger. "To big decisions, may they be the right ones."

"You decided?" Beck asked, knowing that Jessie had been wavering on Tag Jadrien's offer to buy the restaurant for more than a month, succeeding only in getting him to up the amount.

"I like watching him dangle," she said. "And Peyton is so close to finishing that cookbook. Can't give up the ship yet, can I?"

"Then we drink to making Tag dangle," Beck said, tapping the lemonade.

"There's an image I'd like wiped out of my brain," Savannah said under her breath, cracking them all up.

"What we should drink to is good weather," Peyton said, pointing at Savannah's phone. "They are predicting some mighty big storms this month and next."

Lovely snorted. "Coconut Key will survive because that's what we do."

"We are hearty Coconutters," Ava chimed in with a giggle.

"Then I'll drink to good weather..." Beck lifted her glass. "Anything else? Because this divorcee needs a mim—"

"Mom?" Callie came up the back stairs to the veranda. "You got a second?"

"Something I forgot to sign?" she asked.

"Just, um, can you come here for a second?"

The echoes of their last conversation still fresh in Beck's head, she nodded and walked to the stairs, following Callie to the bottom. "What's up?"

"Well, I was just putting all the paperwork in my rental car and a man pulled up and he says he's your contractor."

"*What?*" She looked over Callie's shoulder across the yard to the street where she did indeed see a big, unfamiliar truck.

"I didn't know if you want me to tell him you're, um, celebrating or whatever, but I didn't want him to leave. I know how long and hard you've been looking for a contractor."

"I'll go talk to him." She brushed by Callie, not even bothering to give up the drink, headed right for the front of the house.

As she came around the front stairs, she spotted a man across the property, looking up at the house with his hands on his hips. She slowed her step to study him with the same scrutiny he gave the house.

His hair was thick, tousled, a magnificent shade of silver that could have made him look old, but not with that strong and fit physique. His skin was tanned without being weathered, and when he walked, there was a gracefulness to each step that made her think of dancing or... doing other things she didn't think about too much anymore.

Whoa. Wasn't she just thinking about feeling...swoony?

"Hello," she said, clearing her throat as she came closer. "Is it true? You're a contractor?"

He broke into an easy smile that was both familiar and not quite like anything she'd ever seen before. Her gaze dropped to a cleft in his chin that reminded her of Kenny. Must be a tradesman thing.

"I am. And you're...wow." His gaze dropped over her, then back to her face, the quick check giving her an unexpected jolt. "Beck." He said it with no question in his voice, as if he actually recognized her.

"Rebecca Foster." With the drink in her left hand, she extended the other one and he closed it in a large, warm grip that felt confident and strong. "I'm thrilled you're here."

Thrilled? *Easy, girl.*

His smile wavered as he studied her, really searched her face as if he was memorizing it or...trying to remember something. "Well, hold that thought until you know everything."

She laughed, releasing her hand. "Why? Are you wildly expensive? Not available until next year? Or you just want to wait until after this allegedly bad hurricane season is over."

He didn't answer, his gaze—dark as night and just as intense—locked on her face. "The price could be high. My availability will depend on what you need. And the storms? I have a feeling we're about to have one."

Her own smile disappeared as she inched back, not even sure how to process that response. "I don't know what to say to that."

"My name's Bill, Beck."

"Bill. Well, great. It's nice to meet you, Bill."

"Bill Dobson."

"Welcome to Coquina..." The rest caught in her throat. "Did you say...*Dobson*?"

"So he didn't tell you. Loyal to the core, that kid." He gave a tight smile and nodded, his gaze shifting to the stairs as the front door opened. "There he is." He took a few steps closer and looked up at Kenny. "Surprised to see me, son?"

Son?

Kenny just stared at him, the color draining from his face the way it probably was from Beck's as she stood with her jaw wide open.

They *knew* each other? Kenny Gallagher and *his biological father*?

The door flew open again and Ava launched out like a rocket. "Uncle Bill!"

She leaped into his arms for a hug the likes of which she rarely gave, even new Ava who did hug.

Wait...*this* was the Uncle Bill she always talked about? Kenny's boss and closest friend?

She could feel the whole world shift a little as Kenny came down the stairs, his gaze on her.

"Beck," he said in a gruff whisper. "There's something I haven't told you."

No kidding.

Staring back at him, she did the only thing she could do. She lifted that champagne glass and one eyebrow at the same time. "Here's to family...*son.*"

And finally, she got to drink her mimosa. Good thing, because one look at this new arrival in Coconut Key and she had a feeling she was going to need it.

Want to know what happens next in Coconut Key?
Check out Book Three...*A Season in the Keys*!
Visit www.hopeholloway.com to sign up for Hope's
newsletter to get the latest on new releases, excerpts,
and more!

Read the entire Coconut Key Series!

ABOUT THE AUTHOR

Hope Holloway is the author of charming, heartwarming women's fiction featuring unforgettable families and friends and the emotional challenges they conquer. After a long career in marketing, she gave up writing ad copy to launch a writing career with her first series, Coconut Key, set on the sun-washed beaches of the Florida Keys.

A mother of two adult children, Hope and her husband of thirty years live in Florida and North Carolina. When not writing, she can be found walking the beach or hiking in the mountains with her two rescue dogs, who beg her to include animals in every book. Visit her site at www.hopeholloway.com.